An Immodest Proposal

"When we are finished with the painting, I have another position in mind for you," she said, surprised at the raggedness of her own voice. Artemisia opened her eyes and met his direct gaze.

"Really? What might that be? Something for Mr. Beddington perhaps?"

Bother his fixation with Beddington!

"No, this is something for me," she said evenly.

"What do you need, Your Grace?"

She took a deep breath and jumped into the void. "I find I require a lover."

Distracting the Duchess

Emily Bryan

LEISURE BOOKS NEW YORK CITY

A LEISURE BOOK®

March 2008

Published by

Dorchester Publishing Co., Inc.
200 Madison Avenue
New York, NY 10016

ISBN 10: 0-8439-5870-7
ISBN 13: 978-0-8439-5870-6

Printed in the United States of America.

10 9 8 7 6 5 4 3 2

Visit us on the web at www.dorchesterpub.com.

Distracting
the Duchess

"Beddington holds the key."
—Last coherent message received from
Angus Dalrymple, Esq.,
covert agent for
Her Majesty's interests
on the Indian subcontinent

Chapter One

I'm going to have to shorten his willie."

The artist stepped back from her easel and regarded the offending member with a critical eye. Her name was Artemisia. "Sounds like amnesia," her father had complained when her mother insisted upon the unusual moniker. Artemisia Dalrymple Pelham-Smythe, to be exact. Such a heavy load might have been a burden for some. But Artemisia was a duchess, so most people simply called her "Your Grace."

"Of course, it's absolutely true to life," she said finally, closing one eye and holding her thumb upraised to do a rough comparative measurement. "The proportions are accurate to the model, but critics tend to find well-endowed males in art to be prurient. I can't imagine why. A willie is just a willie, after all. What do you think, Cuthbert?"

"On the subject of *art*, Your Grace, one is of no opinion." Cuthbert set down the silver tray and poured out a steaming cup of tea with extreme dignity. "But if one may be so bold as to suggest, perhaps madam would do well to be more delicate in her speech."

Artemisia took the offered cup and sipped the aromatic blend. It was almost as good as the tea she had grown up with in Bombay.

"I *was* being delicate, Cuthbert. That's why I called it a willie instead of a pe—"

"Your daily reading, Your Grace," Cuthbert interrupted smoothly, handing her a neatly folded newspaper.

Hiding her smile, Artemisia set down her teacup. She knew she shouldn't purposely try to irritate her butler, but his ears turned such a charming shade of purple when she did.

Artemisia ran her gaze over the headlines. "*The Tattler*?" She tried never to read the ubiquitous scandal sheets, and *The Tattler* was the worst of the lot, laden with juicy *on dits* and sly innuendo. "You know I've no time for such drivel."

"Indeed. Then perhaps madam should refrain from giving the writers so much fodder. The article just below the fold could not escape one's notice. Will there be anything else, Your Grace?"

"No, I think that's quite enough," Artemisia said wryly.

The butler bowed and retreated with dignity. Almost as an afterthought, he stopped and turned back.

"A gentleman is waiting to see you, madam."

"Ah! That will be the model Mr. Phelps is sending round today. I'm ready to start sketches of Eros now that Neptune is finished. Nearly finished," she amended, silently reminding herself that there was yet a willie to be shortened.

"It is highly unlikely that this man is one of your young gods." Cuthbert shook his head solemnly. "He dresses like a proper English gentleman."

"There are so many secondhand clothing shops in London, a stable lad can fit himself out like a lord if he wishes."

Artemisia bit her lip. She realized she was sounding just like the writer in *The Tattler* who last week bemoaned the fact that class distinctions could no longer be made by dress—not with so many ladies' maids larking about London as well turned out as their mistresses. It irked her that she should be mouthing the sentiments of a scandal sheet. Artemisia made a mental note not to read *The Tattler* again even if Cuthbert shoved it under her nose.

She consulted the ormolu mantel clock above her fireplace. Even in summer, she burned a fire for the comfort of her models. Goose bumps did not become an Olympian, after all. "Send the man in."

Once Cuthbert closed the French doors to her studio, Artemisia released a pent-up sigh. Perhaps she should encourage him to retire, but the crusty gentleman's gentleman probably wouldn't hear of it. Cuthbert's family had been with the estate for two generations. He had served Artemisia's late husband, the Duke of Southwycke, as his father had served the duke's father before him. Even though his master was dead and Cuthbert not-so-tacitly disapproved of his unconventional mistress, he lived to serve Southwycke. Anything else was unthinkable.

Artemisia donned a paint-daubed smock over her simple day dress and began assembling her materials. Today she'd do a few preliminary sketches and experiment with poses. Once she settled on a composition, she'd transfer her ideas to canvas with her brushes and pallet knife. As she arranged her tools, one of the soft sticks of chalk rolled from the table's edge and she bent to retrieve it. She was so intent on her task, she didn't even hear the door swing open behind her.

Trevelyn Deveridge had been warned that the duchess had a well-earned reputation for the unexpected, but he certainly didn't anticipate being greeted by the sight of her bottom first.

And a bottom as ripe as a plum, he almost said aloud. She wore no crinoline, no contraption of horse-hair and wires to enhance her form, just a simple shift covered by a short smock, nothing to obscure what was a decidedly shapely derriere.

Stick to business, he ordered himself. *You're here to find Beddington, not to see the sights.*

Wiping off his salacious grin, Trevelyn cleared his throat.

"Oh!" She straightened and turned abruptly. Trevelyn's first impression was that the duchess was much younger than he expected and far more comely. Several locks of her raven hair had escaped from the loose chignon, teasing her delicate neck, the curls off on jaunts of their own. She looked as if she'd just risen from a rousing tussle on a feather tick. He flexed his fingers, imagining threading the silky tendrils through them. As if she read his thoughts, a becoming flush kissed her cheeks. Then her delicately arched brows lowered in a frown.

"You're late," she accused.

"Your pardon, Your Grace, but—"

"Spare me your excuses. Surely Mr. Phelps explained that punctuality is essential to your position. I don't want to lose the morning light."

"Clearly there's been a misunderstanding, mum," he began in his best imitation of a rough country burr while he made an old-fashioned courtly leg to her. He'd been trained to adopt an assumed identity when the situation called for one. Trevelyn had already decided this was a job for Thomas Doverspike, his less aristocratic alter ego. "Allow me to introduce myself, an' it please you. I'm—"

"No names, please," she said crisply. "At least, not until the painting is well underway. I find calling you by the title of the work enables us to maintain professional distance." The duchess beckoned him closer with a wave of her slim fingers. "Well, don't just stand there. Come here so I can get a good look at you."

Amused by her abrupt manner, Trevelyn swallowed his retort and strode forward. The first lesson drummed into him when he joined Her Majesty's corps of intelligence officers was to listen more than he spoke. He might learn a wealth of information if he simply let his subject talk. The duchess had obviously mistaken him for someone seeking employment. Once she realized her error, she'd be embarrassed enough to tell him anything.

Even where to find the elusive Mr. Beddington.

She eyed him carefully, walking a slow half-circle around him. Finally she stopped and pinned him with a direct gaze. Her eyes were a deep moss green, and a faint streak of blue chalk was smudged near her temple. The scent of oleander, mingled with oil paint, wafted about her. He inhaled her sweet fragrance, surprised to find his soft palate aching for him to plant a kiss on the chalk smudge.

She shook her head. "No, I'm afraid you won't do at all."

Trev blinked in surprise. Women usually found him most agreeable. "An' it not be too forward to ask, how do I disappoint you, Your Grace?"

"The fault is not yours. I shall have to speak to Mr. Phelps about this. I specifically requested blond curls and a soft, cherubic face for my Eros. While there is a hint of a wave in your hair, the color is definitely chestnut, and the planes and angles of your face are

far too jarring to belong to the god of love. With
those brooding dark eyes and that strong jaw, you're
much more a god of . . ."

She stopped, and her eyes seemed to go out of focus for a moment, as if she was seeing something
other than him. One of her brows arched.

"There's nothing else for it," the duchess said. "You
shall be Mars, my god of war."

"I've been called many things, Your Grace. Never a
god of anything." He inclined his head slightly. "Expect I should feel honored."

"You will," she said with certainty. "When I'm finished, your face and form will be immortal. Now
then—let's begin, shall we? The dressing room is
through that door. There's a robe in there for you.
Remove your clothing—all of it, if you please—and
return in the robe. Pray be quick about it. The sun
waits for no one."

And neither, evidently, did the Duchess of Southwycke. She wanted him naked as God made him, did
she? Trevelyn never expected to have to pose as a
figure model to serve his Queen, but he'd done far
more difficult things for the sake of Victoria Regina.
Besides, when a lady asked so prettily for a gentleman to disrobe, how could he in good conscience
refuse?

*Especially when the lady is a well-favored, wid-
owed duchess,* Trevelyn decided. *No marriage trap
here, even if the session ends in something more involved than etchings.*

He might have thought better of it if the duchess
had been a wrinkled old hag, but a leisurely morning
spent unclothed in the company of a lovely woman
would be far more interesting than the quick interview he'd expected. And if all went well, the job

would certainly provide him with an opportunity to spend enough time with her to glean all the information he sought, probably without her ever knowing his true business.

He squared his shoulders and decided to play the hand dealt him. Trevelyn headed for the dressing room, whistling "Rule Britannia" between his teeth.

The things one does for one's Queen and Country . . .

Artemisia tapped her toe with impatience, waiting for her newest subject to emerge from the dressing room. She could see why Cuthbert had confused him with a true gentleman. His doeskin breeches were soft and clean-looking, but her keen eye spotted the slightest shininess of wear on his waistcoat, and once he spoke, his accent clearly marked him as a young man trying to dress a notch or two above his station.

Pity her time in London had taught her to look for such distinctions. The rules were much more relaxed during her upbringing on the frontier of British India. She was used to gossiping with her Indian nursemaid, visiting the Maharajah's daughters, taking tea with the viceroy's wife and dancing with enlisted men all on the same day. In London, she had to be ever mindful of her place or the scandal sheets would flay her for some breech of acceptable behavior.

Her gaze fell on *The Tattler* still on the tray next to her teacup. She knew she shouldn't, but her curiosity got the better of her.

"Well, let's see what's got the wind up Cuthbert's drawers, shall we?" Artemisia said to the marmalade-colored cat sunning itself on the windowsill. She perched on the settee and spread the scandal sheet across her knees. The tabby leaped from the sill and tiptoed across the back of the settee, hovering near

Artemisia's shoulder to rumble unquestioning approval in her ear. A smaller gray cat crept under the settee to weave about her shins. She leaned down and scratched beneath his chin absently while she read.

> *London's favorite Merry Widow, the infamous Duchess of S, made quite a splash Sunday last—literally. She was found cavorting in the St. James fountain with unnamed associates of the lower sort. The peeress with pretensions to artistic inclinations claimed to be researching how a water nymph feels for her current work in progress—rumored to be a scandalous set of paintings of the entire Greek pantheon in the altogether.*
>
> *Truly, the* bon ton *would delight in shunning the feckless widow, if only Her Grace hadn't stolen the march on London society and shunned it first.*

"At least they got the subject of the paintings right, Castor," she said to the orange cat near her shoulder. "But precious little else. Isn't that right, Pollux?"

She lifted the gray cat to her lap and let him knead her thighs till he was ready to settle in a furry ball. The scandal sheet's words stung. But even to herself, she wouldn't admit vulnerability, so she took refuge in irritation.

" 'Pretensions to artistic inclinations,' indeed."

When she was barely old enough to hold a quill, her *ayah* recognized her innate talent. The Indian nursemaid reported Artemisia's skill to her father, who engaged drawing tutors for his precocious eldest daughter. By the time she was twelve, her portraiture was in much demand among the wildly eclectic British community associated with "John Company" in that remote outpost of the Empire. Now that she was grown, she wanted more than anything for her work to be recognized, not as that of a gifted child, but as an artist in the full bloom of her talent.

So far, London society had done its best to discourage her. The proper range of subject matter for female artists was forget-me-nots or sparrows, certainly not scantily clad or—perish the thought!—naked young men.

"Nude, not naked. There's a world of difference," Artemisia murmured. "Honestly, Pollux, you'd think the *ton* had nothing better to do than peep and snicker over its peers. Busybodies, every one of them."

Artemisia cast the scandal sheet to the floor and purposefully trod it underfoot on her way back to her easel. What did she care what they thought?

And yet her chest ached strangely.

Growing up riding elephants on tiger hunts hadn't prepared her for dealing with the sharp claws of the *bon ton.* When her husband had been alive, his exalted rank and impeccable decorum insulated her from society's scratches. Now that Artemisia was on her own, the self-appointed arbiters of acceptable behavior lost no chance to express their disapproval. The young Duchess of Southwycke was judged decidedly odd. Small wonder she became reclusive. When she did venture out, it was often in the company of those considered far beneath her station.

The romp through the fountain was probably ill-advised, especially since she hadn't anticipated how transparent wet muslin became, but she credited the outing with infusing her *Neptune* with a wonderful sense of motion.

"Ah! There you are." Artemisia looked up when she heard the door hinge squeak. Ordinarily, she'd speak to Cuthbert about such a defect, but now she was grateful for the warning. She was not in the habit of greeting her models posterior first, and the incident had thrown her strangely off balance.

The new fellow sauntered toward her, a tuft of dark hairs peeping from the deep vee in his robe, hands in his pockets as if he were in his own dressing room. Unlike her previous models, he seemed totally at ease.

"Let's just try a pose or two before you disrobe, shall we?" she said, determined to ease him gently into the work. "Most of my models find it more comfortable to get into character prior to—"

"I have my share of faults, Your Grace, but my old gaffer always told me it don't pay for shyness to be one of 'em," he said as he shrugged out of the plush velvet dressing gown she'd provided for him. He let the garment drop to the parquet floor.

He cocked his head at her. "How do you want me?"

Chapter Two

*H*ow did she want him?

"Yes, well, let me think about that for a moment," she all but stammered as she averted her gaze. A quick glimpse of him was enough to quicken her breath. His boldness unnerved her. "Have you done this sort of work before?"

"No, Your Grace, but there's a first time for everything, they do say. Do I still disappoint?"

Heavens, no, almost escaped her lips. She'd rarely seen such a specimen of male beauty. Like most of her models drawn from the working classes, this man was well-muscled, vigorous labor having sculpted his limbs and torso. Yet his skin was smooth and his hands and feet beautifully shaped. His nails were clean and neatly trimmed, enough of a rarity to be remarkable among those who worked to earn their daily bread.

While it never quite made sense to Artemisia, popular notions of male attractiveness currently required small hands and feet. She was pleased to see this man's were not. His fingers were long and powerful, but with a certain aristocratic grace. His feet had high arches and the bones of his ankles formed a strong curve into his thickly muscled calves. He stood proudly, his weight evenly distributed on both feet, his arms relaxed at his side.

He made no reflexive fig-leaf gesture, so Artemisia's gaze followed the thin strip of dark hair that started at the indentation of his navel and led to his groin.

There's one willie I won't whack off, no matter what the critics might say. As she looked at him, his member rose, the smooth skin darkened with engorged blood.

"Please don't be embarrassed," she said quickly. "This sometimes happens."

"Indeed, Your Grace, it happens with regularity," he said with a wicked smile. His teeth were very white.

Artemisia clamped her lips together. With other models, the first session was always awkward. This man, however, seemed totally at ease in his own skin, as if he often paraded nude before strange women.

"From what part of London do you hail?" she asked, wondering if Mr. Phelps had hired a male prostitute for her instead of a model. This man was a bit older than her usual subjects. Based on the sharp delineation of his features, she judged him nearing thirty, though his muscle tone rivaled the younger workmen she'd used on previous canvases. "Where did you say Mr. Phelps found you?"

"I didn't say." The infuriating smile hadn't faded. "How did you imagine your Mars?"

"Right, then," she said, grateful to get down to business. "Mars needs to be contemplating a battle. Turn your head and gaze into the distance. Kindly refrain from smiling, if you please. I seriously doubt the god of war has a sense of humor."

When he complied, she was immediately relieved to be able to look at him without his dark eyes focused on her, hot and knowing. His member was still swollen and potent.

"You want me to just stand here?" he asked, his brown-eyed gaze flicking back to her for a moment.

"Perhaps you should point toward an imagined goal—with your hand, I mean."

Heat crept up her neck and spread over her cheeks. The man had her blushing, for pity's sake. She'd been a married woman. She'd painted any number of men in the nude. An erect willie shouldn't be enough to reduce her to stammering. With her other models, she'd always been in complete control. This man's lack of self-consciousness made her uneasy.

He made a noise in the back of his throat, suspiciously like a stifled chuckle, as he lifted his arm in compliance. "Perhaps Mars should have a weapon of some kind," he suggested.

He already had a formidable one between his legs, but Artemisia took the opportunity to escape to the table at the far end of the room, where she kept an assortment of props in a disordered heap. "Yes, quite right. Good idea."

She hurried back to him with a Greco-Roman helmet, a round shield and a short sword called a *gladius*. He bent his head so she could crown him with the helmet. She was forced to step near him as she adjusted the strap beneath his chin. His lips curved into an inviting smile. Standing this close to him, she noticed the faint shadow of his beard and had to restrain herself from running a fingertip along his jaw to feel the tiny bristles. His heat radiated toward her, and his scent flooded her nostrils. Her mouth went suddenly dry.

"Here." She held out the shield and *gladius,* while

stepping back to a safer distance. "Try a few poses and I'll tell you to stop if I see something I like."

"You don't see anything you like yet?"

Artemisia's mouth tightened into a thin line. He was *enjoying* her discomfort! She should sack the impudent wretch now and be done with him. But he did have the most amazing eyes, and for a dazzling moment she'd glimpsed an image of what a marvelous god of war he'd make. She was loath to give up a perfectly good subject just because he made her squirm in her pantaloons.

She turned from him and settled on the straight-backed chair, her sketch pad balanced on her knees. Work, that's what she needed. Once she was firmly ensconced in her art, he'd become merely a pleasing arrangement of light and dark, lines and angles, not a disturbingly well-made, flesh-and-blood man.

She'd been a widow for nearly two years now, and she had no intention of marrying again. The legal status of a married woman was on par with a child or an imbecile, and she refused to be treated like either. Still, two years was past time when other women might be tempted to take a discreet lover.

Artemisia had no time for such things, she told herself. So much of her life was taken up with her art and what man, however liberal-minded he might be, would want a mistress who spent copious amounts of time with other nude men? She'd made it a firm rule never to become unprofessionally attached to any of her models, so that left her with nothing.

Nothing but squirming in her pantaloons.

She looked up and saw that her new Mars was making practice cuts with the sword, holding the hilt of the blade in an authoritative manner. He tossed the *gladius* up in a rotating flash and caught it cleanly, testing the sword for balance, his movement a study in masculine grace.

"An intimate acquaintance with weaponry, I see. You have served in the military," she observed as she deftly captured the raw-boned angles of his face.

"I've seen my share of battlefields."

A shadow flitted across his features, but it was gone so suddenly, she decided she'd imagined it.

"I admire those who serve their Queen and Country in such a manner," she said. "Would you care to speak about your time in uniform?"

"There's not much to tell that makes fair hearing."

This time she was sure she didn't imagine the brooding darkness that fell over him. Then suddenly one corner of his sensual mouth turned up.

"Why don't you tell me about yourself," he suggested. "Painting fellows in the altogether ain't exactly the done thing, now is it? Most ladies would faint dead away right proper at the sight of a naked man. Have you been doing it long?"

"I took it up again after my husband died," she said, refusing to rise to his bait. She had no need to explain to this forward fellow the allure the human form held for her. The exquisite lines, the depth of feeling, the divine spark of one created in the image of God—no maggoty bowl of fruit could hope to compete with that. "But I can't remember a time when I wasn't an artist. I started out drawing as a child, then tried my hand at sculpture with a certain amount of success."

She was being modest. If he knew anything about art, he'd know a sculpture of hers was housed in a place of honor in the Queen's own collection. It was Artemisia's seminal work, the piece that had guaranteed her reputation as a child prodigy. A reputation

she was now trying to live down by focusing on another medium altogether.

Altogether. In the altogether. Strange that he should
use the same phrase *The Tattler* did about her work.
Perhaps he'd read the scandal-sheet article about her.
She studied his face again.

Several of her models confessed to being illiterate,
but she already knew this man was quite different
from the others. His eyes held a glint of lively intelligence.

"Your accent does not mark you as a Londoner,"
she said as she shaded the tendon that stretched from
his neck to his shoulders. "Did you grow up in the
country?"

"Yes, Your Grace, an' it please you, I'm a Wilt-
shireman."

"Ah, the Chalk Horse country."

"You know it?"

"Of course," she said. The primitive horses high on
the ridges, formed by ancient Britons who cut into
the turf to expose the white chalk, were arguably the
oldest art on the British Isle. "My father told me
about the horses of Wiltshire when I was a child in
India."

"India." His dark eyes flashed as he repeated the
word. "Now there's a place I'd love to see, and no
mistake. The gorgeous East, they call it. But I suppose you didn't much care for it. They do say India's
not a fit place for an Englishwoman."

"Rubbish," Artemisia said. "I was born there. It's
wonderful. An immense land, filled with color and
stunning beauty and peopled with very handsome
races. While I won't minimize its troubles—poverty,
disease and ignorance being chief among them—
they are the very same failings we suffer here. For

every beggar on the streets of Calcutta, there is one haunting the crowded alleys in London."

He cast her a look of surprise. Then his eyes narrowed in frank appraisal. "That's an unusual view, you being a lady of quality and all."

She chuckled. "For my opinions, I suppose you must blame my father. He always encouraged me to speak my mind. Not terribly ladylike, I'm afraid, but the pot is already thrown and fired. Not much help for it now."

"Who was your father that he should bring you up in such an unusual way?"

"No one you'd know. Angus Dalrymple, lately of the East India Company. My father's no titled lord, but he was a great man, nonetheless."

"Was? He's not dead, is he?"

Her Mars seemed truly disturbed by the thought, his dark brow furrowed with concern. Artemisia smiled at him before returning her gaze to her sketch pad. "No, my father is very much alive."

"Just no longer great?" he asked before thrusting his sword through an imaginary foe.

The insolence in his question snapped her head up. In the intimacy of her studio, she encouraged her models to speak their minds, but this was over the line.

The play of light shafting through the tall windows cast delineating shadows on his muscular arms. When he turned away from her, the broad expanse of his back, the ridge of his spine and the two slight indentations above his tight buttocks made her breath catch in her throat at his sheer male beauty.

There was no denying it: Insolent devil or not, the man was magnificent.

She cleared her throat before speaking. "My father

suffers from a strange malady that has disordered his mind. He may not be the man he once was, but his illness in no way lessens my regard for him."

He stopped slicing the sword through the air and tested the cutting edge with the pad of his thumb. "My apologies, Your Grace. I meant no disrespect." He heaved in a deep sigh. "Well, that tears it," he mumbled under his breath.

"Something vexes you?"

"You said I wouldn't know your father, but I have heard of him. Or more rightly, I've heard of a friend of his."

"A friend of Angus Dalrymple's?" Her chalk was flying furiously, trying to capture the look of consternation on his features. She wasn't sure yet which of his many expressions was most suitable for her Mars, but the man's face was so mercurial, going from light to shadow, from sly sensuality to somber reflection. He was a feast for her eyes. "And who might that friend be?"

"Mr. Beddington."

The chalk in her fingers snapped in half. Artemisia swallowed hard as she bent to retrieve the pieces. Surely she hadn't heard him properly. "Who?"

"Mr. Beddington," he repeated.

"And what do you know of him?" She closed her sketch pad and folded her hands, hoping he hadn't marked the tremor in them.

"They say he's a canny man of business, is Mr. Beddington. Any pump the bloke puts his hand to is sure to be flowing with guineas sooner rather than later. Must be rich as Croesus by now, him or whoever he works for."

"And who says these things?"

"Folk what keep an eye on the way of things hereabouts," he said. "Folk in my line of work."

"I know I said no names, but I feel the need to know yours now, if you please."

He made a bow with a small flourish, the gesture casually graceful, as if he were dressed for an audience with the Queen instead of stark naked before a duchess. "Thomas Doverspike, your servant, mum."

"And who is your current employer, Mr. Doverspike?"

"I work for a small counting house off and on, doing odd jobs. But I don't plan on staying there. No, indeed. A Doverspike always has an eye out for the main chance, my old gaffer used to say. I figure a man of Mr. Beddington's stripe could use a fellow with my talents. I'm a dab hand at most anything."

Artemisia didn't doubt it. Odd jobs for a counting house probably made him a bill collector of sorts. After seeing his darker glances, she pitied anyone in debt to Mr. Doverspike's employer.

"So you think this Mr. Beddington is a friend of my father's?"

"More like his particular friend. A bloke don't hear of one's success without the other mentioned in the same breath. Stands to reason they're on friendly terms."

"Nothing of the sort," she said crisply, deciding a judicious slice of the truth might serve to deflect further questions. "Mr. Beddington just happens to be the trustee of my father's estate during his incapacity. No more, no less." She didn't feel the need to add *and my late husband's fortune as well*. Wherever Mr. Doverspike was getting his information, it was much too on point for her comfort. "And what services did you intend to offer Mr. Beddington?"

"Even gentlemen like Mr. Beddington need some-one with connections on the low side of respectable, if you catch my meaning." Mr. Doverspike's smile flattened into a grimace. "Not that being your god of war ain't a fine position, but there's not much future in it, is there? I plan to make something of myself one day, and a bloke like Beddington's just the one to help me do it."

"Your ambition does you credit, I dare say. It's quite unlikely, but *if* I see Mr. Beddington, I will mention you. At present, the post of Mars is all I can offer." For a moment, Artemisia's imagination ran amok with the idea of Mr. Doverspike's less-than-respectable connec-tions. He definitely had a wildness about him, a raw edge of danger.

"My thanks, Your Grace."

Light shafted in shallow pools near the base of the tall windows that lined the south side of her studio, heralding the sun's zenith. The morning was nearly spent and it was time to put aside her sketches. The consideration of light was only part of why she insisted her models arrive early and on time. The last thing she needed was her mother or younger sis-ters having a run-in with one of her young gods. Artemisia might be a duchess, but that wouldn't stop Constance Dalrymple from pitching a fit over what she perceived as Artemisia's lack of decorum and downright fast behavior.

Artemisia could hold her own in an argument, but she preferred to avoid one if she could. What her mother didn't know wouldn't hurt her.

"That's all for today," she said, waving him away. "Pray be more punctual on the morrow. See Cuthbert on the way out for your pay."

"As you wish, Your Grace."

There it was again, the graceful bow that spoke more of courtly dancing than seedy companions. The contradiction between his country speech and his occasional cultivated gesture troubled her. She doubted anyone else would have marked the inconsistency, but art had honed her skills of observation to a fine point.

His interest in Beddington wasn't something to be easily dismissed either. If Mr. Doverspike wasn't such an appealing subject, his curiosity alone would be enough to convince her to let him go. The pointed questions about Beddington were dangerous enough on their face, but when voiced by a decidedly rough-edged fellow, they were even more troubling.

Artemisia couldn't put her finger on it, but there was something not quite right about Thomas Doverspike.

Chapter Three

"There you are, Artemisia dear. Finally." Constance Dalrymple lifted the cup of chocolate to her exquisitely rouged lips. "We were just going over the final preparations for the ball. I need assurance that your Mr. Beddington has the arrangements well in hand."

Artemisia smiled a greeting to her younger sisters, Delia and Florinda, who were yawning over their breakfasts. Their mother kept the girls trotting at a breakneck pace late into each evening, trying to make certain the Misses Dalrymple were seen in the most flattering light at all the fashionable milieus. The London Season was in full blossom. In the quest for husbands for both her sisters, Artemisia was playing reluctant hostess to a masked ball a fortnight hence, a frivolity for which she had little patience and even less interest. But it had to be borne for the sake of domestic peace.

"Mr. Beddington's assistant is bringing over the bills for approval later today." Artemisia sat at the head of the long mahogany table. Maintaining her position as mistress of the household was a constant battle while her mother was in residence. She nodded her thanks to Cuthbert as he set a pot of chocolate at her elbow and poured the frothy delight into an eggshell-thin china cup. "Have no fear, Mother. Your credit at the milliner's is still good."

"You think I'm worried about the money?" Constance's powdered eyebrows shot up. "Merciful heaven, no. Your father, God love him, made certain his lambs should never fret about finances, even though they're now sadly in want of a father's guidance. No, it's the guest list. Have we received a single response?" Without waiting for Artemisia's reply, she hurried on. "I'll have you know, the Viscountess of Shrewsbury positively snubbed me at the opera last night before a wide circle of the best folk. It was most humiliating."

Constance pulled a handkerchief stiff with Belgian lace from her cuff and dabbed at the corners of her dry eyes. Artemisia suspected that if her mother hadn't married Angus Dalrymple, Constance could have had a bright career on the London stage.

"We've had Lady Shrewsbury to tea a dozen times and put up with her pasty-faced little daughter for any number of house parties, and yet she waltzed past me without so much as a how-de-do." Constance gave an injured sniff. "And do you want to know why?"

"No, but I expect you'll tell me." Artemisia sipped her chocolate, hoping Cuthbert would return shortly with a plate of buttered eggs. She made do with a spare breakfast of tea and toast before beginning her work each morning. By the time the rest of the household roused, Artemisia had worked up an appetite. And this morning's session with Mr. Doverspike had roused more than a taste for jam and crumpets.

With a steely glint of triumph in her light gray

eyes, Constance plopped down a dog-eared copy of
The Tattler. "Imagine my horror at seeing your pec-
cadilloes flaunted before the entire *ton*. Your outrageous and lewd behavior is robbing your sisters of a
chance for happiness. Really, Artemisia, it is too bad
of you. What will people think?"

"If people want to believe ill of a person they
will, whether they read it in a scandal sheet or not,"
Artemisia said evenly. "The only thing worse than
being accused of lewd behavior is having it not be
true."

Delia erupted in a giggle that was immediately silenced by Constance's black frown.

"Mother, I have never engaged in lewd behavior."
The Tattler's scathing words still stung her heart, but
her mother's belief in them hurt even more. "Those
who know me can attest to my faithfulness to my
husband, my dutiful mourning of his passing and that
my bed has been cold as a nun's ever since."

Artemisia didn't feel the need to add that her marriage bed had been nearly as chilly as her widow's
bower.

"Honestly, dear, you might temper your speech."
Her mother's brows lowered. "Have a care for your
sisters' delicate ears."

"And have them go to the marriage bed as igno-
rantly as I went to mine?" Artemisia shook her head.
If not for the frantically whispered explanations from
Rania, her beloved Indian *ayah,* the mercifully brief
coupling with her elderly husband would have been
horrifying instead of just painful and embarrassing.
"Knowledge of the world is the best defense against
it. Delia and Florinda deserve better."

"Listen to you," Constance said with a forced
laugh. "As if marriage was a thing to be guarded

against. You did well enough for yourself by it, *Your Grace*." Her mother's tone dripped acid.

Despite the four-decade difference in their ages, Theodore Pelham-Smythe, the Duke of Southwycke, was considered quite a catch for a girl with nothing but precocious artistry and her father's impressive fortune to her credit. Southwycke had gained a badly needed infusion of funds and Angus Dalrymple's eldest became a "by-God Duchess." Few could cross the chasm from well-moneyed nabob to the lofty heights of aristocracy, but the canny Scot had managed it by arranging his daughter's splendid match. Artemisia looked upon the marriage as a sort of last request from her father and went willingly, if unenthusiastically, to the altar.

"If you've no thought for my peace of mind," Constance said with pursed lips, "you might at least guard your behavior in order to allow your sisters their chance at a titled match."

"There's more to life than a title," Artemisia said with a shudder at her wedding-night memories.

For form's sake, His Grace had visited her boudoir once a week. Those hours were most often spent playing companionable chess before her fire. Sometimes Artemisia read the latest installment of Dickens aloud while Theodore slipped into the light sleep of advancing years in his easy chair. The duke became simply "Teddy" to her in those quiet moments, and she mourned his passing as she might a distant uncle's.

"I'll happily settle for 'Lady' before my name, thank you very much," Delia said with a dramatic flourish that was an unaffected imitation of their mother's theatrics. "What more is there?"

"W-well, what about l-love?" Florinda stammered.

"I suspect love is overrated," Artemisia said. Love she was prepared to do without, but lust was another thing altogether. Artemisia was determined never to marry again and lose the freedom of widowhood. However, Rania assured her that the duke's unsatisfactory performance was no measure of all men. Intrigued, Artemisia was giving serious thought to acquiring an experienced lover, especially since her session with Mr. Doverspike that morning left her with a flutter in her drawers that wouldn't settle itself.

Now at twenty-five, even with her title and fortune, Artemisia was firmly on the shelf, especially since her stepson, Felix, would come into his majority in little over a year. Once Felix took a wife, Artemisia would be known as the dowager duchess. That dour title fairly reeked of Epsom salt and stale breath.

Would any man, say even a man like Thomas Doverspike, want to bed a dowager?

But until Delia and Florinda were suitably wed, her parents and siblings would remain in residence. And Artemisia preferred to take a lover to her bed without having to sneak him past the room where her mother and her increasingly delusional father slept.

Since histrionics obviously weren't swaying Artemisia into a more biddable frame of mind, Constance abandoned the pretense of tears and tucked the hanky back into her cuff. "You have a title to shelter behind. But how shall your poor sisters hope to find suitable husbands if your behavior causes us to be shunned by Polite Society?"

"Rest easy, we shall not be shunned. I received word yesterday that the Queen and Prince Albert plan to attend your ball," Artemisia said. Young Queen Victoria had found such rapture in marriage

to her somber German cousin, she heartily approved
of love in general and was charmed by the idea of a
masked affair. "The Russian ambassador has sent his
acceptance as well. Once word slips out that the royals are coming, the rest of the *ton* will batter down
the doors like a herd of stampeding elephants."

"Surely th-they'll have better costumes th-than
that," Florinda said with an innocent stammer.

"Eat your breakfast, girl," Constance said, fanning
herself in her excitement. "Remember what I told
you about speaking out of turn. In fact, it's best if
you don't speak at all, Florinda darling. Men don't
like women who push themselves forward."

She cast a reproving eye once more at Artemisia,
then seemed to remember that her daughter's title
was probably responsible for this glorious coup.
"Just think! The Queen and the Prince here in my—I
mean, your—home. Oh, we have so much to do."
Constance pushed back from the table, pulled a slip
of paper from her bodice and handed it to Artemisia.
"Here are the names of potential suitors for your sisters. They both seem to be eligible and come from
the finest of families, but do have your Mr. Beddington do some investigating, would you, dear?"

Artemisia frowned at the list. "Lord Shrewsbury?
The snubbing Lady Shrewsbury's son?"

"He'd do quite well for our Delia. From what I've
heard, the viscount has had a run of bad luck at the
whist tables of late and is sorely in need of funds."
Constance smiled with feline satisfaction. "Let's see
her ladyship snub me with the Queen looking on."

"And the Honorable Trevelyn Deveridge," Artemisia
read. "A second son?"

"The second son of the Earl of Warre. He should do
nicely for the third daughter of Angus Dalrymple,"

Constance said with a trace of annoyance. "I needn't remind you how influential Lord Warre is in the House of Lords. Even without a title, Trevelyn Deveridge will one day be a man of importance. And his older brother has only managed to sire a string of daughters. Once the earl passes, Trevelyn Deveridge will be only one heartbeat from an earldom."

"Mother, you're talking about a man's life," Artemisia said, tight-lipped with irritation. Constance Dalrymple's stalking of the aristocracy was more bloody-minded than her father's beaters before a tiger hunt.

"Have I said anything untrue?" Constance said with a roll of her eyes. "I'm merely being practical."

Cuthbert arrived with her breakfast in time to save Artemisia from making a reply she might later regret. "Mr. Shipwash has arrived, madam. He awaits your pleasure in the study."

"Mr. Shipwash, Mr. Shipwash. Always he sends an underling. Why on earth do we never see Mr. Beddington himself?" Constance demanded. "I don't care how astute the man is. Surely attending the Duchess of Southwycke is not beneath him."

"I believe the *Valiant* has docked," Artemisia said. "Perhaps he's seeing to the disposition of the tea shipment we've been expecting."

"Still . . ." Constance frowned, then pointed to the paper with the names on it. "Do be good enough to remember my request to him, won't you, dear?"

Despite her growling belly, Artemisia excused herself and left her mother and sisters to stew over their costumes for the coming fete. Once she stepped into the hall, Cuthbert appeared at her elbow.

"Madam, before you begin with Mr. Shipwash, perhaps you would do well to see the other gentleman who is waiting," Cuthbert said softly.

"Another gentleman?"

"Yes, Your Grace. He claims to have been sent by Mr. Phelps. This way, if you please."

Artemisia followed her butler to the parlor, where she found a young man twisting his cap in nervousness. He reeked of gin, but he ducked his head deferentially when he saw her.

"Beggin' your pardon, Your Grace. I'm terrible sorry for bein' late, but the idea of shuckin' outta me skivvies had me all flummoxed. I only meant to stop at the tavern for a minute, to screw up me courage, so to speak. But after a few pints, I sort of lost track of the time."

Artemisia listened in distracted disbelief as she studied the fellow's features. Blond curls wreathed his head like a disheveled halo, framing a cherubically rounded face that was pretty as a girl's. Obviously, he was Mr. Phelps's answer to her quest for Eros, god of love.

But if this was the model she'd expected earlier, who was Thomas Doverspike? And why did he let her believe him to be her next subject? A sinking sensation dragged at her belly. Could he be that nasty reporter from *The Tattler,* come to ferret out her most intimate secrets by masquerading as her life model? It was too horrible to contemplate.

"It'll never happen again, Your Grace," her would-be Eros promised.

"Indeed, it will not," she said crisply. "The position has been filled." Then, because the young man looked so crestfallen, she turned to Cuthbert. "I believe this young man will serve Southwycke better in the stables than my studio. Might we have a position for him there?"

"Most probably, Your Grace," Cuthbert said.

Her erstwhile model stumbled over himself, thanking her for the opportunity to muck out the stalls rather than strip out of his clothing for a few shillings. She left him in Cuthbert's charge and hurried to see Mr. Shipwash.

Artemisia breathed deeply to quell the tremor in her chest as she walked the long corridor to the study. If Mr. Doverspike was a writer for *The Tattler,* it certainly explained his nosiness. His queries about Mr. Beddington became even more troubling.

Well, she'd have to see about this. Thomas Doverspike would be back in her studio in the morning. And she could think of any number of ways to humble a naked, spying member of the press.

"Good day, Mr. Shipwash," Artemisia said with forced pleasantness to the stoop-shouldered gentleman cooling his heels in her paneled study. The masculine room had been the duke's private retreat, but since his death, Artemisia had claimed it as her own. "Be kind enough to close the door and we'll get right to business."

"Very good, Your Grace."

James Shipwash spread the portfolio before her and took notes while Artemisia scanned the documents, nodding his agreement to her changes and answering her queries succinctly. If Mr. Shipwash disagreed, he was encouraged to explain himself. Sometimes Artemisia heeded his advice, and sometimes she brought Shipwash round to her point of view.

"That covers everything, I believe. Oh, before I forget, my mother wished to have the affairs of these gentlemen examined—Lord Shrewsbury the younger and Mr. Trevelyn Deveridge." She handed the slip of paper to Mr. Shipwash.

"How soon do you wish a report?"

"You have until the masked ball. Mother intends to marry off my sisters to these gentlemen. I want to make sure they have at least some redeeming qualities before I see my siblings shackled to them." Artemisia eyed the stack of documents the clerk placed before her. Almost as an afterthought, she added, "While you're at it, see what you can discover about one Thomas Doverspike. Of the three, this request is the most urgent."

James Shipwash wrote down the name in his small ledger. "The other two gentlemen will be easy enough to investigate. I've not heard of Thomas Doverspike. Where shall I begin with him?"

"Check the roster of contributors to *The Tattler*. Then try our contacts in the constabulary. I wouldn't doubt there's a criminal dossier on Mr. Doverspike somewhere," she said as she dipped her pen in the inkwell and signed the first document with a flourish.

Josiah H. Beddington

Chapter Four

$\mathcal{P}$ale dawn sent forth pink attempts to penetrate London's soot-choked sky. Felix Pelham-Smythe, soon to be the next Duke of Southwycke, angrily shook off his footman's attempt to assist him as he stumbled from the gilded barouche. He could spare no time to notice the delights of a new day's birth. Not after the depressing night he'd just spent. Besides, he was fully occupied with keeping himself upright as he made his way toward the nearest door of the manor house.

"*My* manor house," he grumbled. "Though you'd never know it. The place is positively infested with Dalrymples."

Just because he wasn't quite of age yet, his stepmother, who was really only a few years older than he, held the purse strings.

Correction, he told himself: Her guard dog, Mr. Beddington, controlled Southwycke's coffers. Between the two of them, they kept Felix on a short leash.

A damned short leash.

Well, that would change with time. But not soon enough to suit Felix. Hellfire, he couldn't even get Beddington to agree to discuss the wholly inadequate size of his piddling allowance. Everything came down from on high through the great man's assistant, Mr. Shipwash, or Felix's not-so-great stepmother.

"As if Beddington was bloody Moses on Mt. Sinai," Felix slurred. He caught a toe on a paving stone and nearly plunged facedown on the path.

His stomach heaved uncertainly, and he hoped he'd make it to his suite without being sick in public. On second thought, what did he care? The servants needed something to clean up anyway.

Felix emptied his belly behind the hydrangea and felt slightly better for it. His head was beginning to pound, and his mouth tasted like a band of gypsies had danced over his tongue. Barefoot.

Drink wasn't entirely to blame for his malaise. Dame Fortune had been cruel to him at the whist tables of late, and Felix didn't have the guineas to pay up.

Didn't Beddington understand a man had to honor his debts?

If Felix had been unlucky at cards, at least he'd been fortunate in his creditors. Amazingly, Lubov and Oranskiy, the visiting Russians holding his markers, were willing to forgive his losses if only he'd do them one teeny, tiny favor.

Put them in touch with Mr. Beddington.

It was a simple enough request. After all, shouldn't a mere man of trade hop to when summoned by a peer of the realm? Well, almost a peer, at any rate.

However, nothing was simple when it involved Beddington. Felix was sick and tired of having his wishes ignored. He didn't care that Beddington had taken Southwycke's dwindling resources and turned the estate into one of the most prosperous in the Empire. His aloof manner was downright insulting. The man was beyond impudent. As soon as Felix took his rightful place as Duke of Southwycke, his first official act would be to sack Beddington.

But his birthday was months away, and he had the sneaking suspicion that Lubov and Oranskiy might turn out to be much less pleasant if he couldn't deliver the estate's trustee to them.

Felix had no idea why they wanted Beddington. In truth, he didn't care.

He only knew he had to flush the reclusive Mr. Beddington into the open.

And soon.

Artemisia nearly tripped over her stepson's body on her way to the garden. Her nose twitched delicately at the alcoholic fumes rising from his prone form. She could almost hear Cuthbert declaiming that it was "bad form to be found snoring off a debauch in one's garden instead of one's bed."

Artemisia sighed and stepped over Felix, satisfied he'd come to no more harm than a crooked neck from sleeping on cold stone. Farther on the path, she met Naresh, her father's Indian servant. Naresh and his wife Rania, Artemisia's *ayah,* had left their sun-drenched home and followed the Dalrymples to the soggy British island out of loyalty to Angus. If ever they regretted their decision, Artemisia had yet to hear them complain.

"Good morning, Larla," Naresh said, templing his fingers in a graceful greeting. He always used Artemisia's milk name instead of her Christian one. It made no difference to Naresh and Rania that Artemisia was a duchess and should be considered a grand, if unconventional, lady. To the humble Indian couple, she would always be Larla, the first round, little white baby they'd cosseted and adored.

"Is my father in the garden?"

"Oh, yes, by Jove. He is gardening fit to wake the dead," Naresh intoned in his singsong English. "He is sending me to fetch a vase for his roses."

"But it's past time for roses to be in bloom," Artemisia said with despair. "He's delusional, isn't he?"

"Do not let your heart be troubling. Seeing roses where there are no roses is no bad thing. Would you rather he was seeing thorns?" Naresh asked philosophically. "He is calling me by name, and I am thinking he will know yours as well. The master, he is having a good day today."

"Well, Southwycke's future master is not," Artemisia said with disgust. "Felix is passed out on the path again. Please see if you can rouse his valet to put him to bed."

"As you wish."

Artemisia continued on in the pale early light. Southwycke's garden was not fashioned after the popular French style, each blade of grass and leaf neatly manicured. This garden grew in unruly profusion. Most of Artemisia's visitors considered it an untidy mess, but she loved it. The rampant growth reminded her ever so slightly of the thick jungles of India, where one never knew if the next bend in the path would reveal a vine-encrusted, abandoned temple or a troop of monkeys screaming through the canopy overhead.

Artemisia heard her father before she saw him.

"Fetch me those pruning shears. Lively now, there's a good lad."

She covered her mouth in despair. Angus surely must know he'd sent Naresh away. He'd fallen to talking to himself now. Even if the words made sense in a garden, the world generally frowned upon speaking to thin air.

Then Artemisia's ears pricked to another voice. Her father wasn't alone, after all. But who could be with him this early?

She peered around a large clump of pampas grass to see who had invaded her garden.

Bold as brass, Thomas Doverspike strolled over to her father and handed him the set of shears he requested.

What on earth was he doing here? She'd told him to come early, but not at the peep of dawn. And she certainly didn't want him troubling her father.

"Thankee kindly," Angus said. "Now just ye hold this stem still while I nip the bugger off. Got to trim it just so or the vine will run wild."

When Mr. Doverspike did as her father bid, Artemisia was surprised by the sudden warmth in her chest. Perhaps there was some good in the fellow, after all, if he could take time for her poor, confused father. Their heads were bent conspiratorially, the dark hair and the balding pate, hunkered close together. Mr. Doverspike was saying something, but Artemisia couldn't quite make it out. She edged nearer without leaving the shelter of the decorative grasses.

". . . and so if I should say to you, 'The tigress feeds by moonlight . . .'" Mr. Doverspike's tone trended up, turning the statement into a question.

Artemisia's father jerked his head toward the younger man and straightened his arthritic back. "Why, I should say, 'But the bear feeds whenever it may.'" Angus Dalrymple laughed as if he'd just uttered the greatest witticism in the world and clapped his grubby hand on Mr. Doverspike's broad shoulder.

"But it's up to men like us to make sure the bear don't feed at all, eh?"

"Yes, quite," Thomas Doverspike agreed, as if their disjointed conversation about wild beasts made perfect sense. "But to do that, I need the key."

The key to what? Artemisia wondered. The manor house? The duke's strongbox? Good Lord, was the man intending to rob them while they slept?

"Didn't ye get my message? I don't have it." Angus scratched the top of his freckled bare head. "Ye want Mr. Beddington. That's the ticket."

Beddington? The last thing she wanted was for her father to steer this stranger even more toward Mr. Beddington. And what was this nonsense about a message? She'd only met Thomas Doverspike yesterday herself. Her father couldn't have sent a message to a man none of them knew. Angus Dalrymple was sliding further into the dementia the doctor warned them was only going to worsen with the passage of time.

And he certainly didn't need someone like Thomas Doverspike giving him a push down that dark road by playing along with his delusional games.

"Mr. Doverspike, a word with you." Artemisia pushed through the grass like a lioness springing on an unsuspecting gazelle.

Her father turned his pale blue gaze on her and smiled, his face a wreath of wrinkles. Constance had wanted to confine him to Bedlam, but Artemisia wouldn't hear of it. The conditions at the hospital for the insane were deplorable. As long as her father didn't do himself or others any harm, she would see him cared for at home.

"Larla, me heart. Give the auld man a kiss, then." His Scottish accent always deepened when he was feeling sentimental.

She gave him a dutiful peck on the cheek and continued to glare at Mr. Doverspike.

"So ye already know Tommy-boy, here, do ye? Weel, that's grand, then, isn't it?" Angus said genially, then turned back to Doverspike. "How did ye happen to meet me Larla?"

"Tommy-boy" dipped in that infuriatingly smooth bow of his, one brow arched in amusement. Artemisia's face felt so hot, she wondered why steam wasn't leaking from her ears.

"Larla?" Mr. Doverspike said quizzically. "That name is a right puzzlement, guv. I only know the lady as Her Grace, the Duchess of Southwycke."

"Weel, we can fix that right now. Doverspike, this is me firstborn and the apple of me eye, Larla Dalrymple. Her mother gave her the name Artemisia—after her father, Artie Campbell, ye ken—and old Theodore Pelham-Smythe pitched in the duchess part . . . haven't seen him around much of late, have I?" Angus paused and worried his bottom lip for a moment. Then he shrugged off the mystery. "But to me she'll always be me Larla. Won't ye, sweeting?"

Her father slipped his arm around her waist and tugged her close to plant a dry kiss on her temple. Gently, she disengaged herself. Her family relationships were not fodder for the likes of Thomas Doverspike. Especially since now she was convinced he must be a reporter of some ilk trying to learn more of the family's intimate secrets. To trade on her father's misfortune—truly, members of the press had no shame.

"Father, Naresh will be back to help you momentarily. Mr. Doverspike and I have some business to discuss," she said with a pointed glance that dared

him to dispute her word. "We haven't time for pleas-
antries just now."

"Och, and more's the pity." Angus shook his balding head. "If ye haven't time, ye haven't anything."

"Very wise," Mr. Doverspike said with a mischie-
vous glance at Artemisia. Did the man just wink at
her? "I suspect you are a philosopher of sorts, Mr.
Dalrymple."

"Angus, son. I'm too old to stand on ceremony.
Call me Angus." He waved them off. "Hurry on with
yourselves then. Only mind the python on the path
as ye go."

Python, indeed. Artemisia shook her head. The
only snake in this garden was the unconscious Felix.

And possibly the mysterious Mr. Doverspike.

Artemisia was relieved to see that Naresh had col-
lected her stepson and bundled him off to his bed
before Mr. Doverspike had the pleasure of seeing a
future peer foxed out of his mind.

Doverspike followed closely behind her, humming
a tune she didn't recognize. Probably a shockingly
ribald drinking song, but at least it allowed her to
know he was there.

Once, on a tiger hunt, Naresh told her that wild
creatures had a sixth sense that allowed them to feel
when eyes were upon them. Was Thomas Doverspike's dark gaze focused on her right now, probing
her secrets, looking for a point of weakness? A delicious shiver tickled down her spine and settled at its
base.

This will never do.

She stopped, turned back suddenly and bumped
right into him. He reached out to catch her as she tottered. Her whole body was pressed tight against him.

Dressed *en dishabille* as she was, without stays and whalebone to buttress her form, she could feel every solid plane of him. The broad expanse of his chest, his tight, flat abdomen, even his muscular thighs, and his . . .

Artemisia gulped as she realized what other part of Mr. Doverspike became suddenly rock hard.

"He's right, you know." His voice was a low rumble, like the purr of a full-grown tiger. He smelled of the wild, too—all wood smoke and rose clippings and green, growing things. "He's absolutely right."

Who is? Artemisia wanted to ask, but the words got caught up in her throat. She didn't trust herself to speak for fear an unruly shiver would slip out with her words.

" 'If we haven't time, we haven't anything.' " He studied her face with unhurried absorption, making no move to release her as he ought.

It was one thing to reach out to catch her when she was in danger of losing her balance, but it really was positively indecent the way he was holding her now—so close she could feel his heartbeat, feel her own quickening into the same racing rhythm.

A woman could sink into those dark eyes and never be heard from again. Artemisia felt herself begin to tumble into them. If she tilted her head, he might very well kiss her.

This will most certainly never do.

Artemisia shoved against his chest, and he released her immediately. She stomped away from him toward the house.

"You're wrong, Mr. Doverspike," she called over her shoulder. "For some things, there is not enough time in the world."

Chapter Five

$\mathscr{A}$t first Trev thought he'd overplayed his hand and scared her shy of him. Still, he thought he sensed a moment when her body melted into his before she shoved him away. He really shouldn't have held her so close, but damnation, she felt good in his arms.

He feared he'd been sacked as well as rebuffed, but clearly the duchess meant for him to follow. Else she wouldn't continue to glance back at him.

"Come along, Mr. Doverspike, don't dawdle."

"Oh, that's right," he drawled. "The sun waits for no one."

"Precisely." She sailed through the halls to her sun-lit studio, claiming the space by right and sweeping all lesser mortals out of her way.

Without further instruction, Trev slipped into the changing room, peeled out of his clothes and donned the comfortable robe. He took several deep breaths before he rejoined Her Grace, willing his lust into quiescence.

The duchess might have once been a married woman, and from the number of covered canvases in her studio, he was sure she'd painted a veritable pantheon of naked men. Yet the way her green eyes flared with alarm when he held her close was more reminiscent of a virgin.

She was seated with her drawing accoutrements at the ready when he emerged in his robe. Light from the floor-to-ceiling windows behind her bathed her in luminescence, gilding her dark hair with the luster of polished jet. Fashion favored blond curls, but they seemed insipid to Trevelyn compared to Lady Southwycke's dusky beauty. Her head was bent over her sketchbook, completely absorbed in her work. She was so lovely, his member rose of its own volition, despite his determination against just such a reaction.

Then she looked up, the disdain on her pouty lips reminding him how little she thought of him, and his erection shriveled.

That's for the best, he thought as he went to collect his helmet and *gladius.*

"No, no props today." She stood to adjust her easel. "I only want to capture your basic lines without any distractions."

No distractions? The woman herself was a walking distraction. He'd bet any amount of guineas she didn't know how the light behind her diffused through her thin morning gown, rendering it nearly transparent. He could see the outline of her shapely legs quite clearly. For one who prided herself on keen observation, she didn't look to herself very often.

Or maybe she did. Maybe she was completely aware of the allure of the unobtainable and used that knowledge against her models with sadistic ruthlessness. Was she certain none of the baseborn fellows she employed would dare raise so much as their eyes toward her, even though their rampant cocks showed no such reticence?

"Mr. Doverspike, whenever you're ready we can begin," she said evenly. "I seem to recall your claim that you were not shy, so if you please . . ."

She let the command dangle unspoken in the air. Trev began to mentally count backward from one hundred in an effort to maintain control over his body. He drew off the robe and let it fall to the floor.

Her green gaze slid over him, critical and unflinching. He forced himself to breath normally. *92, 91 . . .*

Did she feel anything at all when she looked at him? Even the slightest flicker of desire? Or was he just a sentient bowl of fruit as far as she was concerned, an interesting problem for her to resolve in lights and darks?

"If you find the studio too chilly, I can ring for Cuthbert to stir up the fire," she offered.

"No, I'm fine, thank you." The idea of another person, even a servant, witnessing his struggle to master himself was too distressing to contemplate. He welcomed the slight chill in the room at this point.

88, 87 . . . Her gaze dipped to his groin, and he ground his teeth. *83, 82 . . .*

Her brows drew together in a frown as she bent to her work. The scooped neckline of her morning dress fell forward, giving him a clear view of the hollow between her breasts. He flexed his fingers, trying to banish the thought of plunging them into her bodice to explore the luscious peaks and tender valley.

76, 75 . . . Despite his best efforts, his body roused to her.

"I'm most pleased to see that you've become accustomed to my presence," she said without looking up from her renderings. Then she turned her penetrating gaze on him. "Oh!" The hint of a satisfied smile twitched her lips as she flicked his erection with a fleeting glance before returning her attention to her sketch pad. "Well, give it a bit more time and this will all seem quite normal to you."

"Care to wager on that?" he murmured between clenched teeth.

She appeared not to have heard him, for she continued scratching her chalk over the paper with deft, sure strokes.

"For someone who hasn't much to say now, you certainly were quite talkative in the garden." Her eyes flashed back at him, this time with repressed irritation. "Since my father fell ill, we've tried to speak to him in sensible ways, even when he makes little sense in return. Perhaps you thought you were being kind by indulging in fanciful wordplay with someone whose mind wouldn't know the difference—"

So she'd overheard the exchange of code between himself and Angus Dalrymple. Whatever else might have slipped her father's mind, he still responded to the set phrases of the Corps properly. Trev didn't want to endanger her by revealing the true nature of his conversation with her father, so it was best to let her imagine what she would of him.

Even if it was the worst.

"Let me advise you, Mr. Doverspike, I don't appreciate your making sport of the afflicted."

"That was never my intention, I assure you," he said.

"Then what is your intention?" she demanded, her cheeks dashed with crimson. "Asking unnecessary questions, accosting an old man in his garden—just what is your game? Are you gathering a few more tidbits for those gossipmongers you write for? If you make my father a laughingstock, I promise I'll instruct my solicitor to sue you and your miserable employers for every pot of ink they possess."

"What?"

"You may drop the pretense, Mr. Doverspike. I know Mr. Phelps did not send you to me. The real model came later yesterday, too far gone with drink to be of any use." She narrowed her eyes at him, daring him to deny his subterfuge. "All those questions about my father and our trustee—you aren't employed by any counting house. You write for *The Tattler,* don't you?"

Trevelyn smirked in surprise. He'd been on the receiving end of *The Tattler*'s sharp lash more than once. He had no more use for that yellow rag than she obviously did.

"I promise you faithfully that I do not write for *The Tattler* or any of its competitors. I abhor them."

"Careful, Mr. Doverspike," she said in a voice laced with strychnine. "Your Wiltshire accent is slipping. Now, who are you and why are you here?"

Funny how being stark naked made it harder to hide behind an assumed persona. Trev's mind churned furiously for a plausible ruse.

"I . . . oh, hang it all, you might as well know that I am responsible for your real model's morning debauch. I chanced to meet him over a pint, and he told me about this job. All he had to do was stand around in the altogether, he said." Trevelyn shrugged. "It sounded a much easier way to turn a coin than my usual employment, so I helped him into a rum pot and took his place."

"And your accent?"

"I thought you probably used country bumpkins for this post, so it made sense to sound like one." He cocked his head at her. "But truth to tell, this job is not so easy as it looks."

The sincerity in his tone seemed to soften her anger.

"No, I suppose it isn't," she conceded. "But why were you talking with my father?"

"Does one need a reason to strike up a conversation with a pleasant old man?" A dollop of flattery never hurt, and Trev knew he could be charming when the occasion called for it. "Truly, I didn't see the harm in humoring him with a bit of nonsense. It will not happen again."

She sniffed, apparently mollified by his answers. "Indeed, it will not. I encourage my models to speak their minds with me, but I would appreciate it if you did not seek out my father again. From now on, kindly present yourself to Cuthbert instead of skulking around in the garden. There are those who would consider your actions this morning on the order of trespass." She sent him a frosty glare. "That is how I will consider them if they are repeated."

"Yesterday you chided me for being late. Today I was early and you're still unhappy." Trev decided a good offense would stand him in better stead than a good defense, and Her Grace had just encouraged him to speak his mind. "Is there anyone who can please you?"

It occurred to him that he had yet to see a smile of real pleasure on her lips. He'd like to be the man to coax one there.

But for now, he had to remember his place. He was Thomas Doverspike, a common fellow who'd worked his way into her presence through guile. And she was a duchess, after all. As Trevelyn Deveridge, he might seek to charm her, but Thomas Doverspike needed a job. And he'd just been insolent to his employer.

"I ask your pardon, Your Grace. I misspoke." He ducked his head deferentially. She regarded him for a few moments, her brows knitted together as if she were trying to weigh him for veracity.

"No, you didn't. You said exactly what you thought," she finally said. "No one has done that to me in a long time."

"I'm sorry if I offend."

"No, you're not," she said with a tight grin. "And I'm not sorry either. In fact, it's rather refreshing to hear the truth from someone. I *am* hard to please. But it's only because I care so deeply about my work and am rarely satisfied with it. I suppose that perfectionism spills over into other things."

"I'm sure your paintings are quite wonderful."

"But you wouldn't know because you've never seen them."

He shook his head.

"No one has. I am doing the entire Greek pantheon, and until I finish with the major gods, I won't have a showing. It's rather like a symphony: No one would be satisfied with just the first movement. Each painting will be part of a larger whole."

"Then you intend to sell them all together?"

"Sell them? Why would I do that?" she said with a frown.

"The usual reason is to make money."

She shrugged. "Fortunately, I have no such need."

"Then how will you ever know if your paintings are any good? I mean, unless someone is willing to plunk down a bag of guineas for them, how do you measure their worth?"

"Art is measured by how it affects those who view it," she said.

"And how does painting the gods affect you?" His voice was huskier than he'd intended.

She drew a few lines on her sketch pad as she pondered. The duchess didn't seem to sense his underlying question. He drew a relieved breath.

"The gods were men idealized," she finally said. "Don't we all seek perfection?"

"So what you're telling me, Your Grace, is that you're looking for the perfect man."

Chapter Six

ooking for a perfect man?" Her cheeks bloomed with fresh color. "Certainly not. Besides, perfection is only an ideal. It does not exist in men. I can only strive in the creation of it."

"And thus trump even the Almighty." He raised a brow at her. She looked back to her sketch pad, but as Trev watched, her knuckles whitened around her chalk. Clearly, he'd struck too close to the mark. Then, slowly, her mouth curved into an enigmatic smile.

"Sit down, Mr. Doverspike," she ordered with calm.

"On what, Your Grace?"

"On your posterior, of course. Mars did not have overstuffed armchairs, you know."

He did as he was bid, feeling even more ridiculous seated on the cold floor than he did standing. If he sat with his knees raised, his ballocks would dangle between his legs on the polished oak. If he sat with his legs straight before him, he'd feel unnaturally stiff, like a wooden marionette whose strings had been cut. He crossed his legs, Hindu-fashion, but felt too exposed by half.

The duchess sighed. "Let me help you," she said. "I experimented with a pose last night in my sketching. Place your weight on one hip, legs to the side."

She left her sketch pad and came to stand over him. It was a maneuver clearly designed to make him feel small.

He stared up at her without a blink, determined not to let her best him. "How do you want my arms?"

"Lean on one palm," she suggested. "No, a little farther. Here, like this, Mr. Doverspike." The duchess knelt and positioned his hand away from his body so his torso was stretched into a reclining pose.

"You know, I've never been naked with a woman who didn't call me by my Christian name," he said. "Under the circumstances, I don't suppose you could call me Thomas?"

"It is precisely because of the circumstances that I must call you Mr. Doverspike," she said. "And besides, you aren't naked. You are nude."

"Feels naked to me."

Her face screwed into a puzzled frown as she leaned forward and took his other hand. The heady floral fragrance she wore tickled his nostrils. Was that lilac or oleander, or some exotic mix of the two?

"I'm not quite sure where I want this other hand," she said.

The neckline of her gown fell forward again as she leaned toward him. Trevelyn had a suggestion for where he could put his hand, but he wisely kept it to himself. His fingers tingled at the nearness of her breasts. He began to mentally count from one hundred again to gain mastery over his response to her.

"Why did your father call you Larla? I know that's not your given name."

She looked at him sharply. "Larla was my baby name. It's not important."

"It must be to him if he still remembers it. What does Larla mean?"

Her lips twitched in a brief smile as she put his hand first on his hip and then palm down on the floor before him. "When I was a child, my *ayah* always said we all have secret names, names that call to our true selves."

He watched her lips as she spoke, captivated by the play of her pointed little tongue against her teeth and lips. Secret names. Did she suspect he wasn't really Thomas Doverspike? For a moment he regretted the necessity of deceiving her.

"And if you learned that secret name and its meaning," she went on, "you'd know that person as well as if you climbed into the same skin."

He'd be satisfied with just getting next to her skin. As she fussed around him, what he could see of her was flawless, smooth and pale. He couldn't help wondering about the parts he couldn't see.

"Then by that reckoning, I'm halfway to knowing you, Your Grace. Now I only need discover what Larla means."

Trevelyn knew he was being brashly forward, but how could she expect a man to sit around wearing nothing but a smile and not feel some degree of familiarity? Especially when she leaned over him, casually arranging his limbs and adjusting his posture to suit her.

"What do you think it means?" she asked as she moved his right hand from one spot to another.

Her delicate fragrance beckoned to him. When she shifted, he was rewarded with another tantalizing peek at the tops of her breasts, pale, rounded mounds of perfect flesh. Would her nipples be pink and sweet as sherbet or ripe and rosy as berries? He closed his eyes and began to count backward again.

This time, in French.

Her touch was warm, and where her fingers nudged and prodded a shower of sparks sizzled over his skin. For a moment he imagined her hand wandering over his groin. He bit the inside of his cheek. If he let his mind tread that road, he'd be well on his way to disgracing himself before her, spilling his seed like a callow youth in the first throes of lust.

"Doesn't this affect you at all?" he asked, giving up trying to quell his swelling erection. "If it doesn't, I'm guessing Larla must mean ice maiden."

"There's no need to be insulting," she said with an unmistakable catch in her voice, a breathlessness that told him his nearness had moved her. "Just because I'm not helpless with lust over your nude body does not mean I'm without feeling. I bridle myself for the sake of my art."

"And you're always in control?"

"I must be."

"Care to put that notion to the test?"

She bit her lip and looked away, determined to ignore his question. "Oh, botheration!" she finally exploded. "I can't decide where to put your right hand."

"I've an idea." He reached up and placed his hand along the side of her neck, his fingers gentle on her nape. She gasped but didn't jerk away. Slowly, he pulled her head down till her breath was a moist warmth on his face. Her lips were parted, her eyes wide. She made no move to free herself.

Trevelyn closed half the distance between their lips, watching her intently. She held her breath for a heartbeat or two; then a soft moan escaped her lips and her astonishing green eyes fluttered closed.

He took her mouth, tasting, questing. Her lips trembled beneath his, then softened. When they parted, he slid his tongue in to explore her luscious secrets. To his delight, she actually suckled him for a moment, then twisted her tongue with his in a warm, wet joust.

Definitely no ice maiden.

Trevelyn sat up straighter without releasing her mouth and cupped her cheek with his left hand. Her skin was as exquisitely soft as he'd imagined it would be. He trailed his fingers over her silky smoothness, down her neck to brush the tops of her breasts with feather-light strokes. He toyed with the hollow between them, sliding his fingers in and out of her bodice. Then he cupped one of her breasts in his hot palm. Her nipple was hard beneath the sheer muslin of her simple dress.

She grasped both his shoulders and pushed herself away from him.

"Mr. Doverspike!"

"Larla," he whispered.

She scrambled to her feet. "Kindly remove yourself this instant."

He stood and cocked his head at her. "You're giving me the sack because you enjoyed kissing me?"

"Yes. I mean no," she stammered, realizing she'd admitted to warming to his kiss. She backed away several paces. "I mean this should never have happened. There are certain proprieties that must be observed."

He looked down at his bare body. His cock bobbed merrily. "How can there be any propriety when one of us is naked as Adam?"

"You don't understand anything about art." Deep in her throat, she made a noise of frustration. "You're making a mockery of everything I'm trying to accomplish."

He cast her a sideways glance. "You arrange matters so you spend long hours alone with naked men in circumstances that demean them. I think you need to ask yourself what it is you're really trying to accomplish."

Her eyes flared, then narrowed. "Get out."

He bent to retrieve his robe and caught a flash of movement. Behind her, he saw a figure at one of the windows.

A man was grappling with an awkward black box on a tripod. It looked suspiciously like daguerreotype equipment. If that blighter had captured him kissing the duchess on one of those copper plates . . .

"I mean it, Mr. Doverspike. I want you gone this instant, do you hear?" She stamped her aristocratic foot like an empress. "At least do me the courtesy of looking at me when I speak to you."

Trev shrugged on the robe and knotted the sash at his waist, never taking his eyes off the man at the window. The photographer realized suddenly that he'd been discovered. He snatched up his equipment and took to his heels.

"Excuse me, Your Grace." Trevelyn pushed past her and mounted the sill. He threw open the window and turned back to her. "I'll return shortly so you can continue to tell me how much you dislike me and want me gone."

He dropped out of the window and disappeared into the wilds of the duchess's overgrown garden.

Chapter Seven

Clarence Wigglesworth had struck gold more surely than the horde of fools rushing off to the wastes of California. The images he'd just captured of the Duchess of Southwycke and her low-born model were priceless. It was more than he'd dared hope for when he convinced his editor to invest in this expensive daguerreotype equipment. Thank fortune, the newest cameras allowed the exposure time to be sliced from fifteen minutes to only one. Still, that kiss had been a protracted affair. Now Clarence's foresight and ingenuity were about to pay off. Handsomely.

For a moment, Clarence wondered if the duchess would pay him more for the daguerreotype than *The Tattler*. No, he told himself, he was a journalist, not a blackmailer. The public deserved to see one of the peers of the realm practically in flagrante delicto, taking advantage of a poor, common fellow. Though truth to tell, it looked as if the bloke welcomed the duchess's abuse. Still, the public had a right to know that the high-and-mighty's feet were also made of clay. The titled gentry were just as weak, just as ordinary in their vices as anybody else.

Oh, how misery loved company.

And Clarence now had proof of Her Grace's weakness. If only he could remember the way back through this higgledy-piggledy mess of a garden to the gate at the rear of the property. His informant had left it unlocked and the directions to the part of the house where the duchess kept her nefarious "studio" were most explicit. He'd been curious to see art in progress.

Art, indeed.

So that's what the upper crust calls it, he thought. Looked to him like a good old game of hide the sausage in the making. What he'd seen through the window was no more artistic than what went on in your average bawdy house, though to his sorrow, he could rarely afford to visit those establishments of fleshly bliss.

It was worse, actually, he decided. After all, in Her Grace's studio it was the *man* who was groveling naked on the floor.

That turn-about was enough of an affront to his sensibilities, but then when the duchess knelt down on the floor with him, well . . . it was shocking.

Deliciously shocking.

Now if he could just—

The sound of feet pounding after him down the well-worn path interrupted his thoughts. Clarence glanced back in time to see the duchess's model bearing down on him. The man's robe flapped about him like a demon's tattered wings. Panic gave Clarence extra speed, but the fellow caught up to him, grabbed him and threw him to the ground.

His precious equipment clattered to earth as he rolled with his half-dressed assailant, finally coming to rest beneath the incensed artist's model.

"What do you think you're doing, skulking about a

lady's home like a two-penny peeper?" The man rolled Clarence onto his stomach, ground a knee into his spine and pinioned both his hands behind him.

"I'm no peeper. I'm a member of the press, a writer for *The Tattler*," Clarence whined, twisting his neck so he could eye the man who had him subdued in so demeaning a fashion. "I'm only doing my job. . . ." He stopped long enough to study his attacker for a moment. "Lord Deveridge?"

"No, that would be my brother," the man said.

Clarence remembered that the Earl of Warre had two sons—twins, if his memory served. So this must be the unlucky younger one. "Damned shame to miss a title by a matter of minutes, eh, guv?"

"That's none of your concern. If you wish to be released without having your face rearranged, give me your name and be quick about it."

Deveridge smiled as he spoke, but it was a cold smile, and Clarence didn't doubt he was in danger of a beating.

"Wigglesworth, Clarence Wigglesworth," he said, screwing his courage to the sticking point. "You may have been born a gentleman, but I can take a bloke like you down a peg with just a few strokes of the pen. Best you remember that. You don't want to tangle with a member of the press."

"If you reported on the work of Parliament or the deplorable condition of drains in the city, I'd agree with your characterization of your employment. But I've only apprehended a sneak thief."

"I never stole in my whole living life," Clarence protested. Apples from vending carts and the occasional hot bun didn't count.

"You steal people's good names, people who've not done you any harm, assassinating their characters with the poison that drips from your pen." Deveridge leaned down menacingly. "You will not write another syllable, good, bad or indifferent, about the Duchess of Southwycke."

"But—"

"If a breath of scandal touches Her Grace in that rag you write for, believe me, you will answer for it."

"What will you do? Sue me? I rarely have more than two coins to rub together." Now that he recognized the man as an aristocrat, Clarence felt a little bolder. What did these cultured types know about scrabbling to make a living in London? "What can you threaten me with that's worse than an empty belly?"

"Mr. Wigglesworth, I never make threats. I make promises," Deveridge said with a wolfish grin. "I don't care a fig what you might write about me, but if you sully the duchess's name in any way, I'll kill you."

Judging just by his tone, Deveridge might have been making a comment on the weather, but the casualness of his lethal promise made it all the more chilling. Clarence felt his throat constrict.

"Now that we understand each other, allow me to assist you to your feet." Deveridge stood and offered Clarence his hand. "Pity about your equipment. I hear those things are deucedly expensive." He strolled over and yanked the damning copper plates from the daguerreotype.

For one or two heartbeats, Clarence considered fighting the man for his hard-won coppers, but Deveridge's cold-blooded promise still threatened to loosen his bowels.

"Now, if you're interested in a true journalistic effort," Deveridge continued pleasantly, "might I offer you a tip?"

Clarence gathered up the remains of his photographic debris, his chest heavy. His employer would have his hide for this debacle. "No, thanks. You've done quite enough for me already this day."

The man shrugged in a lordly way. "Suit yourself. I was only going to suggest you make the acquaintance of Basil Philpot, the bailiff for the House of Lords. He knows everything that happens there, on and off the floor, and is quite voluble after only a pint or two. He'd be a good source for a real journalist."

"I *am* a real journalist," Clarence said. "You just don't like my brand of news. Don't you understand, we have to give the public what they want?"

"Perhaps it's time someone gave them what they need," Deveridge said softly, shoving his hands into the pockets of his robe. "Good day, Mr. Wigglesworth. I'm sure you know the way out." He strolled away as if he'd only been taking the air in the duchess's wild garden. Then he stopped and looked back at Clarence with a wintry glare. "Remember my promise."

Clarence swallowed hard and nodded. If he wrote another scurrilous word about Her Grace, he had no doubt Deveridge would make his promise good.

Artemisia swiped away the last of her tears just in time. Mr. Doverspike was climbing back through the window. She sniffed loudly and hoped to heaven her nose wasn't red.

"How can one hope to have a civilized discussion with you if you insist on escaping out windows?" she blustered in an attempt to hide that she'd been crying. "Well? What have you to say for yourself?"

"You said you wanted me gone." He shrugged and

spread his hands in a self-deprecating gesture. "The truth is, you had a reporter from *The Tattler* at your window just now. He and I had a little chat in your garden."

"Is that what—" Artemisia's breath hissed over her teeth. Her day was going from bad to worse. "Then he was at the window when we—"

"Yes, but don't fret, madam. I am in possession of some coppers that will never see the light of day." He pulled the fading daguerreotype plates from the pocket of his robe. The images were shadowy, but she could definitely make out two forms in a shocking embrace. The reclining nude was rampantly aroused, and though the image was blurred, his hand was definitely reaching for her breast.

Mr. Doverspike was right: He wasn't nude, he was naked. Blatantly, unabashedly as bare as Adam, and the answering warmth between her own legs reminded her she'd been playing with Eden's fire.

"This is dreadful." Her mother would be furious. The publication of a damning article in *The Tattler* would probably coincide with Constance Dalrymple's masked fete. "Even without a picture, there'll be a piece about it, and my reputation will be thoroughly ruined. Not that I care so much for myself, but my sisters will suffer horribly for my indiscretion."

"I doubt it," he said smugly. "There will be no article. We came to a not-so-gentlemanly agreement. The reporter in question will refrain from writing about you."

"How can you be so sure?"

"If he doesn't, I won't allow him to continue breathing."

She looked askance at this astounding statement.

She'd sensed danger seething about him, but would he truly do murder for her?

He cocked his head. "I told you I have contacts on the low side of respectable, Your Grace."

She took a deep breath, trying to quell her rioting insides. "Very well. I thank you, Mr. Doverspike, for your help in preserving my honor. Now, if you will kindly get dressed and see yourself out. . . . Please leave an address with Cuthbert where I can send the rest of your pay. I release you from my service."

"What? You haven't finished the painting."

"No, and I never shall." Tears pricked at her eyes again, but she blinked them back. "Please just go."

"Why?"

"I think that's painfully obvious. A line has been crossed, one that is inviolate, between an artist and her subject."

"Just because I kissed you?"

"Because I *allowed* you to kiss me. The fault is mine and you have my profoundest apologies, but I cannot continue to work with you."

"Rubbish," he said. "You hold yourself to an impossible standard. Do you think for a moment the old masters of the canvas didn't have more than a passing acquaintance with their subjects?"

Her cheeks burned. She'd always suspected that was the case. How else did artists capture the expressions of longing and the knowing looks if there hadn't truly been some *knowing* going on?

"Nevertheless, I must ask you to leave."

Mr. Doverspike's mouth hardened into a tight line. "You'll at least give me a good character, I hope."

"Certainly, I'll be happy to write a general letter of reference and send it round with your pay."

"That wasn't quite what I had in mind. I was hoping you'd introduce me to Mr. Beddington and recommend my services to him."

Beddington. Not again. She thought she'd deflected his interest in Mr. Beddington. "That is not something I'm at liberty to do."

"Seems to me you're at liberty to do whatever you jolly well please, Your Grace."

"What could I possibly say to Mr. Beddington about your services? 'Here stands Thomas Doverspike. He takes off his clothes well and frightens members of the press witless.' "

"Hopefully not at the same time."

A laugh erupted from her lips. "No, I daresay. Not at the same time."

"And yet, I've taken my clothes off and frightened *you* witless, haven't I?" He took a step to close the distance between them.

Fright wasn't exactly the right word. Her insides jumped at his nearness, every pore in her body alive and tingling. She could still taste his kiss. She turned from him lest he see how difficult drawing a breath had become for her. "Please leave, Mr. Doverspike, I beg you."

She heard the soft pad of his bare feet on the hardwood and drew a sigh of relief. He was going. Then the sound of rustling pages made her turn around. The man was leafing through her sketch pad.

"What are you doing?"

"Just seeing what we've accomplished together here." He turned the paper sideways and screwed his face into a frown. "Do I really look that ridiculous?"

He pointed to one of the studies depicting him with

the helmet and sword, chest puffed out, military bearing severely at odds with his nudity. It did seem a tad overdone to her, now that she considered it afresh.

He flipped the page. "Oh," he said, his tone thoughtful. "This is what you were trying to do this morning."

"Yes." It was her preliminary sketch of his reclined figure. There was tension in his shoulder muscles as her Mars leaned despairingly toward an unobtainable prize. "Mars is always depicted in military splendor, victorious and virile. I thought I'd take an entirely different tack on the subject. When two forces meet on a field of battle, one side is always declared the loser. This is the god of war in defeat."

"More often than not, both sides lose," he said softly. "Of course, there are some battles that can't be avoided. I've fought in a few. But most wars are just mud and blood for the blokes who must fight them. In this sketch, you've hit upon what war truly is—failure and loss and utter stupidity. Whatever you do, Your Grace, you must finish this work."

"I can't," she said. "You inspired it."

"I inspired failure and loss and utter stupidity?"

Against her will, he drew another laugh from her.

"There, you see," he said. "If we can laugh together, we can work together." He held up the sketch for her to see. "This is important, madam, more important than how little esteem you have for me. This says something about war that no one else has had the courage to say. If you fail to see it through, this vision will haunt you for the rest of your artistic life." He handed the sketch pad to her. "Isn't that worth putting up with me for a little while longer?"

The problem wasn't that she had too little esteem

for him, but rather too much. She'd have to learn to control her response to him if she was to make this work. Still, he was right about the sketch.

"Very well, Mr. Doverspike. Kindly remove your robe and assume the position. The sun will not wait."

Chapter Eight

Her Mars groaned and shifted slightly.

"Don't move," Artemisia ordered. "You'll change the way the light strikes your upraised arm."

"If I don't move, my upraised arm is like to fall off," he complained.

She glanced at the mantel clock. "We have been at this for the better part of an hour," she conceded. "Very well, let's take a break. The tea should still be hot, and I asked Cuthbert to bring round some extra scones. You'll find them under the silver tray."

Thomas Doverspike rose to his feet and donned his robe before helping himself to the offered pastries. Artemisia draped the canvas to keep dust from settling on the fresh paint. With countless coal fires burning, London was ever so much dirtier than Bombay. She poured out two cups of tea, laced his with an extra lump of sugar just as she'd learned he liked it and poured a smidgeon of cream into hers.

"How's it coming?" he asked between cramming bites of the flaky scones into his mouth.

"It's taking shape." Artemisia blew on her tea to cool it before she sipped. She slipped a hand around to massage her lower back. Life models weren't the only ones who suffered muscle cramps.

"Can I see it?"

"Not until it's finished."

She'd made amazing progress on the painting in a few short days. This was going to be an important work. She could feel it in every stroke.

Her paintbrush fairly flew, but she was a stickler for detail, and while parts of the figure leaped off the canvas, other portions were still flat and two-dimensional. Thomas Doverspike's lean musculature was a delight to duplicate and his skin glowed with buoyant health, but she'd left his groin area fuzzy and indistinct. She considered draping him there. A judicious sash or fig leaf would solve the problem, but her artist's heart damned her for a coward. He was beautiful in all his parts. Even in defeat, Mars was still a virile male. It would be less than courageous if she covered him just because the sight of his willie tied her knickers in a knot.

He still experienced rampant erections, but she refrained from direct comment on them. She never tired of looking at him though, the skin over his enraged phallus tight and straining, dark with engorged blood, his ballocks drawn up in a snug mound. She found herself wondering what his shaft would feel like. Would it be smooth in her hand? Warm? The thought made her cheeks burn, and something primitive flared to life in her belly.

She had to think of something else. "Now that you've had a bit of time to get used to it, are you finding your job easier?"

"Why do you ask?"

"A while back it sounded as though you found serving as my model demeaning," she said. "I hope you've changed your thoughts on that."

He shrugged. "Until you've shucked out of your

skivvies and stood there, you wouldn't understand. I guess you'd have to try the job yourself to know what it's like."

"I beg your pardon?" She'd surely misheard him.

"That's not a bad idea, actually," he said, dusting the crumbs off his hands. "It would be a nice rest for both of us. We could trade places and I could draw you for a while."

She almost choked on her tea. "Very funny. For a moment, I thought you were serious."

"I am."

She set down her teacup. "Ludicrous. You're no artist."

"Well, you have me dead to rights there," he said. "I've no eye for composition like you, but I'm not such a bad draftsman. Here, I'll show you."

He fetched her sketch pad and chalk and with a few deft strokes captured Pollux napping in the window, his furry feet tucked beneath his body in a manner that Artemisia thought made him look like a kitty loaf.

"Not bad," she admitted. His lines were clean and sure, the figure of her cat in near perfect proportion.

"I did a bit of mapmaking in the service," he explained. "Well, how about it, Your Grace? Shall we turn and turn about? I promise not to give you three . . . eyes."

"Mr. Doverspike, this is entirely irregular. It just wouldn't be proper for someone in my position," she protested. "It would be . . ."

"Demeaning?"

"Not at all," she said, irritated to have been caught by her own argument.

"Then what's stopping you? Are you afraid?"

"Certainly not," she lied. Then, because she believed that whatever else art was about, it was about truth first of all, she swallowed hard and nodded.

"I must admit I was a bit afraid myself at first," he said.

She scoffed. "You? Mr. Shyness-is-not-one-of-my-faults?"

"Sometimes the only way to face your fears is to ignore them and push through," he said. "Being naked—your pardon, I mean *nude*—before someone you barely know is daunting. But in this case, you know me."

Did she? She still wondered about Mr. Doverspike. She liked him well enough, but he was too self-possessed for a common worker, too subtly dangerous for a member of the gentry. Even though he'd spent time nude in her presence for more than a week, he was still a puzzlement to her. Her skills of observation were higher than most, but she still couldn't discern the secrets of another human heart.

She tried to dismiss memories of his kiss from her mind, but sometimes it rose unbidden. It was like recalling a whirlwind, one that swept reason before it and left devastation in its wake. No doubt looking at his sensual mouth was clouding her judgment now, since she was actually entertaining his outrageous suggestion.

"I'll never be able to explain to you what it's like," he said. "If you truly want to know what it is you're asking of your models, you have to experience it for yourself." He raised a brow at her. "If you dare."

If she didn't do as he suggested, he'd continue to accuse her of demeaning him. The infuriating man had boxed her into a moral corner where she couldn't refuse.

"I'll be right back." She headed for the dressing room. By the time she closed the door behind her, her belly was writhing like a net full of eels. She took a deep breath. She could do this. After all, she did expect her subjects to do this very thing without a qualm. In the interest of fairness, she should know how they felt.

Her hands shook as she removed her paint-spattered smock. The simple muslin day dress came off next. She was down to her chemise, stays and drawers, and realized she couldn't go forward. She was unable to unlace her own corset.

"Are you all right, Your Grace?"

"Yes, I'm fine," Artemisia said, irritated that her voice trembled. *Bloody French dressmakers*. She'd long believed fashion made fools of everyone. How could it be that a grown woman couldn't even undress herself? She hadn't thought of this when she agreed to this farce. Now she'd have to admit she couldn't go through with it.

"Do you need help with your stays?" The sound of his voice told her he was just outside the door.

"How thoughtful of you to offer." She should have realized he'd be intimately familiar with the undressing of women. He wasn't about to let her off on a technicality. She opened the door a crack.

"Yes, Mr. Doverspike, I would appreciate your help," Artemisia said, as if it was the most natural thing in the world for him to assist her with her corset. She was committed now, and the last thing she wanted was for him to see her falter. She turned her back to him, certain he'd know what to do.

She held her breath as he tugged at the knot. When it came free, his fingers worked their way up her spine, pulling her laces loose on each set of eyes.

She realized suddenly that he'd have to lace her back up when they were finished.

She removed the corset and her breasts fell free beneath her thin chemise. She was able to draw a deep breath but didn't feel up to turning to face him. What might she read in his brown eyes now?

"Thank you. I can manage from here," she said quietly.

He withdrew from the small room and left her to face her fears. She lifted her chemise over her head and lowered her drawers. What would he think when he saw her? She wished she provided a mirror for her models. She longed to check for imperfections.

She looked down at herself. Her nipples were at full alert, and if she slipped a hand over her slightly rounded belly to the dark curls at the apex of her legs she suspected she'd find them damp. Her heart pounded and she felt an answering throb in her groin.

Really, this was the most outrageous thing she'd ever done, she decided. She didn't have to go through with it. All she need do was slip back into her drawers and chemise and call for Mr. Doverspike to relace her stays.

But then he'd know her for a coward and a hypocrite. How could she expect her models to do something in the name of art that she was unwilling to do herself?

Artemisia took down the second robe from its peg and slid her arms into the capacious sleeves. She pulled it tight around her, the feel of velvet against her bare skin a surprise. She'd worn any number of velvet gowns before, but with all the layers of undergarments—drawers, chemise, corset, petticoats, crinolines—the soft fabric barely touched her skin and certainly not in such intimate places. The texture rubbing against her naked bottom was positively decadent. She decided she liked it.

"Do you require further assistance, Your Grace?" Mr. Doverspike asked through the door.

"No, thank you," she said, determined to brazen this out. She drew a deep breath and opened the door.

The look of surprise on his face was almost worth the flips her stomach was doing.

She padded to the center of the room. "Well, don't stand there gaping. If you intend to draw me, you'll need more than a handful of fingers. My sketch pad is yours, and you'll find fresh chalk in the top drawer of the little desk."

He quickly retrieved the items and seated himself in her straight-backed chair, crossing one ankle over his knee to cradle the sketchbook. "Whenever you're ready," he said, one corner of his mouth twitching with a suppressed grin.

Suddenly all the levity drained from his features and his eyes went darker. Artemisia felt the heat of his gaze even through the thick velvet. Surely he'd scorch her when his view was unfettered by the robe. She looked down, seemingly fascinated by the swirling grain in the dark hardwood, unable to meet his eyes. She fiddled with her lapels, inching the fabric off one shoulder. Anticipation rippled through her, but now that the moment had arrived, Artemisia wasn't sure she could go through with it. She was about to admit defeat when he cleared his throat.

"You haven't asked how I want you," he reminded her, his voice husky.

She looked up at him, realizing that he'd be the first man to see her in the nude. Her late husband's pitiful poking exploration of her flesh was done in total darkness. Funny that this stranger should know her in a way the man whose name she bore never had.

"How do you want me?" she asked in a small voice.

His lips moved as if he started to say something, then thought better of it. "Turn around, facing away from me," he finally said with gentleness. "It'll be easier."

She obeyed, her heart beating a furious tattoo on her rib cage. She forced herself to take a deep breath.

"Now, let the robe fall slowly from one shoulder. That's good. A little more."

The velvet brushed over her skin, followed by a breath of air as she bared her back to him. Down her spine, past the curve of her waist, the robe cut a diagonal across her figure as it fell to her wrist on the left side.

"Let the robe drop to your elbow on the right. Bend that arm and lift it slightly," he suggested, his voice strangely tight.

He was draping her, she realized, as elegantly as any painter might arrange his subject, using the folds of fabric to create opposing lines and textures. Thomas Doverspike might claim not to be an artist, but he certainly had fine instincts.

The fabric dipped to expose her buttocks. Was that his sharp intake of breath she heard? Heat lightning raced over her skin, leaving her feeling warm and rosy. The top of her crevice tingled as she imagined his gaze exploring her derriere.

"Can you make a quarter turn?" he asked in a hoarse whisper.

"Like this?" She pivoted slightly, realizing he'd see

one of her breasts from that angle. The knowledge made her nipples pucker.

"Perfect," he said with reverence.

Even though she knew he didn't mean anything by it, Artemisia was inordinately pleased by his choice of the word. *Perfect.* She'd been called lewd and feckless and outrageous by people who didn't understand her dedication to her art. No one had ever called her perfect. Her insides did a jig.

She turned her head to look over her shoulder at him.

"Yes, that's it! Don't move," he said with excitement. His dark head bent over the sketchbook and the chalk scritched over the page. "You're beautiful, Larla."

Artemisia's breath caught in her throat. She didn't even mind his casual use of her milk name. It felt right. He found her beautiful.

She relaxed into his unabashed approval, enjoying the warmth radiating from her belly each time he looked up at her. The admiration in his gaze set her skin dancing as he followed the curve of her spine from her nape downward. When he focused on her bottom, she imagined the pale mounds must be pinking under his regard. Her nipples were drawn so tight, if she hadn't been ordered to stand still she might have pressed her own palms against them to ease the ache.

So this is what it feels like, to be admired, to be accepted, to be beautiful and perfect in someone else's eyes. To be a work of art.

Artemisia's spirit soared. As she bared her body, she exposed her soul as well. She closed her eyes for a moment and felt herself fly free.

Suddenly she realized this was no longer about art.

Perhaps it had never been about art. She wished she'd been brave enough to drop her robe for him head on. She wanted him to see her—all of her—to have his dark gaze search out all her secrets and pronounce them perfect and beautiful.

And not just his gaze. She wanted his touch. She could almost feel his hand, the way he'd slid it from her cheek when he kissed her, down her neck to the tops of her breasts. When his square, capable fingers brushed her nipples, she thought she'd burst out of her skin. What if that hand continued trekking south, over her belly and into the patch of dark curls? Would he find her fair?

And his kiss . . . Her lips tingled to feel his mouth on them again. What if his lips wandered to other places?

She felt a growing moistness between her legs and scented a whiff of her own arousal, musky and sweet at the same time. Surely he must smell it as well. She gathered her courage and cleared her throat.

"When we are finished with the painting, I have another position in mind for you," she said, surprised at the raggedness of her own voice. She opened her eyes and met his direct gaze.

"Really? What might that be? Something for Mr. Beddington, perhaps?"

Bother his fixation with Beddington!

"No, this is something for me," she said evenly.

"What do you need, Your Grace?"

She took a deep breath and jumped into the void. "I find I require a lover."

Chapter Nine

Mr. Doverspike laid down his chalk and rose to his feet. "Don't tempt a man wearing nothing but a robe, Your Grace."

"It's no temptation," Artemisia said, still turned slightly away, watching him over her shoulder. "I mean it."

He walked toward her, sinuous and slow, like a tiger stalking a roe. She wanted to face him squarely, but sudden apprehension rooted her to the floor. She hadn't meant she wanted him to make love to her right now. There was so much to be done on the painting, and it might color her perceptions of him to change their relationship in such a profound way. And yet she couldn't find her voice long enough to call a halt to his advance. She knew she should pull the robe back up around her, but it seemed she'd misplaced the will to move.

Thomas—she thought of him as Thomas now—stopped behind her, his breath warm on the back of her neck. His hands rested lightly on her shoulders, then smoothed their way down her arms. He lowered his mouth to her neck, first kissing, then suckling her flesh. She'd never felt such a delicious sensation. Her whole being throbbed as he consumed her.

"Mmm. So sweet," he murmured, before nuzzling her ear and taking a tender lobe between his teeth.

Artemisia leaned into him and felt his body, hard and strong, against her softness. As he planted a string of baby kisses on her nape, his hands slipped around to tease the undersides of her breasts. Feather-light, his fingers moved with maddening slowness. She longed for him to claim her breasts with his palms, to heft their weight and, please God, to soothe the ache in her nipples with a rough touch.

She thought she knew what desire was. She'd wake from time to time with a yawning emptiness, a vague discontent that left her adjusting her knickers in frustration. She never imagined this torrent of sensation, this unassailable urge toward something dark and forbidden. Now she simply *wanted*, unable to name her desire. Sharper than hunger, the relentless throb between her legs threatened to drive reason from her mind.

A small whimper escaped her lips when he covered her breasts with his blessed hands.

"Shh," he urged. "It will be all right. I'll make it all right."

One set of her body's demands was assuaged, but a new group queued up, clamoring for his attention. Her skin shivered under his touch, tendrils of pleasure shooting up and down her limbs. When his fingertips traced the curve of her ribs, the small muscles barely beneath the surface contracted with joy.

He turned her to face him and claimed her lips, pulling her against his body. She could lose herself in his kiss.

But she knew she mustn't. With Herculean effort, she pulled herself from his embrace.

"No, please," she said, even though her body rebelled against her will. "This isn't the time or place."

"Don't you remember what your father said? If we haven't time, we haven't anything. Here and now is all any man or woman can lay claim to," he countered, placing his hands on the narrow expanse of her waist and tugging her close.

"No, Thomas." She gathered up her robe to cinch it around her rioting body. "We must wait until the painting's finished."

"Why?" He parted her robe, clearly disinterested in her answer, and slid his hands in to caress her breasts. She couldn't find the will to cover herself again, not when he tormented her with his thumb circling a pink areola. Then he dipped his head to claim a nipple with his mouth.

"Oh!" A jolt of desire streaked from her breast to her womb. She had to explain something to him, but for the life of her, she couldn't remember what. His tongue twirled circles around her sensitive nipple, robbing her of rational thought. When he switched to her other breast, she grabbed a slice of sanity and held on.

"We must wait. Once the painting is finished, then I can set you up in a nice little town house, someplace in Mayfair, I think," she said breathlessly. She buried her fingers in his dark hair. Her legs were trembling so, it was a wonder she was still upright. "Close enough to be convenient and far enough to be discreet."

"Set me up?" He straightened to his full height.

"Of course." Artemisia craned her neck to look up at him. Her nipples demanded his mouth once more, but he hadn't reduced her to begging. Not yet. "Isn't that how these things are done?"

"What do you mean by 'these things'?" His eyes narrowed.

"Just as I told you. I intend to take a lover. I wish that lover to be you." She pulled her robe closed, gathering her shredded dignity with it. How could he run so hot and then so cold in mere seconds? "I would agree to a generous stipend, of course."

"A stipend," he repeated.

"That way you wouldn't have to continue working for the counting house."

"So I'd be available whenever you need me," he said flatly. "To perform for your pleasure when you wish."

"Exactly, clever boy." She wished he didn't sound so doubtful about it. She could already imagine furnishing a little love bower, a place apart from the rest of the world, where she and Thomas could plumb the depths of delight without fear of interruption or discovery. "We could even draw up a contract, if you like. Some men do when they take a mistress, I've heard tell."

"I see." He ran his hand through his hair, but one lock fell back down on his forehead. She reached up to push it away, but he grasped her hand and held it tightly.

Too tightly.

"So I'm to be available to rut with you on command?"

"There's no need to be vulgar." She tried to pull her hand away, but his grip was firm.

"What if we agree on a good roll thrice a week and maybe a quick swive or two as needed?" he suggested, his face hard as English oak. "I'm pretty good with my hands, I'm told. Perhaps we should write a diddling now and then into the damned contract, too."

"Why are you so angry?"

"Because, madam, I am unable to enter into a *service* contract of that nature with you," he said coldly.

"You don't find me attractive?"

"That is beside the point."

"Then what is the point? Men enter into this type of arrangement with women every day of the week." She finally worked her hand free. He'd left her knuckles red and aching. "Why are you making everything so difficult?"

"Because, Your Grace, you are not a man and I am not a woman. I cannot be your kept mistress."

"Semantics, Mr. Doverspike."

"Reality, madam." He knotted the sash at his waist. A muscle in his jaw worked furiously. "And now, if you would please clothe yourself, I will assist you with your corset. Then I find I must absent myself from this house before I do something I will later regret."

His dark eyes glinted dangerously. Then he turned and waved a hand toward the tall windows, where the sun was reaching its zenith and disappearing over the manor house's steep gables.

"As you can see, Your Grace, we have already lost the light."

Chapter Ten

"The manifest of the *Valiant*, the disposition of her cargo and the final tally of profit from the latest voyage—I believe you'll find everything as you hoped, Your Grace." James Shipwash slid the thick file across the desk to Artemisia.

She was meeting him in the small suite of offices she kept near the wharves instead of in her study. Mr. Beddington had to keep up appearances, and a business address was part of them.

It was a tidy collection of spaces, an anteroom where Mr. Shipwash did his work, Mr. Beddington's inner sanctum where they held their weekly conference and a storeroom to house the records the business generated. During day-to-day operations, James Shipwash ran interference on the occasions when someone tried to call on Artemisia's nom de guerre. It was simple enough for Shipwash to tell a visitor Beddington was unavailable or had just stepped out.

Mr. Shipwash pushed his spectacles up on the bridge of his nose. "Even with the week's delay on account of squalls off Bermuda, the *Valiant* has produced more profit than we projected. If I may be so bold as to say, taking on that coffee shipment was a stroke of genius, madam."

Artemisia leafed through the ledgers of neatly

totaled columns and sighed. Once the world of business had excited her almost as much as her art. Perhaps it was the clandestine foray into a man's world under the guise of Mr. Beddington that gave the enterprise its spice. She certainly had a knack for it, a definite gift for predicting which cargo would bring the most coin once it was brought successfully to market. But lately, the facts and figures of trade failed to stir much enthusiasm in her.

Perhaps because Mr. Doverspike had shown her that there were some masculine realms into which she could not enter, no matter how moneyed or well-intentioned she was. A woman could not keep a man as a man might keep a mistress.

At least, not that man.

But why should it matter who paid the rent on a love nest if both the birds were content to flock there together?

Evidently, it did matter. It mattered a great deal. Thomas Doverspike had not returned the following morning for his sitting, or any morning since. The canvas of Mars remained in shrouded seclusion.

And the painting would have been good, she thought with bitterness. Strong and controversial in theme, her Mars was just the sort of work that would catapult her to the pinnacle of the art world's attention.

But now it would never see the light of day.

Why did Thomas Doverspike insist on being so difficult?

She shifted her attention back to the ledgers. At least numbers were easier to understand than men.

"This looks fine, Mr. Shipwash." She turned her gaze to the window, where a spiky forest of naked masts bobbed in the Thames. "Be good enough to draw up a list of exportable items for the return trip to the Caribbean and the Americas by Thursday next and I'll make my decisions then."

"Very well." He gathered up the report and filed it in one of the polished mahogany cabinets. "Now, as to the other matter you asked me to investigate . . ."

"The other matter?"

"The gentlemen, madam," he said. "Here is a dossier on each. As you can see, Lord Shrewsbury's son has debts in excess of ten thousand pounds to proprietors of various gaming hells."

Artemisia waved that away. It was the bargaining chip her mother was counting on to arrange the match between the viscount's son and her sister Delia. Ready coin was the surest way for a moneyed commoner to marry into a title.

"Shrewsbury the younger is fond of drink, mad for foxhunts and absents himself from Parliament as often as he can."

"In short, he's a model British peer," Artemisia said cynically.

"There is nothing to urge against his suit of your sister," Mr. Shipwash admitted.

"On the contrary, my sister is the one pursuing him. And if I know my mother, she'll see the match made if for no other reason than to repay Viscountess Shrewsbury for snubbing her at the theater," Artemisia said. "And what of Trevelyn Deveridge?"

Mr. Shipwash frowned. "He's a bit of a chancer, madam. Second son and all. Served admirably enough in the military, but resigned his commission under unspecified circumstances. He seems not to have any visible means of support other than the miserly pittance his father, the earl, doles out. Yet he lives well. No unusual vices, other than what might be expected in a healthy young man."

Artemisia took the cryptic remark to mean that Mr. Deveridge fancied light women. She knew her mother would not consider that a detriment as long as the gentleman hadn't contracted the French pox. "He's young?"

"Nearly thirty, I'd say," Mr. Shipwash said. "It's noised about that Lord Warre is not terribly pleased with his youngest offspring."

"Why not?"

"I'm thirty years of age myself, Your Grace," Mr. Shipwash said. "My place in the world is established. I have a wife and child and meaningful work that engages me thoroughly. Trevelyn Deveridge is a man who might have been an earl but for an older twin. Now, he's a ship without a rudder."

"Well, if that's all he lacks, Constance Dalrymple will supply him with direction in short order once he marries Florinda," Artemisia said with a rueful chuckle. She could almost pity the faceless Mr. Deveridge. "Thank you, Mr. Shipwash. I will present these reports to my mother."

"I must apologize, Your Grace, for my failure on the other matter." When she frowned quizzically, he continued. "Thomas Doverspike. The man is a vapor. I consulted the constabulary, but he has no history of arrest. None of the counting houses in London has heard of him. I found no trace of him for good or ill."

"Did you check the parish records in Wiltshire, as I instructed?"

"Yes, madam. We only found one Doverspike in the shire," he said. "Ezekiel Doverspike of Amesbury."

"He wasn't able to tell you about Thomas Doverspike?"

"Since he's been dead for nearly eighty years, he

was rather unhelpful," James Shipwash said with drollness.

Artemisia swallowed her disappointment. The man she knew as Thomas Doverspike was gone. For some reason, he must have lied about his name. Whoever he really was, she would never find him now unless he wished to be found. After their last parting, she held out little hope of that.

"I think I should also inform you that several people have been here asking for Mr. Beddington," Shipwash said. "All within the last week."

Artemisia arched a brow. One query a month was more usual and easily dealt with. "Who was here?"

"Your stepson, for one. He was most insistent, battering down the door to this office when I refused him entrance."

"I'm sorry Felix troubled you so. Was he the worse for drink?"

"I fear so, madam. He was here to demand a larger allowance and would not be denied entry into this office. Fortunately, there is a rear door, so I was able to convince him that Mr. Beddington had stepped out that way."

"More money is not going to solve his problem." Artemisia leaned her cheek upon her palm. "Felix needs to stay away from the gaming hells or he'll bankrupt the estate once he comes into his full inheritance. See our solicitor this week and tie up what assets you can in a binding trust until he turns thirty-five. Unless he learns to behave like an adult, he needs to be protected, even from himself."

"I wonder if there aren't others he needs protection from as well. Two Russian gentlemen—and I use the word very loosely—were here asking to see Mr. Beddington in order to settle Lord Southwycke's debts."

Mr. Shipwash adjusted his starched collar in a nervous gesture. "They gave me the impression they could be quite unpleasant if the funds are not forthcoming."

"Did they threaten you?" A flutter of alarm coursed through her chest.

"Not in so many words, Your Grace, but . . ."

"If they return, pay them what they ask, Mr. Shipwash," she said. "We can afford to lose the money. We cannot afford to lose you."

A timid smile lifted his lips.

"Was that all?" she asked.

"There was a fellow looking for employment—a Terrence Dinwiddie."

"Perhaps you could use an assistant, if you think this fellow trustworthy," she said. "Especially if those Russian gentlemen return, it might be safer for you to have someone else here."

"Dinwiddie was a stoop-shouldered, nearsighted blighter. Spectacles thick as bottle caps. He'd be no deterrent to even a mouse."

Artemisia stifled a smile. Mr. Shipwash fit that meager description himself.

"He'd be no use in a crisis and besides, I'd not trust him with your secret," her assistant said. "There was something about him, the way he kept insisting he speak with Mr. Beddington. I didn't like the look in his eyes. And his accent seemed to change once or twice."

"His accent?"

"He had a bit of a Scottish burr at first, but then, when I convinced him Mr. Beddington wasn't here, the accent faded ever so slightly. It was so quick, I might have imagined it, but the fellow left a bad taste in my mouth."

Terrence Dinwiddie. Thomas Doverspike. Both of them affected accents and both sought to gain an audience with Beddington.

Artemisia gnawed the inside of her cheek. She was being fanciful in the extreme, grasping at the slightest chance to think of Thomas again. It wasn't just the painting, she realized, though it was hard to discount the importance of finishing what she started. The truth was, she missed the man.

Did he miss her, even a little?

"Was Mr. Dinwiddie a young man?" she asked.

"No, his hair was streaked with gray," Mr. Shipwash said. "I expect he'll be back to see if we'll take him on."

"Well, use your own judgment on the matter," she said. "There is enough work here for three men. You really could use an assistant, even if it's not this Dinwiddie. If you have someone to run errands and meet with merchants, he could conceivably *miss* seeing Mr. Beddington for quite some time."

"That's true." Shipwash put a finger to his lips and nodded. "If you recall, madam, you did keep me in the dark for almost a month, sending all your instructions by courier and receiving my reports the same way. Most prudent and quite clever."

"I'm just thankful I found you, Mr. Shipwash," she said honestly. "You are the backbone of this enterprise. Mr. Beddington wouldn't be able to function without you."

His ears went scarlet under her praise.

"Look at the time," Artemisia said with a glance at her pendant watch. "I must be going."

"You have other appointments?"

"No," she said with annoyance. "I have to prepare myself for the masked ball Mother insists I host. I still have no idea what I'll wear." She chuckled. "For tuppence, I should go as Mr. Beddington. I could stuff my hair under a beaver hat, bind my chest, dress in one of Father's old suits and smoke a cigar in public. That would teach her."

Mr. Shipwash's eyes went round as an owl's, clearly scandalized. "But, madam . . ."

"Don't fret so. I may have a reputation for outlandishness, but it is sadly ill-deserved," she said. "I'm sure Rania has something arranged for me that will be far less controversial."

She left the office and returned to her waiting coach. As the carriage moved away from the curb, a pedestrian caught her eye. He moved with sure, confident steps, his posture upright. Her carriage was too swift for her to see his face, but something about his gait reminded her of Thomas Doverspike.

Artemisia rapped on the roof with her umbrella handle, signaling the driver to stop. She switched seats so she could look back through the window at the man. Even though he carried himself like a young man, a gray queue fell down his back. Sure enough, he turned in at Beddington's office and mounted the stairs. Then, just before he rapped on the door, his shoulders fell in an arthritic slump and he seemed to age twenty years.

He turned his head, and she was given a clear view of his profile. She narrowed her eyes, wanting to be certain.

"Hmph!" Even though he wore thick glasses, there was no mistaking his mouth. It was the mouth that had visited her dreams and wakened her with frustration and a fleeting brush of pleasure. It was the same mouth she'd been painting on her Mars.

Part of her wanted to turn back and confront him.

Part of her held back in trepidation. Clearly, he had no interest in seeing her again, else he would have kept his sittings. But why was he lurking about Beddington's office in disguise?

She not only didn't know his true name, she really didn't know him at all. Perhaps she should order Mr. Shipwash to offer him a position if only to keep an eye on him and learn what the dratted man was up to.

She shoved aside the thought that such an arrangement might also afford her a chance to see him again. He so obviously didn't wish to see her. A woman had to maintain some shred of pride, after all.

Artemisia leaned back into the crushed velvet upholstery and rapped twice on the ceiling. The carriage lurched forward, adding to the uncomfortable downward spiral in her belly. She'd bared herself to this man, been willing to take him to her bed and trust herself to him. What a fool she'd been.

Whatever game he was about, she was done playing.

Chapter Eleven

*A*h! It suits you, Larla." Rania clapped her thin hands together. "I knew it would. Look at yourself. You are more radiant than a Maharajah's daughter. A veritable moon of beauty."

Artemisia stood before the full-length mirror and saw an Indian princess in a graceful sari staring back at her. The shimmering fabric draped her form, allowing a slice of her bare midriff to peep out in scandalous flirtation. Even though her breasts were supported by the snug, short-sleeved half-blouse, without whalebone stays she might as well be bare-breasted. Ordinarily, she'd be shunned for appearing in public in such a state of undress, but the *ton*'s rules governing polite behavior were temporarily suspended for the duration of a masquerade.

She made a quick turn on the balls of her feet, just to reassure herself that the yards of fabric were securely tucked into the drawstring waistband of the thin petticoat beneath the red silk. No undergarments could be worn with the sari because it was slung low on her hips. The swish of silk on her bare thighs was most erotic.

Rania had insisted Artemisia wear her hair loose and flowing. It fell in a dark wave past her shoulders and down her back to hover in slight curls at her waist. That was fine with Artemisia. The love mark on her neck left by Thomas Doverspike—or whatever his name really was—had not yet faded completely. She'd swathed herself with fichus for the past week in an attempt to hide the telltale mark of passion. Now her own hair would provide a covering. If Rania noticed the raw spot on Artemisia's skin, at least she was discreet enough to refrain from comment.

Beneath the red silk, Artemisia's ankles were adorned with thin bangles, and she sported a ring on the second toe of her right foot. A ruby was lodged in her belly button, and long strings of beads dangled from each ear. Another ruby rested between her brows, suspended from an elaborate headpiece.

"Now for the veil," her old nursemaid said, as she hooked the sheer fabric behind one of Artemisia's ears. The veil wouldn't conceal her identity, but attendees of masked balls frequently feigned ignorance of other revelers' true selves in order to behave outrageously with impunity. "I wish we had time to lace your hands with henna, but even without it, you will be the sun of glory."

"First I'm the moon. Now I'm the sun. Surely there must be a star or two we could toss in." Artemisia smiled at Rania's fulsome praise.

"Assuredly, my heart. Oh, I am ever so glad you have cast off your widow's weeds." Rania adjusted the veil, letting the bangled edges clink merrily through her fingers. "Red is a much better color for you—the color of rejoicing, the color for a bride."

"I will not marry again," Artemisia said with firmness. She and Rania had trod this road many times, but she'd never been able to convince the older woman that she was much better off without a husband. "I like belonging to myself."

"So you say, Larla." Rania tossed her a knowing look. "And yet if you should find the right man, I'm thinking you would be pleased to belong to him."

"Only if the man was pleased to belong to me as well. Men do not give themselves up as easily as women."

She'd have been pleased to belong to Thomas Doverspike for a time. Her belly still flipped when she thought of him. They'd been a hair's breadth from becoming lovers. But now that she knew he was not to be trusted, she congratulated herself on her narrow escape. And yet the heaviness in her chest damned her for a liar.

Strains of violins tuning up reached her ear. The supper hour was over and the ball was about to begin. She'd begged out of the meal, but her mother insisted she appear as hostess for the main festivities. She picked up the hand-held mask, a bejeweled and plumed affair on a long wand, with which she could shield her face should she feel the need.

"'Once more unto the breach, dear friends,'" she quoted sourly.

"Wipe that pained expression from your face, my dove. Rejoice in your youth and your beauty," Rania admonished. "Assuredly, they will fade quickly enough."

Here and now is all any man or woman can lay claim to.

When would she stop hearing Thomas in her head? When would she stop looking for him around every corner? She gave herself a small shake. She was stronger-minded than this. It was time she started behaving like it.

Constance Dalrymple's grand fete was well underway by the time Artemisia made her way down the curving staircase to the ballroom. The decorators she'd chosen under the guise of Mr. Beddington had outdone themselves. The room was a swirl of color. Murals of the Taj Mahal, the onion domes of St. Petersburg, Big Ben, the pyramids of Giza and a dozen other exotic sites graced the walls. Yards of silk festooned the columns at the entryways, and gas lamps burned brightly.

The guests themselves added to the riot of patterns and garish hues. Knights and ladies, sheiks and harem girls, Japanese warlords and geishas, a smattering of American Indians and one cowboy, all decked out in splendid excess. When the *bon ton* rose up to play, they did it with style and vigor.

"Artemisia, where have you been?" Her mother jostled through the press to join her. "The Queen is here already."

"Where is she?"

"Over by the punch bowl as Elizabeth the First. The Prince is Sir Walter Raleigh, and that fat fellow with them—"

"The one dressed as Henry the Eighth?"

"He's the Russian ambassador, Vasiliy Kharitonov," Constance said in a stage whisper.

"You don't have to whisper. He knows he's the Russian ambassador," Artemisia said. "Doesn't it seem odd to you, Mother, that the Russians should send an ambassador to the English court when everyone knows they have designs on British interests in Asia?"

Constance frowned at her. "What has that to do with anything? Our only concern is that our guests enjoy themselves. *All our guests.*" Her mother squinched her eyes and made a sour face. "Honestly, Artemisia, if you start talking politics you will embarrass the life out of me. I want you to go over there and charm the royals, and I mean now."

Artemisia wanted to ask why her mother didn't go herself, but she already knew the answer. Only Artemisia had a title. Of course, that didn't keep Constance from ordering her about.

Artemisia had learned long ago to choose her battles with her mother. As long as what Constance Dalrymple wanted wasn't too far removed from Artemisia's own wishes, she was pleased to comply.

She stopped before Queen Victoria and dipped in a graceful bow, hands pressed palm-to-palm in keeping with the character of her costume.

"*Namaste,*" she intoned. "Welcome, Your Majesty. Your luminous presence in my humble home brings light to all."

The Queen accepted this superlative as her due and smoothly introduced Artemisia first to her beloved Albert and then to the Russian ambassador.

"Lady Southwycke," Victoria said. "I was just telling his Excellency, Ambassador Kharitonov, that you are an artist of no little renown."

"Your Majesty does me honor."

"Not at all." The Queen waved her hand imperiously. "The ambassador was admiring the little equine statuette on the piano. If I am not mistaken, that piece is your work."

"Yes, it is," Artemisia said. "In fact, it is the companion piece to the one my father sent Your Majesty from India. My father said he couldn't resist keeping one for himself."

The ambassador lifted the statuette and peered at it through his monocle. The small horse was frozen in time, caught rearing its front legs, its mane and tail flying.

"Is very fine, very fine, *da*," Kharitonov said, pronouncing *very* as if the word were *wary.* "In my country, I breed horses for Russian cavalry, and it pleases me, collecting of horse sculptures. Part of collection I bring. Perhaps you come see sometime." He hefted the statue. "Is for sale, *da?*"

Artemisia blinked back her surprise. "No, Excellency, I never sell my work." She hoped her father would forgive her if he ever became aware of what she was about to do. Her only defense was that the grasping Russian had forced her into doing the politically expedient thing. "However, allow me to make a small present of it. Please accept this poor statue with my compliments."

The Queen patted her hands together in a soundless clap. "*Brava,* Lady Southwycke. However, never let it be said that we are less generous than our subjects. Ambassador, you may expect the companion statuette from our own collection to be sent to your lodgings on the morrow."

The ambassador stammered his thanks to both women. Artemisia excused herself lest the ambassador ask if anything else in her sumptuous home was for sale and made her way back to her mother's side.

"Oh, you were brilliant, darling," her mother cooed. "The Queen positively lit up when you were speaking. Whatever you said, it was the right thing. I'm sure everyone noticed."

Artemisia basked in her mother's rare praise and watched the dancers assembling on the smooth hardwood. Her sister Florinda was decked out like a peacock, literally. The fantail plumage spread out on either side of her hips, making it difficult for her to negotiate even the simplest of steps.

But Artemisia's gaze wasn't fastened on her sister.

She watched Florinda's partner with growing consternation. He was dressed as a musketeer, a fleur-de-lis pattern on his tunic with a plumed cavalier's hat cocked at a rakish angle over his dark hair. He wore a black domino covering the top part of his face. Artemisia couldn't place him exactly, but something about the man's posture sent warning bells clanging along her nerves.

"Everyone is having a lovely time," her mother gushed, returning a wave to a matron across the dance floor. "You may tell Mr. Beddington I'm pleased. I did send him an invitation. Is he here?"

"Oh, yes. I'm sure he's here someplace," Artemisia said. "You know, Mother, part of the charm of a masquerade is not knowing who is behind the mask."

"Well, I hope to heaven Florinda knows who's behind that musketeer's mask and manages not to make a fool of herself by stuttering like an imbecile," Constance said. "She's partnered with the young man I intend for her."

"Trevelyn Deveridge?" Artemisia narrowed her eyes at the man dancing with her sister. "You should know that Mr. Beddington reported some troubling unanswered questions about his military service. It seems he may have left the corps under less-than-ideal circumstances."

"That doesn't concern me in the least."

"It might matter to Father."

"What your father doesn't know would fill the library at Oxford." Constance gave her a toothsome smile for the benefit of anyone who might be watching. "Angus has nothing to say about the girls' matches. Besides, in the case of the Honorable Mr. Deveridge, his stint in the military doesn't matter one iota. It's his familial connections that are important, and his father, Lord Warre, cuts a wide swath through Parliament."

"I didn't know you were political," Artemisia said with a frown.

Constance laughed musically, as if her daughter had just uttered a witticism. "It's not the politics; it's the power. That's all it ever is, really. The Dalrymple name is joined to Southwycke, but you must admit, a dowager duchess only counts for so much. Once the house of Angus Dalrymple is entwined with both Shrewsbury and Warre, I defy anyone to ever snub me again."

Artemisia bit her tongue. Even though they were discussing her sisters' futures, as usual, her mother had managed to turn the situation so it was about her. Artemisia tried to remind herself that her mother had grown up barefoot in a Highland hovel. That might account for being overly self-conscious about her station—or lack thereof.

Still, it wouldn't hurt for Constance to think of her girls for once.

The string ensemble struck up a stately gavotte, and Artemisia looked back to Florinda and her dancing partner. The gentleman bared his white teeth in a dazzling smile. Then he bent in a courtly bow and finished it with a flourish. He excused himself and retreated from the dance floor.

Artemisia gasped and had to force herself to close her gaping mouth. The man her sister had been dancing with, the man her mother claimed was Trevelyn Deveridge, had just bowed as smoothly as that wretched pretender, Thomas Doverspike.

Chapter Twelve

Trevelyn pushed his way through the throng, making obligatory acknowledgments as he passed members of the *ton* he recognized beneath their costumes. He'd never been too fond of masquerades, but his father was keen on his attendance at this one. The earl had all but shoved him onto the dance floor with that tongue-tied little peacock.

Lord Warre had tried numerous times to see him wedded to a socially prominent wife. So far, Trev had eluded capture, but there had been some near misses over the years. As long as he was careful not to compromise some darling debutante, Trevelyn planned on enjoying his bachelorhood for the foreseeable future. After all, he wasn't destined for the earldom. It wasn't as though he needed to sire an heir and a spare.

His work in Her Majesty's Secret Service, which he took pains to be sure his father knew nothing about, nearly made being single mandatory. Especially once he made the transfer to the Delhi office. A man couldn't disappear into tribal regions to play the Great Game for months at a time if he had a memsahib and a passel of little ones depending upon him.

Besides, the girls his father shoved him toward—he

couldn't think of the simpering creatures as women—seemed even shallower than ever since he'd met the unconventional Duchess of Southwycke. There were more layers to her personality, and surprising sensuality, than a dowager has petticoats. He'd have been delighted to peel them back one by one, but not as her kept fancy man. As Trevelyn Deveridge, he'd have had no objection to making her *his* mistress, but as Thomas Doverspike, he was still furious that she thought she could own him as if he were one of her damn cats.

Part of his mind recognized the inconsistency in that view, but he wasn't prepared to examine it more closely. If not for the urgency of locating Beddington, he'd avoid her completely.

Angus Dalrymple was no help, even to himself. The duchess was cagey and secretive about her trustee. Mr. Beddington had shown an almost wraith-like ability to disappear into thin air. Trevelyn had practically met Lady Southwycke coming out of the office door in his guise as Terrence Dinwiddie. But when he arrived at the business address of J. S. Beddington, Esq., the only person in the well-appointed suite was the bespectacled James Shipwash. Lady Southwycke surely hadn't spent the better part of the morning closeted with Beddington's assistant. He'd met with another dead end.

A suspicious dead end.

Beddington holds the key. Since Angus Dalrymple trusted him with it, surely the man must realize its vital importance. If the key wasn't found soon . . .

To escape the press of people, Trevelyn slipped into the duchess's dark studio. He slid the bolt home behind him to make sure of a few moments peace. With his luck, one of the debs would follow him in and claim he took liberties, and before he knew what was what, he'd be led down the aisle.

The strains of the string ensemble and the nattering small talk that reminded Trev of a gaggle of geese faded behind the closed door. The smell of oil paint and chalk and the sweet, lingering scent of oleander, the fragrance the duchess always wore, greeted him. It was almost as if she was there in the dark. He brushed away the unwelcome longing that thought stirred.

With only the light of the moon shafting in the long windows, the room was awash in shades of gray. The canvases of Her Grace's work stood around the room shrouded with white linen to protect them, like so many disembodied souls. Curiosity niggled at him. This might be his only chance to see "Mars." He crossed over to the draped easel nearest the windows, pulled back the covering and stared at his own likeness as the god of war.

In battle, Trevelyn had done his part and been commended for valor more than once. In the midst of smoke and blood and cannon fire, a man couldn't think. He could only act. But he'd never become inured to the suffering of the wounded and dying. It was what had led him to resign his commission. His records had been sealed lest the numerous honors drew undue attention to him, and he embarked on a career in intelligence. With the right information in the right hands, he'd help avert future bloodshed.

The background of the painting was fuzzy and indistinct, but the figure of Mars nearly leaped off the canvas. Somehow, the duchess had managed to capture his sense of needless waste and despair in a few thousand brushstrokes. The expression on the god of war's face was grim. His muscles were strained and taut, his long limbs stretched out as if on a rack of agony, cleanly defined by her deft hand. He was just about to pronounce the unfinished work a masterpiece when his gaze swept the torso of Mars.

The duchess had rendered his balls pea-sized and his penis the length of a cigar butt.

A very short cigar butt.

"Something vexes you about my painting?"

She stepped from the shadows into a silver pool of moonlight. He should have trusted his instincts and his nose when he first entered this dark lair.

Much as he'd hoped to avoid her this evening, still he had to admit she was dazzling. The jewel on her forehead winked at him. And, good Lord, was there one in her belly button as well? The pale skin of her bare midriff made his palms burn to touch her there, to feel the silken softness of her abdomen.

She was as enchanting and exotic as the Eastern princess in Richard F. Burton's salacious missives from Aden. Reportedly, the princess neglected the short-sleeved half-blouse beneath her sari, her breasts proudly displayed for all eyes. Trevelyn dared not let his mind wander that route as he gazed at the duchess. But his mouth went suddenly dry.

"*Bon soir,* Your Grace." Trevelyn affected a thick French accent, in keeping with his costume. The Gallic nasality should mask his voice's normal timbre. He hoped that even though he saw through her disguise quickly—by Heaven, there was little enough of it—she'd have no reason to associate a musketeer with her erstwhile model. "What makes you think something vexes me?"

"Possibly the little snorting sound you made a moment ago," she said with poisonous sweetness as she came to stand beside him, seemingly as intent on the canvas as he had been. "I don't usually allow my work to be seen before it is finished, but since my model for this piece has disappeared, it's likely this one will remain forever in its current state."

The thought of his image depicted with minuscule genitals for eternity bothered him more than it should have.

"Are you sure this is an accurate likeness, madam? The model seems somehow . . . disproportioned."

"Really?" she said with incredulity, stepping forward to squint at the offending portion of the canvas. "It's exactly as I remember him."

"Indeed?"

"Indeed," she affirmed. She drew herself up to her full height and removed the filmy veil covering the lower half of her lovely face. She extended a regal hand to him. "You seem to know who I am, my fine D'Artagnon. I can return the compliment, though we've yet to be properly introduced. You are, I believe, the Honorable Mr. Trevelyn Deveridge, son of the Earl of Warre, are you not?"

"Your Grace does me honor." He bowed over her offered fingertips and brushed a kiss on her knuckles, hiding his disappointment that she'd ferreted out his true identity. She was clearly furious with his alter ego for deserting her. If things were different between them, he'd have turned up her palm and pressed his lips into her soft hand. "Surely a second son is unworthy of your notice."

"Oh, there's where you're wrong. You've done a great deal that's come to my notice. In addition to being Mr. Deveridge, you are also Terrence Dinwiddie, a stoop-shouldered, graying scribe in want of a position."

He froze.

"Though why you should solicit employment at the office of my trustee, I can't imagine. Not receiving enough of an allowance from the Earl, are you?"

"Your Grace, I—"

"Or perhaps you were dissatisfied with your wages here. Is that it, Mr. Doverspike?"

She smiled at him, her teeth silvered by moonlight. It was the feline smile of a tabby directed at a mouse she intends first to toy with, then to devour.

"Have there been any other incarnations, or did I get them all?"

He straightened and met her smoking gaze. "There are others, Your Grace." Some of his disguises were far less salubrious than Doverspike and Dinwiddie. Several extortionists and one wife-beater were still quaking over their run-ins with the ruthless Tobias Dunsworth. He took a step toward her. "But you've no cause to have met them. Not yet, anyway."

"You're not terribly good at it, you know," she said. "If I can see through you, your disguises can't be that effective."

"Before I saw the unfortunate proportions you've given your Mars, I would have said your powers of observation were keener than most, Your Grace," he said smoothly. "In truth, you are the first to connect me with either of those alternate identities."

"Are you a criminal, Mr. Deveridge? Or were you merely trying to learn more about the family you intend marrying into?"

Trevelyn swallowed hard. "What?"

"You needn't be so circumspect. Mother assures me the arrangements are nearly complete."

"Arrangements for what?"

"Your betrothal to my sister Florinda, of course," she said. "I suppose I owe you a word of thanks. I must say, I now understand your reluctance to become my lover, since you are destined to become my brother-in-law. This canvas of Mars is somewhat awkward, though. I never expected to paint a family member in the nude."

"Naked," he corrected as he took another step closer. Her scent worked its way to his brain and drove caution to the winds. "I was naked. And so were you, madam. Gloriously, splendidly naked."

He thought the pulse beat at the base of her throat spiked a bit.

"Yes, well, under the circumstances, I shall have to rely upon your discretion in that unfortunate matter," she said, her confident bearing slipping. "Pray banish that episode from your memory. I certainly have."

"Liar," he said.

Her eyes flared at him. "You, sir, will not insult me in my own home."

"The truth is no insult." He grabbed her and pulled her close. She struggled but couldn't break free of his arms. "And this is the truth between us, Your Grace."

He covered her mouth with his. At first her lips were hard and unyielding, and she pummeled his chest with her fist. She almost convinced him that her protest was genuine. But just when he was about to concede defeat and release her, he felt the stiffness drain from her body and she relaxed into his.

Her mouth softened and her lips parted, an unspoken welcome. He claimed her mouth with his tongue, first in gentle exploration and then in bold thrusts. Her fists uncurled and she grasped the shoulder tabs on his tunic, tugging him closer.

His hands found her waist and pulled her tight against his aching groin. His fingers played in the indentation of her spine, tracing the length of her exposed flesh. Everywhere he touched she was warm, almost feverish.

God love the Hindus for inventing the sari, he thought as he plucked the gem from her navel and explored that secret space with his thumb. She moaned into his mouth.

He began unwrapping her, pulling the end of the sari that was draped across her breasts.

"No, please," she whispered.

"There are a hundred people on the other side of that door." He continued to slide the silk over her shoulder. "The only way you'll convince me you truly want me to stop is to scream."

He cupped her chin and sampled her lips again. She was sweeter than spun sugar. "What's it to be, madam?"

She looked up at him, her eyes enormous in the moonlight.

"I won't scream."

"I promise you'll have no regrets," he said.

Chapter Thirteen

Artemisia couldn't bring herself to move. She trembled as Trevelyn continued to draw the silk drape over her shoulder. The fabric caressed her skin, but it was nothing compared to the caress of his gaze. He tugged at the long strip of cloth, easing it from the waistband of her thin petticoat. The silk gave way and she felt the sari slide around her. She stood still, hardly daring to breathe. Fire raced through her veins. Reason told her this was the path to perdition, but for the life of her, she wouldn't stop him.

"What are we doing?" she whispered in disbelief.

"What I've wanted to do since the moment I first saw you," he said with a quick brush of his lips on her temple. "When you waved your luscious bottom in my face."

Heat seared her cheeks. The man had unsettled her from the very first as well. So much so that even though she knew what they were doing was the worst kind of foolishness, she felt compelled to plunge ahead.

As he continued to unwrap the sari, she turned from him to speed her disrobing.

"If you were prepared to keep me as your lover, you must have wanted this too," he said softly.

She stopped turning, her face away from him. "Only

since the day you first announced you weren't shy," she admitted.

The last of the silk sheared away, and she stood in only the tight half-blouse and straight petticoat. He lowered his lips to her neck. A rivulet of pleasure coursed over her skin as his fingers found the lacing at the back of her bodice. With great gentleness, he spread the opening and pulled up the blouse. She lifted her arms in surrender, and her breasts sprang free as the garment slid over her head.

He reached around and cupped her breasts. No teasing touches this time. He held her, his palms hot beneath them. He thrummed her nipples with his thumbs until they became stiff peaks of longing. She whimpered at the crackle of heat lightning that seared her from her breasts to her womb. She'd ached for him to hold her this way. The joy of his touch now was almost more than she could bear.

She was bereft when his blessed hands left to slide down her ribs, the surprising calluses at the base of his aristocratic fingers nicking her skin, setting off a chain of sparks in their wake. He grasped her hips and pulled her close so she could feel his hardness. Artemisia surprised him, and herself, by arching her back and pressing her derriere against him.

He groaned.

A thrill of power rushed through her and settled in her groin. She was the focus of his desire. As such, she had the power to please or thwart him, to grant him pleasure or dash his hopes. She reveled in the measure of control this gave her. Then he kissed her shoulder and worked his way up her neck to suckle her earlobe. Her control quickly slipped away.

She'd never felt more tinglingly alive. Every square inch of her skin was charged with anticipation. She waited for his touch, the deft flick of his fingertips, the moistness of his mouth, the warmth of his palms as they slid over her.

He tugged her petticoat over her hips and let it drop to pool at her bare feet. She was glad her costume required her to go without drawers. His hands found her buttocks, teasing the crease beneath each round cheek, then cupping them and kneading the tender flesh. Artemisia's heart pounded between her legs.

Slowly he turned her to face him. His gaze traveled from her face down to her moonlit breasts, over her ribs and narrow waist to the flare of her hips. Her breath hitched as he studied the triangle of dark curls at the apex of her legs. His mouth lifted in a satisfied smile.

"You are nothing short of magnificent," he said with reverence. Then he bent his head and paid homage to her breasts.

His breath warmed her nipples, teasing them with the nearness of his mouth. His tongue drew circles around her areolas. When he finally took one into his mouth, her knees nearly buckled.

"This will never do," she said, stepping back.

He gave her a confused look.

"I like you better *naked*."

"Never let it be said I failed to fulfill a lady's wish," he said with a grin. With her help—and sometimes hindrance, when she insisted on kissing him instead of tugging at his clothing—he peeled out of his costume.

Her Mr. Doverspike was no longer merely an aesthetically pleasing collection of lines and planes, a puzzle of light and shadow. He was naked, bared body and soul. She reveled in the sight of him, hard, strong and undeniably male.

"Oh, Thomas, you're beautiful, and I never told you."

"Your eyes always did, even if the words never came. And it's Trevelyn, Your Grace," he said as he enfolded her in his arms. The warmth and frisson of his bare skin on hers was heaven itself. "Call me Trevelyn. Or Trev, if you like."

"Oh, yes, Trev. I definitely like." She was surprised at the huskiness in her tone. "I suppose given the circumstances, it is rather ridiculous for you to call me 'Your Grace.' Perhaps you'd better call me Artemisia."

"No, if you'll allow me, I think I'll call you Larla," he said with tenderness. "It's your secret name, and I intend to discover all your secrets in short order."

He scooped her up and bore her to the fainting couch in the corner. There he laid her down with gentleness. Then he stood over her, his hot gaze claiming every inch of her.

Artemisia stretched languidly, the velvet beneath her bare bottom a pleasure in its own right, inviting him to look his fill. She felt wanton and wild and desperately wicked. Her whole being throbbed, but the ache between her legs was so intense, she almost spread them for him, almost begged him to take her right then and there.

She bit her lip to keep from it.

He knelt beside her.

"You are mine, you know," he said. "I claim you this night."

"This night I am yours," she agreed. She swallowed hard, wondering what he was going to do with her. She shivered in anticipation.

He kissed her once more, softly, almost chastely. Then he abandoned her lips and his mouth roved over her—under her jaw, the tender ticklish curve of her armpit, the bend of her elbow, the breathless spot on her ribs. He filled the indentation of her navel with his tongue.

She writhed beneath him.

He took her nipple between his teeth and bit down. Not enough to draw blood, but enough to make her buck with desire. Her womb contracted once in sympathy with her breast.

His hand slid over her abdomen and cradled her sex. Her mound throbbed under his palm, and when he slid a finger along her folds, he found a warm, wet welcome. His fingertip grazed a sensitive spot and she jerked at the shock of pleasure that coursed through her.

Her breath came in ragged gasps.

"Shh, Larla," he whispered. " 'Twill be all right, you'll see."

She quieted as a child might while being soothed after a bad dream. Her solitary life had been the nightmare, though she'd never acknowledged it. She'd been so cut off, not just from other people but from herself as well. She had no idea her own body could take her on such a wild, careening ride of peaks and valleys.

Trev played her senses as a virtuoso violinist might play a Stradivarius. He was a consummate guide for this pleasure odyssey. Looking up into his desire-darkened eyes, Artemisia realized she trusted him.

Trusted him implicitly.

When his hand began moving, she closed her eyes and let him lead her through a dark place to an unknown destination. She sensed the precipice ahead as a blind woman senses a drop in the path before her, but she didn't hold back. If she should fall, she instinctively knew he'd be there to catch her.

Perhaps the fall was the whole point.

He started to withdraw his hand. Someone was crying. It took her a moment to realize the small sounds of distress were coming from her own throat. His skillful fingers danced her near the promised relief and then whisked her away.

She was prepared to beg him to continue pleasuring her with his hand, to send her over the edge to destruction or paradise. The intensity of longing was so strong, she almost didn't care which lay at the bottom of the long drop, so long as the unbearable need was stilled.

But then she felt his mouth on her and all coherent thought fled.

"Larla," a voice called from a great distance. "Larla, where are ye, lass?"

I'm here, she wanted to say, but she couldn't seem to make her mouth work. Her world spiraled down to an ever-tightening circle of blissful agony. Every muscle in her body clenched in concert with her womb.

"Artemisia, your mother is looking for ye," the voice said from closer at hand, perhaps just on the other side of the studio door.

Good Lord! My mother! And that disembodied voice belonged to her father.

"Stop, oh, please stop," she said with supreme effort. She grasped Trevelyn's hair and pulled his head up from between her legs. "Someone's coming."

Trevelyn blinked stupidly at her, like a man in the thrall of a hypnotist's trick.

Her body's intense need retreated in the face of oncoming panic. She pushed him off her and scrambled to her feet.

"I've been such a fool. There's a party going on

beyond that door. Anyone might stumble into this room," she said as she struggled into her petticoat and pulled the tight bodice over her head. The unresolved ache between her legs pounded with each beat of her racing heart. Her hands trembled.

"I locked the door behind me," Trev said.

"But still, what if someone heard us in here?" Her face burned with the thought of the sounds that had escaped her throat while in the grip of passion. "What was I thinking?"

"You weren't." Trev ran a hand over his face and through his disheveled hair. "And neither was I. I ask your pardon, Larla. Here, let me help you with that."

He turned her around and cinched the lacing on her bodice tight. Then he bent and helped her wrap the sari around her body in sensuous folds. Each flick of his fingers was agony because she wanted more than anything for him to be helping her disrobe again instead.

Embarrassment heated her cheeks. She could hardly stand to look at him.

"Larla! The bear's getting ready to leave," her father called. "Come bar the door behind him. Where are ye, sweeting?"

Her heart sank. Angus Dalrymple was talking off his head in public. If he kept this up, her mother would start insisting he be sent away again.

Only a few moments ago she'd been euphoric, drowning in a flood of new sensations. Now she was utterly adrift.

"Larla?" The doorknob rattled, but the old man wasn't able to open it. "Are ye there, child?"

Trevelyn slipped a finger under her chin and turned her face up to his. He dropped a quick kiss on her nose.

"We'll make a better job of things next time," he said. "May I call on you on the morrow, Your Grace?"

Next time. The shining promise hovered in her mind. "Please do. If you don't, I shall be forced to call on you."

"Shall I come as Thomas Doverspike or myself?"

She smiled wickedly, thinking of the minuscule genitals on her Mars. "Send Thomas. Now that I think on it, I believe there's a problem with the painting. It isn't at all accurate to the model."

"Phew!" Trev swiped his brow in mock relief. "I'm glad to hear you say so."

The door shivered under her father's attempts to open it. Thank God Trevelyn had slipped the bolt behind him, but the door wouldn't withstand a determined battering.

"Go," Trev said.

She fidgeted with her veil and finally managed to catch it behind both ears. "What about you?"

"I'll dress and rejoin the party in a few minutes. If you've been missed, it will do your reputation no good for us to be seen returning to the ballroom together." He lifted her hand to his lips. "Save a waltz for me."

"All of them," she promised.

Chapter Fourteen

$\mathcal{D}$on't know what's got your mother's knickers in a knot, but she's in a great *stramash*," Angus muttered to Artemisia as they walked arm in arm toward the ballroom. The gaslit corridor was lined with revelers. His rheumy eyes darted from one masked face to the next. "Too many hungry people in the house. Who let them all in? Where's that Naresh? He should know better than to let so many beggars in at once. We can't bloody well feed all England."

"Hush, Father," she whispered. "It's a party for Delia and Florinda. These people are our guests."

"A party? Weel, that's different, then. For the girls, ye say? Anything for me lambkins, ye know that. But these guests do seem a wee bit odd, do they no'?" Between one step and the next, her father transformed into a magnanimous host. He slapped a hand on the back of a medieval knight. "Are ye enjoying yourself, then, me fine sir?"

Artemisia found Naresh serving by the punch bowl and waved him over. The slim, elegant Indian was dressed all in white with a purple plume tucked into his tall turban.

"Keep Father out of mischief, please," she said to Naresh softly.

"That had been my every intention this night, but

your lady mother set me to work serving up the drinks." Naresh inclined his head toward the circle of tittering matrons. Constance Dalrymple was holding court in the center of their fluttering fans. "She has an announcement she will wish to be making and I'm thinking it must be a terrible one. All her guests must have a drink in hand to bear the hearing of it."

"No, Naresh, it's something that requires celebration," Artemisia explained. "She'll be calling for a toast."

Delia's match with Lord Shrewsbury's son must have been finalized. Constance Dalrymple couldn't wait for the banns to be read to announce the upcoming nuptials to the cream of the *ton*. Her mother must be delirious with joy.

Artemisia couldn't begrudge her this moment. Especially since Constance didn't know her hopes for Florinda and Trevelyn Deveridge were in utter ruins. Surely there was another cash-poor eligible bachelor with aristocratic connections who would accept a nabob's daughter. It was better than slogging along in threadbare gentility. Artemisia would set James Shipwash on the hunt first thing Monday morning.

Across the room, her mother swept toward the musicians like a stately galleon, the crowd parting before her in anticipation. She leaned to whisper to the first violinist, who acknowledged her by tipping forward at the waist in a stiff seated bow. He sped up the last rondo and finished the piece with a bravura flourish.

The crowd clapped politely.

"Thank you, my friends," Constance Dalrymple said, as if the ovation was for her. Her color was high, even accounting for the extra paint she was wearing, and her eyes over-bright. "My daughter, Her Grace the Duchess of Southwycke, thanks you for further ennobling her home with your presence. If I could find her in this press, no doubt she'd be delivering this news, but unfortunately, during a masquerade people are sometimes misplaced."

There was smattering of giggles. Part of the unspoken rules of a masked ball was that just as identities were temporarily lost, so one might lose one's inhibitions. Hadn't Artemisia proven that in those torrid moments with Trev? She wondered how many of her guests had availed themselves of the garden or wandered into one of the great house's many empty rooms in search of the same wanton pleasure. She shifted uneasily. The drumbeat low in her belly had yet to be silenced, and she fancied she caught a whiff of muskiness mixing with the scent of oleander swirling about her person.

"At any rate," her mother went on, "I have the most exciting news to share. My daughter Delia has just accepted the suit of Baron Malcolm Cholmondley, son of Viscount Shrewsbury."

No, the Viscount has accepted the fact that from now on Father's money will be settling his son's markers at every gaming hell in London. But Delia will have a title, bought and paid for, Artemisia amended grimly to herself. She doubted there was much point in trying to encourage her future brother-in-law to more prudent behavior, even once the knot was firmly tied.

A rustle of conditional approval, mixed with ill-concealed annoyance, fluttered around the room as the crowd digested Constance's news. Some society matrons already thought the daughters Dalrymple had bagged more than their share of the nobility with Artemisia's dearly departed duke. Now Constance could add a baron to her list of Season trophies.

"Oh, but that's not all! The Earl of Warre wishes to address you as well." Constance dipped in a low curtsy as a tall, straight-backed gentleman approached.

Lord Warre was dressed as a Moldavian prince, resplendent in a red satin-lined cape. He removed his domino and flashed a fine set of teeth to the assembly. With his iron-gray hair and snapping dark eyes, he still cut a dashing figure despite his years. In the strong lines of his features, Artemisia recognized the bone-deep attractiveness echoed in Trevelyn. Her chest constricted.

What in the world might his Lordship have to say to this gathering of revelers?

"As most of you know, my son and heir, Theobald Deveridge, has been happily married for several years," his Lordship began. Artemisia's gut twisted with foreboding. "However, I've yet to see my second son suitably shackled with the bonds of matrimony."

Polite laughter greeted this obviously tongue-in-cheek remark.

"But tonight, I have the privilege to formally announce the betrothal of my son Trevelyn to Miss Florinda Dalrymple. I know you will all join me in a toast wishing them every happiness."

The distinguished gent lifted his fluted wineglass and the rest of the company followed suit.

Artemisia was nearly sick on the spot. She knew Florinda would do her mother's bidding, no matter what, but how could they have announced this without Trevelyn's knowledge?

There was only one explanation.

He knew.

It was the only thing that made sense. Young women were bartered away like pawns on a chessboard every day, but a man did not wed without his consent. In her mind, she ran through their brief conversation in the studio, before his honeyed words and sinfully delicious kisses turned her body into his willing ally. When she'd accused him of spying on the family he intended to marry into, he'd feigned ignorance. But she realized now he'd offered no denial.

Even though Trev was bound to marry her sister, he'd still nearly succeeded in seducing her. If not for her father's unwitting intervention, her ruin would have been complete. How could she have been so stupid?

She saw him then on the far side of the crowded room, standing silhouetted in the dark doorway, like a fallen angel up from the pit, intent on dragging the unwary down with him. He turned his masked face toward her.

Bile rose in the back of her throat as she fled the crowded ballroom.

Chapter Fifteen

Early the next morning, Trevelyn burst into his father's walnut-lined study without bothering to knock. The family's solicitor, Mr. Weatherby, startled at the interruption and cringed back into the red leather wing chair.

"Good morning, son," his father said in his usual unflappable style. "You're up rather early for someone who didn't make it home before dawn."

Trevelyn hadn't dared come home earlier for fear of losing control and throttling his sire.

"Father, I need to speak with you." He labored to keep his tone civil. "Now."

Mr. Weatherby gathered up his sheaf of paper. "We can continue this at a more opportune time, my lord."

"Nonsense," the earl said. "Whatever my son has to say to me can be said in your hearing. What has taken possession of you, Trevelyn? You seem to have completely forgotten what little manners you have. Your behavior at the Southwycke home last night was unconscionable. You might at least have stayed long enough to accept congratulations from the other guests on your impending marriage."

Trevelyn clenched his teeth and clasped his hands behind his back. The urge to hit something—or someone—was so strong, he didn't trust himself to let his arms dangle at his sides. Trev's eyes burned in their sockets.

Mr. Weatherby turned a sickly green. "Really, my lord, I should give you two a moment—"

"Mr. Weatherby is correct. When you hear what I have to say, I think you will also prefer this conversation be private," Trevelyn said.

The solicitor scrambled to his feet, ready to beat a hasty retreat.

"Sit down, Weatherby. You and I haven't concluded our business yet, and I have no intention of postponing necessary proceedings for my son's frivolities."

Mr. Weatherby sank into the chair and pressed himself into the leather like a rabbit going to ground, caught between two terriers.

"Trust me, Father," he said. "I'm feeling anything but frivolous."

"Well, out with it, then. We haven't all day. Unlike slackers with no livelihoods, Mr. Weatherby and I have work to do," Lord Warre said with undisguised contempt.

"Very well. You were warned," Trevelyn said, taking a deep breath. "You, sir, are a bastard."

Mr. Weatherby looked as if he'd just swallowed a herring whole. Lord Warre's mouth twitched almost imperceptively, but otherwise he showed no reaction.

"I assume," the earl said, "this has something to do with your betrothal."

"There is no betrothal and you know it." Trevelyn tightened his fists. The impulse to knock that smug look off his father's face was almost irresistible. "I've barely spoken three words to the Dalrymple chit. You do not have the power to force me to wed."

"That's where you are mistaken," his father said. "I have it on good authority that you did more than say three words to the girl. You were seen entering the same room a daughter of Angus Dalrymple had just ducked into. The two of you were alone for a goodly length of time, quite long enough for her to be thoroughly compromised, or you're no son of mine."

"But that was—" Trevelyn bit off the words. Obviously, his father's informant didn't stipulate which Dalrymple daughter was with him unchaperoned. Trev wouldn't brush Artemisia with the taint of scandal by naming her.

"You brought this on yourself through carelessness." Lord Warre's voice took on the conciliatory tone Trev recognized as the one his father used when he was lulling a member of an opposing party into complacency. Usually, just before the earl hoodwinked his unwary adversary completely. "If it had been an opera dancer or some light-heeled doxie, I'd look the other way. But a virgin with aristocratic connections—"

"You mean a father with deep pockets," Trev said bitterly.

"There's no need to be vulgar." The earl tugged down his waistcoat. "When the girl's mother told me her daughter was missing and you were also, it was incumbent upon me to see that you do right by her."

"Father, you wouldn't know the right thing if it bit you on the ass."

The earl raised his hands in frustration to Mr. Weatherby as if to say "You see what I must endure," and then looked back at Trevelyn.

"You are nearly thirty years old." His father raised an aristocratic hand and ticked off Trevelyn's faults on his slim fingers. "You resigned your commission.

Politics hold no interest for you. The world of trade is obviously not suitable for a Deveridge. You are clearly not cut out to be a man of the cloth. You have no purpose, no sense of yourself, son. A wife steadies a man, helps him find his place in the world. I would not be the man I am today if not for your mother."

"Perhaps with a wife of one's own choosing that would be true," Trev conceded, wondering for the first time what the duchess would say if he offered to make her his wife instead of his mistress. The duchess didn't seem the type to turn into a biddable spouse. She'd probably give him that direct stare of hers and announce, as she did when she first met him, that he "wouldn't do at all."

Trev also wondered if his hard-edged father might have been a much different man had his wife lived longer. Trevelyn's mother had died when he and his brother were six, trying to bring their stillborn sister into the world. She might have brought some softness to Lord Warre and acted as a buffer between him and their sons. But she left her men too early. Pain over her parting set them at odds with each other in a caustic circle with no end.

"I have not compromised Miss Dalrymple," Trevelyn insisted. "And I will not marry her."

"Then you leave me no choice." The Earl of Warre rose majestically to his full height, forced to look up slightly to meet Trevelyn's gaze. "If you blacken the family name by refusing to honor my troth, I will cut you off, sir. Not a penny. Not a roof to shelter beneath. Not so much as a cup of broth will come to you from me or those who serve me. You will be dead to me. Your brother Theobald will be my only son."

Trev held his father's unblinking gaze for the space of several heartbeats.

"So be it." He turned on his heel and strode to the door. He stopped under the lintel and looked back at the earl. His father hadn't moved a muscle, but Trev thought he suddenly appeared much older. If he could only tell his father, if the earl knew the true nature of the work in which Trevelyn was engaged, perhaps he'd think better of his youngest son.

Trev's life did have purpose. He was dedicated to gathering the intelligence that would avert unnecessary warfare and save the lives of countless British soldiers. But to do that, he needed a reliable means of validating the information, and that meant finding Beddington's damned key.

But Trevelyn couldn't tell his father what truly occupied his days and nights. He couldn't tell anyone. With a lodestone of regret lodged in his chest, he turned and strode out of the house that had been his London home since before he could walk.

He'd garnered half a dozen commendations for valor from his commanding officers, but his father was the only man whose approval he craved.

The man whose approval he would never earn.

"Oh, Your Lordship, this is terrible, simply terrible," Mr. Weatherby said. "You surely can't let him go like that."

"I can't believe he'd be so stubborn." The earl leaned his forehead on his palm for a moment, his eyes closed. "My hands are tied. I can't retract my ultimatum. Surely he'll think better of his present course."

"What if he doesn't?"

The earl skewered his solicitor with a steely gaze.

"Then I must do as I have promised and disinherit him."

"But, milord, he doesn't know. You never told him. Trevelyn has no idea what he just renounced."

"No, he doesn't," the earl said. "And I fear he never will."

Felix Pelham-Smythe stepped from the smoke-filled darkness of the gaming hell into the stark brightness of early morning. Clammy sweat dotted his brow. He should have remained at his blasted stepmother's masquerade, for all the good it did him to sneak off to play last night. He'd hoped a change of game from whist to hazard would result in a change of his luck, but such was not the case.

He was now indebted to the cursed Russians for triple his yearly stipend, and the duchess repeatedly ignored his pleas for an advance. He'd tried to explain to Lubov and Oranskiy that he'd have the money. They need only wait a few months till he came into his own. Hellfire, he'd even pay them whatever usurious interest they cared to demand.

But the Russians weren't prepared to wait. He needed to come up with a scheme to get the money. Quickly. That, or he had to produce Beddington for them. In truth, they seemed more keen on Beddington than the guineas they were owed, and that was fine with Felix.

The devil of it was, he could never catch the man, let alone introduce the Russians to him. Every time Felix made the effort to travel down to the wharf to beard the elusive lion in his den, Beddington had conveniently "just stepped out." He was met by the great man's assistant, Mr. Shipwash, with vague promises of Beddington's return at a later time.

As if a future duke had nothing better to do than cool his heels in a grimy little office waiting for an underling to deign to appear. Really, it was too insulting.

Still, insult was better than injury. The Russians were capable of almost anything.

"I show you little souvenir from last man who owed me so much money," Oranskiy had said.

Then Lubov pulled a jar of formaldehyde from his pocket. It contained a severed finger. Felix feared he'd void his bladder on the spot.

"Sometime, when he have long wait, Lubov cut off more than finger," Oranskiy said with an evil smile. "But we reasonable, Lubov and me. Just give us Mr. Beddington . . . before Lubov have long wait."

The unhealthy combination of too much cigar smoke, enough alcohol to drop a horse and totally justifiable terror made Felix double over and empty his stomach into the gutter. If anyone was going to have something sliced off, better Beddington than him.

It was time, he decided as he climbed unsteadily into the waiting barouche, for drastic measures.

Chapter Sixteen

Trevelyn stopped by the small suite of rooms he kept as Doverspike and changed into Thomas's threadbare castoffs. After his sleepless night, he looked even more ragged and unkempt than usual in his guise as Doverspike. It was early enough that the duchess should be working in her studio. He planned to keep his appointment with Artemisia as if nothing untoward had happened. But after the way she'd fled the ballroom when his father made his cursed announcement, Trev knew he had some explaining to do.

He only hoped she'd let him do it.

He banged the knocker twice and received no response. Then he drummed his knuckles on the imposing door of the duchess's home and was greeted after a few moments by the butler.

"Hullo. Cuthbert, ain't it?" he said in his best country burr. He smiled ingenuously, hoping to slide by the man's eagle eyes and continue to pass as Thomas Doverspike long enough to work his way into the duchess's studio.

"Quite, sir." The proper gentleman's gentleman inclined his head slightly. "If you will be so good as to follow me, please."

The butler turned and walked in the opposite direction of Artemisia's studio.

"That's the wrong way, guv," Trevelyn said. "I'm here for Her Grace."

"Indeed, *Mr. Deveridge.*" Cuthbert never slowed his stately pace. "Madam gave specific instructions regarding you, sir. This way, if you please."

So, she'd given her butler his real name. The game was definitely up. Trevelyn trailed Cuthbert through the empty ballroom, now cleared of all evidence of a late-night revel, and down a hall lined with suits of armor and portraits of past Dukes of Southwycke. The ancient peers seemed to glare down at him as he trod by them.

Cuthbert paused a moment before the French doors leading into the solar and cast him a scathing look. The butler was too well-trained to voice his poor opinion of Trevelyn, but the frosty glance plainly said he'd been weighed in the balance and found sadly wanting. Trev wondered how much Artemisia had confided in Cuthbert and how much he had deduced from his own observations.

Small wonder servants were always the best source of information in any great house.

The butler rapped smartly on the door, and Trevelyn heard Artemisia's soft "Come."

The solar was the exact twin of her studio on the far side of the expansive house. Floor-to-ceiling windows bathed the room in early morning light, but the space seemed strangely bereft without the hodge-podge assortment of paints, pots and chalk that were the staples of her artwork. Instead of the scent of oil paint and canvas, this room smelled of lavender and slightly musty Brussels lace and, of course, her.

The duchess was seated on one of a pair of match-

ing settees with her cats, Castor peeping from behind
her skirts and Pollux snugged against her hip. A
book was open on her lap and she held a china cup
to her luscious lips.

Trev was used to seeing her in her paint smock,
totally unfussy and all business. The Indian princess
costume last night cast her in the most exotically al-
luring light, and stark naked she was the finest thing
he'd ever seen. But he was unprepared for the sight
of Artemisia in the guise of an English rose.

She wore the latest Parisian fashions with casual
elegance, the lines of her dress molded to her curves,
her breasts modestly concealed with a filmy fichu. A
tasteful strand of pearls looped her neck, and a gem-
encrusted brooch winked over her left breast. She
was every inch a duchess, and he knew he looked
like a vagabond from Fleet Street.

"Good morning, Mr. Deveridge," she said. "Pray be
seated. Will you take tea? Cuthbert can fetch some
fresh scones, if you like."

"No, that won't be necessary. Just tea, please."
He'd expected stormy recriminations, not this stony
civility. As he perched uneasily on the opposite settee, he noticed faint smudges of fatigue beneath her
green eyes. They gave him hope. Perhaps he wasn't
the only one who'd lost sleep last night.

"That will be all, Cuthbert," she said crisply.

"Very good, madam." The butler gave a sharp bow;
then for Trevelyn's benefit, he continued, "I shall remain within easy call should you require anything."

He pulled the double doors closed behind him.
Trevelyn didn't doubt Cuthbert remained standing at
the keyhole, ready to protect his mistress from any
and all threats.

"Larla—" he began.

"Mr. Deveridge, I seem to have forgotten how you take your tea," she interrupted, giving him a sharp set down. There would be no secret names used during this interview. "One lump or two?"

The glance she cast him as she poured out a steaming cup suggested she'd rather give him lumps on the head than in his tea.

"Two, please," he said, God help him. How could he hope to bridge this chasm of excessive manners?

She plopped the sugar into the dark liquid and stirred it with barely restrained viciousness.

"Thank you." Trev accepted the cup and saucer from her pale hand. He wondered fleetingly if she'd thought to lace the sugar with strychnine.

He raised the cup to his lips and drank manfully. *So far, so good.*

"About what happened last night . . ." he said, unsure how to begin.

"A masked ball is always marked by flights of fancy," she said as coolly as if she commented upon the weather. "A night filled with surprises, was it not?"

"No one was more surprised than I."

"I take leave to doubt that," she said in a tone dripping poison.

"Madam, I had no idea my father was planning to make that announcement."

"That I will believe," the duchess said. "It would be extremely bad form for one to seduce the elder sister on the same night one plights his troth to the younger. After all, one must pace oneself."

"I made no pledge to your sister." Trev raked a hand through his hair in annoyance. "This is some scheme hatched by your mother and my father for God knows what reasons. By Heaven, a single dance constitutes my familiarity with the girl. I barely know the chit."

One of her brows lifted in reproof. "Careful, Mr. Deveridge. You are speaking of my dearly loved sister."

"I realize that and I mean no disrespect to her, but you must believe me when I say I had no knowledge of this supposed engagement." He placed the china teacup and saucer back on the low, ivory-inlaid table that stretched between them. "I have no intention to marry. Not ever. Not to your sister or anyone else."

A shadow passed behind her eyes and for a moment he wondered if she was expecting him to say something different, to make some sort of declaration to her. Given the degree of intimacy that had developed between them—Heaven help him, he could still taste her—it would not be surprising for her to expect a proposal of marriage. Part of him would be willing to give it, he realized with a start, if not for his covert work in the Great Game. It wouldn't be fair to expect a woman to accept the risks he was planning to take.

She sipped her tea, snatching a glance at him from beneath her lowered eyelids.

"Probably a very wise course for one such as yourself, Mr. Deveridge. I seriously doubt you'd make a faithful husband for any woman." She looked away from him. "However, the deed has been done. Your father has declared your intentions before the entire *ton* and I, for one, will not allow you to make a mockery of my sister by trying to wiggle out of your obligations."

"If my father made the announcement, then perhaps he should be the bridegroom. The man is a bachelor, after all," Trevelyn said.

She skewered him with look of distaste. "And a man three times the bride's age."

"As was your late husband," he reminded her.

"I will thank you to refrain from commenting upon the duke. It is clear you know little of honorable men and even less of women." Her lower lip trembled, and she drew a deep breath. "Anyone who could so toy with another's affections and then fail to live up to his commitments . . ." She was unable to finish her thought for the tears she was trying to blink back.

Trev moved quickly to her side and gathered her in his arms. "Larla, I'm so sorry."

"Don't call me that." She balled her hand into a fist and pounded his chest once, but she didn't pull away from him. "You've no right. All you've done is lie to me from the moment I first laid eyes on you."

"Truly, I never meant to hurt you. If you believe nothing else, I beg you to believe that," he whispered into her neck. She smelled so tantalizing, all fresh and dewy; it was all he could do not to eat her up. "I have no name for what it is between us but I can't seem to stay away from you."

He covered her mouth with his, hunger flaring white-hot inside him. More than anything on earth, he wanted this woman. If he wasn't able to bury himself in her sweet flesh soon, he was sure madness would descend upon him in earnest.

The memory of her nipple in his mouth, the catch of her breath as he stroked her, the bare thought of the taste of her wet mound sent his cock into a frenzy of aching lust. He couldn't get enough of her.

At first she answered his kiss with desperation, thrusting her tongue into his mouth. His hopes soared. But when he slid a hand under her skirt, she fought free of him. Her face was flushed with longing, but she scrambled to her feet and put as much distance between them as she could.

Wide-eyed, she looked at him with something re-
sembling horror. "Get out of this house."

"Larla—" He moved to embrace her.

"No, I mean it." She put out her arm to stop him. "If
you come any closer, I shall cry out and Cuthbert will
call the constable. I will see you hauled before the
magistrate on charges of attempted rape, I promise."

It wasn't her threat that stopped him. It was the
terror in her eyes. Had he become such a ravening
beast? No, he realized; she was afraid of herself and
the way her body responded to his.

"It would be no rape and you know it," he said.

She narrowed her eyes at him. "Insulting me will
not save you from prison."

"Lying to yourself will not change the truth," he
said with as much gentleness as he could muster
given his state of frustration. "Whatever else is true,
this much is certain: I am not engaged to Florinda. To
continue that farce is to court disaster. Do you think
there's the slightest chance you and I could see each
other at family gatherings and not eventually tumble
into the same bed?"

"I asked you to leave."

"I will go as you request, but know that I will not
wed your sister."

"After your behavior this morning, sir, I will do all
in my power to make certain of that," she said. "I
presume you still possess enough decency to allow
Florinda to claim she rejected you."

He nodded. "Whatever tale you wish to circulate, I
will be happy to corroborate."

Trevelyn turned and walked toward the door. He
stopped with a hand on one of the ivory knobs.
"Whatever this is between us, Your Grace, it will not

go away just for the wishing. Somehow you have marked me, and I believe your heart bears a similar mark. I am at your disposal, madam. If you should require my services, however slight, inquire for me at the Golden Cockerel on Tydburn Street."

"That will never happen," she said with vehemence. "I wouldn't know which name to use."

Chapter Seventeen

Once Trevelyn left, Artemisia allowed herself five full minutes to regain her composure before she rang for Cuthbert. With nothing more than a kiss, the infuriating man had reduced her to a light-heeled wanton. Her family, her position, her art—everything faded into insignificance in the white-hot flare of passion ignited by Trevelyn Deveridge's mere presence.

Naresh told her once that all the souls on earth chose their own king. Whether it be a mate or drink or a taste for opium, whatever one yielded to became one's master.

Artemisia refused to be a slave to lust. After all the nudes she'd painted, hadn't she proved she could look upon a man's body in a detached, professional manner? None of her other models had driven her to such outrageous extremes.

It was just this one man who gave her fits.

Well, that was easily remedied. She'd take steps to exorcise Trevelyn Deveridge—or Thomas Doverspike or Terrence Dinwiddie or whatever he bloody well wanted to call himself—not only from her life, but her family's as well. She couldn't bear to contemplate a lifetime of looking at Trev over a Christmas pudding with Florinda by his side. With or without her mother's blessing, the first order of business was to locate a suitable replacement as Florinda's intended. She gave the bellpull a vicious yank.

"You rang, madam?" The unflappable Cuthbert appeared in the doorway.

"Send for the barouche to be readied. I must visit Mr. Beddington on an urgent matter."

A frown of disapproval wrinkled Cuthbert's brow. "I regret to inform you that Master Felix departed the ball late last night and has not yet returned with the barouche."

"Very well," she said, her lips tightening into a thin line of censure. Felix was another problem she'd have to deal with, but later. Her duty to her sister came first. A new marriage agreement needed to be negotiated quickly so Florinda's broken engagement to Trevelyn could be announced in the same breath. Artemisia wasn't prepared to examine the downward spiral in her gut whenever she thought about Trevelyn marrying anyone, least of all her sister.

"Go out to the street and hail a hansom for me, if you please," she told Cuthbert. "I have business that will brook no delay."

In short order, Artemisia was jostling over the cobbled streets in a hired cab toward the offices near the wharf. As the hansom clattered through the narrow streets, Artemisia watched London waking. Fishwives nattered in strident clumps as they set up their stalls. The aroma of fresh bread competed with the less wholesome stench of the night soil wagon that still made the rounds in the undeveloped area of the wharf.

When the carriage stopped before Mr. Beddington's office, she asked the driver to wait.

"How long you expect to be, madam?"

A new fiancé for Florinda. A new backbone for Felix. A different continent for Trevelyn Deveridge—

no, not even that much distance was guaranteed to give her peace.

How long would it take to set things to rights? Artemisia wondered.

"Consider yourself engaged for the entire day," she told the cabby before bustling into the office. That should at least give her a good start at rectifying things.

"Good morning, Mr. Shipwash," she called out as she hung her cloak on the coatrack inside the thick oak door.

No greeting came in answer.

She turned around and quickly surveyed the anteroom, where James Shipwash did his work. Usually tidy to the point of obsession, the room was now a shambles. Sheaves of paper were scattered across the floor like maple leaves in autumn. Mr. Shipwash's inkwell lay on its side, a pool of black spreading unchecked across the surface of his desk.

A clatter came from the inner office, as if a chair had been shoved violently to the floor. A dull thud followed, sounding for all the world as if someone had fallen face-first on the smooth hardwood.

"Mr. Shipwash?" she said uncertainly. Artemisia had never used her assistant's Christian name before, but she felt so uneasy, this seemed no time to stand upon ceremony. "James? Are you there?"

A groan came from the next room.

Artemisia hurried into Mr. Beddington's office and found an even worse state of disarray. Drawers had been yanked from file cabinets and documents strewn about in drunken disorder. Above the desk, an oil painting depicting the Hindu god Shiva had been sliced and hacked repeatedly and now hung in tatters. A tingle of apprehension fingered Artemisia's spine.

She noticed an unusual pair of boots sticking out from behind her massive burled walnut desk. A prone figure sprawled next to her overturned chair. Her breath hissed over her teeth.

"Felix!" she exclaimed, recognizing his curled-toe boots as part of his Harlequin costume from the previous night. She knelt beside him and placed a hand on his ribs to check for a breath. His chest expanded shakily. "Good heavens! Are you injured?"

Her stepson rolled over and dragged himself into a sitting position. One of his lapels had been ripped from his jacket and his right eye sported a swelling purple bruise. When Artemisia tried to help him to his feet, he waved her away angrily.

"Give me a moment," he said in a surly tone. The reek of several types of spirits wafted about him, and Artemisia spotted a stain or two on his checkered waistcoat that proclaimed he was wearing bits of last night's supper.

"Felix, what went on here? Where's Mr. Shipwash?"

"Where's Beddington is more to the point," Felix said. "It's him they want, not Shipwash."

"What do you mean? Who wants Beddington?" Her belly roiled in panic. "What are you doing here so early? Tell me exactly what happened."

"I came by because I can't get Mr. Uppity Beddington to deign to answer my requests. Really, madam, it's too horrible to bear, the way the man ignores my plight." Felix gave an injured sniff, and Artemisia noticed blood crusted around one nostril. Someone had connected at least one ringing blow to her stepson's face, but she had no time to offer him tea and sympathy.

"Felix, please go on. Who did this to you?"

"How should I know who they were?" he demanded.

"Beddington doesn't exactly include me in all his dealings, does he now? Won't even speak to me about my financial requirements."

Artemisia pursed her lips, refusing to be drawn into yet another argument with Felix about the state of his allowance.

"Well, Shipwash starts to give me the usual ridiculous tale of Beddington not being available when in come these big chaps. They wanted Mr. Beddington too, but of course the old piker's nowhere to be found. It upset them plenty, let me tell you." Felix swiped his nose on his sleeve. "I don't know what business Beddington's gotten himself into, but these fellows were not the sort you'd invite for clotted cream and crumpets."

Artemisia cast back in her mind, trying to imagine why someone would be after her alter ego. Assuredly, Mr. Beddington drove a hard bargain in the marketplace. His reputation for shrewd dealing might garner some resentment—especially if it was discovered that Mr. Beddington was actually a woman!—but Artemisia had cheated no one. This unprovoked attack made no sense.

"What did Mr. Shipwash do?" she asked.

"He told them to leave their cards and Beddington would get back to them. Set them off something fierce. Not that I blamed them at first. This man Beddington is positively infuriating. He controls every farthing of my income, and do you know I've never even seen him face-to-face?"

"Please, Felix, you're wandering off the subject." When his nose started to bleed again, she handed him her embroidered handkerchief. "Where is Mr. Shipwash?"

"I'm getting to it. One of the mugs starts swinging

and knocks Shipwash flat and the other one begins tearing through everything like a whirlwind. I tried to stop them, but this is the thanks I got." He pointed to his swelling eye.

"What were they looking for?"

"They kept saying something about a key," Felix said, holding his head with his hand.

Artemisia shook her head in bewilderment. There was a goodly sum in the strongbox for day-to-day use in the business, but the lion's share of South-wycke's wealth was held by the Bank of London. Hadn't she told her assistant to pay the threatening men who'd come trying to collect Felix's debts? Were these even the same men? If they were, her stepson wasn't admitting it.

"A key, you say. Did they think there was a safe with valuables on the premises?"

"No, they just want some blasted key. Beddington will know what they mean." Felix mopped his nose with her scented kerchief and then shoved the soiled cloth into his pocket. "It's all they want."

A key. Something about that odd request niggled her brain. Someone else had asked about a key. Trevelyn as Thomas Doverspike and her father had spoken about one in that cryptic conversation she'd overheard in the garden. Yes! When Thomas—or Trevelyn, or whatever the bloody man's name was!—asked about a key, her own father told him he wanted Beddington. She'd taken the statement for the ramblings of a deranged mind. Now she wasn't so sure. But what key could they possibly mean?

"You haven't answered my question." She turned her attention back to her stepson, who still sat splay-legged on the floor. "Where is Mr. Shipwash?"

Felix cleared his throat and raised himself unsteadily to his feet. He was unable to meet her gaze. "They took him."

"Good heavens! You mean to say he's been abducted?"

Felix nodded. "Kidnapped, I should rather say. They only left me behind to deliver their message. Guess they didn't know who I was or they'd have taken a far more important hostage. They said Shipwash would be unharmed so long as their demands were met."

"What do they want?" Artemisia clasped her hands before her to still their trembling.

"They want Beddington," Felix said. "Or, more precisely, this key he supposedly has. Beddington must show himself in the crypt of St. Paul's at midnight tomorrow. With the key, mind." Felix raised an admonitory finger to emphasize the key's importance. "It's no good coming without it, they said. And they were very particular about not calling in the authorities. If they see so much as a shadow of a bobby, the deal is off."

"What . . . what if Mr. Beddington can't come or hasn't got any key?"

"Then in that case, I hope James Shipwash's soul is in order," Felix said gravely. "Ordinarily, I'd judge these chaps as untrustworthy in the extreme, but on this point I'd not doubt them. If Beddington doesn't show, or he doesn't produce the key . . ." Felix let silence hang above them like the sword of Damocles. "They promised to feed Mr. Shipwash to the fishes."

Felix stood in the doorway of Beddington's office and watched his stepmother bundle herself into the waiting hansom. She was in a state and no mistake. It was almost worth this shiner to see her face blanch whiter than a fish's belly.

Almost.

Who'd have thought the bespectacled Shipwash would have such a devastating left hook in him? The clerk had surprised Felix and his confederates with his fighting spirit when the Russians began taking the rooms apart.

Felix fingered his bruise and drew back when the pressure caused additional pain. Shipwash's lucky punch was going to devastate his appearance for at least a fortnight. How was a man supposed to move in the best circles when he looked like he'd been on the short end of a drunken brawl? He'd have to curtail his activities till the bruise faded enough to be covered by rice powder.

Damn shame Shipwash had to strike him like that. Felix held no animosity toward Beddington's assistant. When he agreed to help the Russians with their plan, they warned him that it was dangerous to release a hostage alive, even once the demands were met. Still, it wasn't as if he'd plotted for Shipwash to die. He'd fully intended somehow to arrange for the man's safe passage to Australia or India or some other pox-ridden outpost of the empire once this sorry business was concluded. He'd meant to see to it that Shipwash lived.

But now he couldn't.

Chapter Eighteen

Artemisia found her father in the wind-blown garden, humbly sweeping the first of the autumn leaves from the stone path as if he were merely a gardener instead of a duchess's sire. The sight gave Artemisia pause.

Angus Dalrymple had been such a robust man, of penetrating intelligence and full of joie de vivre. To see him now, so reduced by his malady, nearly broke her heart. It was an insult against nature.

It was tempting to blame the Almighty for her father's predicament. When Angus came down with a blindingly high fever, at first it had seemed enough for him just to survive the illness. The family was elated when the fever unexpectedly left him. Then, when it became apparent he'd been permanently impaired and would likely continue his downward slide, her mother turned bitter. Even the vicar stationed at their cantonment had been little help. He cautioned against questioning the will of God.

As if God had purposely struck her father down. The vicar's version of God seemed too capricious and evil to be named a Superior Being.

Surprisingly enough, it had been Naresh who'd helped Artemisia make peace with her father's condition.

"All life is precious," Naresh told her. "Your father, he is still one of the happiest of fellows. Surely a merry heart is pleasing to your God. All the time your father was in my country, he worked like a *pukka* devil, never stopping to enjoy the bounty of his labor. Now he rests. Who is to say this life is less worthy than his previous one?"

At that moment, Angus must have sensed her presence for he lifted his head and smiled at her. It was a smile of childish simplicity, and her heart constricted at the sight.

"Hello, sweeting," he said. "What brings such a pretty lady to me garden?"

She returned his smile, not certain whether he knew her or not this day, since he used an endearment instead of her name.

"Good morning, Father," she said. "I need to speak with you on a matter of some urgency. Please, sit with me."

Angus obliged and settled beside her on the iron-work bench with a long sigh of contentment. As Naresh had observed, he was clearly enjoying himself.

"Some weeks ago, a young man visited you in the garden," Artemisia said. "A tall gentleman, dark hair and eyes. Do you remember?"

"A young man, ye say. Hmm." Angus tapped his temple in thought. "We see so few visitors these days, just sparrows mostly. Seems like a body would remember a young man among them. What with him having no feathers to speak of."

Despair clawed at her throat, but she swallowed back the sob. "He helped you prune the rosebush."

Angus squinted, as if straining to see the young man in his mind's eye.

"And he spoke to you." Artemisia tried to remember the exact words Trevelyn Deveridge had said to her father. "Something about the tigress feeding by moonlight."

"But the bear feeds whenever it may," her father said reflexively. A glint of understanding flashed in Angus's pale eyes, then faded as quickly as it appeared. He gave her a puzzled grimace. "Aye, I think I mind him. What does the young man want?"

"He's looking for a key," Artemisia said, grasping at the hope her father would remember something useful. "Please, Father, try to think. It's dreadfully important."

Angus frowned for a moment; then a smile spread over his wrinkled face. "Beddington's key!"

"Yes, that's it precisely." Relief flooded her chest. "Where is Beddington's key?"

Angus patted her cheek and chuckled. "Why, with Mr. Beddington, of course. Bless me if ye aren't a bit simple, lass."

Since her father fell ill, Artemisia had borne the weight of her family's well-being. While she relished taking on the decisions and enjoyed the measure of control her position afforded, suddenly, with Mr. Shipwash's abduction, she felt the full burden. Now she was even responsible for whether her assistant lived or died, and for the first time, Artemisia didn't know what to do. Her face crumpled in misery.

"There, there," Angus said when he noticed her distress. "I didn't mean that, Larla. Ye mustn't pay any heed to an auld man's ramblings. Of course ye're a right sharp lassie, and I'll have words with any as tries to deny it."

He put a wiry arm around her shoulders and pulled her close. Nestled against his chest, she was

comforted by his familiar scent, brandy and pipe tobacco with an undertone of hedge clippings.

"Oh, Father, what am I to do?"

"Just lay yer head, lass," he crooned as he patted
her hair with a callused hand. "Bide ye awhile. Surely
there's naught needs doing at present."

Artemisia allowed her head to sink into his shoulder. For a few moments she'd obey him. It would
give her time to think. Dry leaves scuttled across the
path before them, whispering their dying secrets to
the dull grass. *Winter is coming,* they seemed to say.

Winter comes to us all, Artemisia thought bleakly.

In the winter of Angus Dalrymple's life, he had no
more advice to offer her. But he'd given her plenty
when he was able, and it was time she put his teach-
ing to good use.

Logic: That was what this knot wanted. Someone
thought Mr. Beddington was in possession of a key
of some sort and, given the object's obvious signifi-
cance, would presumably know what key was meant.
Since she was Beddington and hadn't a clue, there
clearly had been a misunderstanding somewhere.

She needed more information.

The trouble was the only other person who'd ever
mentioned a key was Trevelyn.

She sat bolt upright.

That was why he asked so many questions about
Mr. Beddington, why he was so insistent about meeting Beddington. Trevelyn Deveridge was looking for
the mysterious key as well.

For a dark moment the thought that he might have
had something to do with Mr. Shipwash's abduction
crossed her mind.

No, it couldn't be.

Trevelyn had been trying to seduce her in the solar

while James Shipwash was being kidnapped. And he had offered to assist her in any way possible. Even in the heat of rebuffed passion, the offer had seemed genuine.

Surely the lust he'd stirred in her hadn't impaired her judgment that badly. At any rate, her father was no help. Trevelyn Deveridge was suddenly her only option.

"I must be going, Father." She patted his forearm and stood.

"And where be ye off to in such an all-fired hurry?"

"I'm going to visit Tre—Thomas Doverspike. You know, the young man who helped you with the roses."

"Och, aye. Fine fellow that." Angus nodded sagely. "I remember now. Tommy-boy. I liked that laddie." He snapped his fingers as a fresh thought descended upon him. "Say, a handy lad like that, maybe he'll help you find that key you're looking for."

"From your lips to God's ear, Father," she said as she pressed a kiss on Angus's high forehead. "From your lips to God's ear."

Chapter Nineteen

The Golden Cockerel on Tydburn Street turned out to be a clean, well-run public house. The scent of freshly baked bread, meaty stew and the yeasty smell of ale brewing in the back rooms greeted Artemisia when she pushed through the brass-trimmed double doors into the crowded common room. Faces blackened from shifts spent in the nearby mines turned as one to assess her. Then, because time on their meal break was short, the men fell back to eating with relish.

"Hallo, mum." The round-faced matron behind the gleaming bar dipped in a bulky curtsy. With flour smudges on both cheeks and an ample waistline, she bore the markings of an excellent cook. "We don't usually cater to folk of quality, but if you're for a hearty meal and a stout pint, I reckon we're the best to be had in London."

The tantalizing aroma reminded Artemisia that she hadn't had a bite since her spare breakfast early that morning. Still, how could she think of food when James Shipwash might be under duress for her sake?

"No, thank you. I'm here to see—" Artemisia stopped short. It didn't seem likely Trev had let slip that his father was the Earl of Warre while he was living among salt-of-the-earth commoners. Was he

Thomas Doverspike or Terrence Dinwiddie, or some other incarnation here? Trevelyn had failed to tell her what name she should use to inquire after him. "That is, I believe a certain gentleman lives here."

"No gentlemen live on Tydburn Street, luv." The woman eyed her with speculation, taking in the fine cut of her form-fitting bodice and three-flounce skirt. "Leastwise none what Your Ladyship might have cause to make acquaintance with. What does your gentleman look like?"

"He looks like me," Trevelyn's voice came from the dark staircase in the corner. His booted tread set the old steps creaking. He was still shrugging on his jacket as he crossed the room toward her. "In which case, you're right, Mrs. Farthingale. She's not looking for a gentleman."

The matron loosed a belly laugh that set her whole being jiggling.

Artemisia shoved down the feeling of relief the sight of him sent through her veins. She must still tread cautiously, she reminded herself, until she could ascertain his motives.

"Hallo, cousin," he said loudly for the benefit of Mrs. Farthingale before he brushed Artemisia's cheek with a chaste kiss. "I happened to see you from my window and thought I'd better come down to meet you. This is something of a surprise. I hope nothing's amiss. How fares Auntie Florinda?"

In the blur of events since she'd spoken with him early that morning, she'd completely forgotten about his betrothal to her sister. Social entanglements seemed much less urgent in the face of Mr. Shipwash's abduction and the mystery of Mr. Beddington's key.

"She's fine," Artemisia said, realizing he was trying

to shield her from idle gossip. A woman visiting a man's private rooms without a proper escort would be deemed shockingly fast. A relative was a different matter altogether. "But Uncle James has taken a turn for the worse."

"Has he, then?" His brows knit together in concern and, to her eyes at least, genuine puzzlement. He turned toward the proprietress of the Golden Cockerel. "Mrs. Farthingale, send up some of that delicious stew of yours, if you please, and a jug of your best ale—not the weak stuff you sell to the miners, mind you. This is my cousin, Hortense Doverspike. She'll dine with me in my rooms."

He grasped Artemisia's elbow and shepherded her toward the stairwell.

"Hortense?" she hissed. "You couldn't think of a better name than Hortense?"

"Hush!" he whispered. "The only thing bigger than Mrs. Farthingale's waistline is her nose. She's into everyone's business, and I don't think you want her in yours."

He didn't say another word as he showed her into his apartments and locked the door behind them.

"So this is where an earl's son comes when he wants to pretend he's not," she observed tartly as she looked around the room.

The furnishings were spare, only a couch and a straight-backed chair with a trunk situated between them to act as a serving table. The room was spotlessly clean but totally without charm.

Or a woman's touch, she thought with a flash of relief.

Through an open door into the adjoining room, she glimpsed his bedchamber. A simple string bed was covered by a well-worn quilt. Artemisia jerked her gaze away. The last thing she wanted to think about in this man's private rooms was his bed.

Trevelyn remained silent, waiting for her to tell him why she'd come. Artemisia didn't need to glance at her brooch timepiece to know that not many hours had passed since she ordered him out of her sight. He must think her changeable as a weathercock.

He motioned for her to sit on the serviceable couch but didn't take a seat himself. Instead he leaned against the wall and peered from behind the thick damask curtains up and down the street. Did he think she'd been followed?

"I presume, madam, your visit has a purpose," he finally said, raking a hand through his hair.

"You told me to call upon you should need arise," she said. A dark curl escaped his attempt to push it back and fell over his forehead. Artemisia was nearly overcome with the urge to smooth his hair back for him. Looking at him, standing there with his arms crossed over his chest, something dark flared in her groin. Need definitely arose, but she didn't think that was what he meant when he'd offered his assistance. She suppressed her reaction to him with difficulty.

"Yes, well, I require clarification on one or two points." Artemisia cleared her throat and removed her velvet-trimmed bonnet, signaling that she was prepared to stay as long as it took for her to be satisfied with his answers. "On the morning you accosted my father in the garden—"

"I think *accosted* is rather harsh, Your Grace." Trevelyn sat down on the straight-backed chair and hooked an ankle over the other knee. "Mr. Dalrymple and I simply enjoyed a pleasant conversation."

"That's what I wish to speak with you about," she said, adjusting her skirt so it spread evenly on both sides of her hips—anything to avoid his direct gaze. "You mentioned a key, I believe."

"Perhaps," he said. "We also spoke of roses, and before you leaped from behind the pampas grass, I think your father gave me a short dissertation on aphids and assorted other pests."

"No," she said. "You discussed the feeding habits of the tigress and the bear. Rather an odd subject for an English garden, wouldn't you agree?"

He shrugged.

"Then my father directed you to seek out Mr. Beddington, though I believe that was your intent from the first," she said, not wanting to divulge more than she must. "Mr. Deveridge, you know something about this key. Why are you seeking it?" She leaned forward in her seat. "Please tell me what you know. It's of vital importance."

He narrowed his eyes. "Why?"

They were interrupted by a light rap at the door.

"That'll be our stew," he said as he went to let the matron in.

His landlady had brought more than stew. A fresh loaf of brown bread, still warm from the oven, with a saucer of clotted cream and a pot of gooseberry jam, a jug of ale, rich and dark as ordered, and "a spot of tea for the lady."

The aroma of the food was heaven itself. When Mrs. Farthingale set the heaping tray before her, Artemisia decided it would do Mr. Shipwash no good if she fainted dead away from hunger. She thanked the good woman and joined Trevelyn in sampling a mouthful. The taste did full credit to the delightful smell.

"I assume you hail from Wiltshire, same as your cousin here. You know, I've an old maid aunt as lives

in Amesbury," Mrs. Farthingale said. "What part of
the shire will you be coming from then, Miss Doverspike?"

"I'm sure Hortense will enjoy visiting with you
after she's had a chance to refresh herself," Trevelyn
said as he stood and maneuvered the woman to his
door. "She'll see you later, then, Mrs. Farthingale.
Thank you."

After he closed the door behind her, he put an ear
to the crack to listen for his landlady's lumbering
tread.

"About the key—"

"Shh!" he ordered with an upraised hand.

Artemisia waited for him to rejoin her. "You were
telling me about the key."

"No, I wasn't." He sat back down and spooned the
piping hot stew into his mouth. Artemisia restrained
a smirk when he was forced to wash it down with a
liberal swig of ale. "I was asking why you wanted to
know about it."

"Very well," she said. "If you must know, Mr. Beddington's assistant, Mr. Shipwash, has been abducted
and is being held until some key is delivered in exchange for him."

"The devil you say." Trevelyn put down his bowl
and spoon and started pacing. "Any idea who's done
this thing?"

"No. I hoped perhaps you might know."

"Me? How could I know?" Trevelyn asked.

"Since you are obviously seeking this object, you
might know who else has an interest in it." She
raised an inquiring brow at him.

He brushed off her question. "Why don't you ask
Beddington? He must have a clue."

"No, he doesn't."

He covered his mouth with one hand for a moment, clearly pondering the matter. "Whatever he may have told you, I have good reason to believe Mr. Beddington has the key. Allow me to offer my assistance. I will be happy to deliver the item for you and retrieve Mr. Shipwash. When is the exchange to take place?"

Artemisia gave a short laugh. "You must think me simple. Why should I trust you to give up an object I know you've been seeking yourself?"

"Flawlessly logical." He conceded her point with a half smile. "However, if you've come to me for help, you must realize that you have to trust me."

She looked into his dark eyes and, with everything in her, she wanted to trust him.

"How can I?" she whispered. "You lie as easily as you breathe."

He sat back as abruptly as if she'd slapped him. He stared at her for the space of several heartbeats, then down at the floor, his brows wrestling with each other.

"Very well, madam," he said. "It appears I must trust you."

GET UP TO 4 FREE BOOKS!

You can have the best romance delivered to your door for less than what you'd pay in a bookstore or online. Sign up for one of our book clubs today, and we'll send you **FREE* BOOKS** just for trying it out...**with no obligation to buy, ever!**

HISTORICAL ROMANCE BOOK CLUB

Travel from the Scottish Highlands to the American West, the decadent ballrooms of Regency England to Viking ships. Your shipments will include authors such as CONNIE MASON, CASSIE EDWARDS, LYNSAY SANDS, LEIGH GREENWOOD, and many, many more.

LOVE SPELL BOOK CLUB

Bring a little magic into your life with the romances of Love Spell—fun contemporaries, paranormals, time-travels, futuristics, and more. Your shipments will include authors such as KATIE MACALISTER, SUSAN GRANT, NINA BANGS, SANDRA HILL, and more.

As a book club member you also receive the following special benefits:

- **30% OFF all orders through our website & telecenter!**
  (Plus, you still get 1 book FREE for every 5 books you buy!)
- **Exclusive access to special discounts!**
- **Convenient home delivery and 10 days to return any books you don't want to keep.**

There is no minimum number of books to buy, and you may cancel membership at any time. See back to sign up!

*Please include $2.00 for shipping and handling.

YES! ☐

Sign me up for the **Historical Romance Book Club** and send my TWO FREE BOOKS! If I choose to stay in the club, I will pay only $8.50* each month, a savings of $5.48!

YES! ☐

Sign me up for the **Love Spell Book Club** and send my TWO FREE BOOKS! If I choose to stay in the club, I will pay only $8.50* each month, a savings of $5.48!

NAME: _____

ADDRESS: _____

_____

TELEPHONE: _____

E-MAIL: _____

☐ **I WANT TO PAY BY CREDIT CARD.**

☐ VISA   ☐ MasterCard.   ☐ DISCOVER

ACCOUNT #: _____

EXPIRATION DATE: _____

SIGNATURE: _____

Send this card along with $2.00 shipping & handling for each club you wish to join, to:

Romance Book Clubs
1 Mechanic Street
Norwalk, CT 06850-3431

Or fax (must include credit card information!) to: 610.995.9274. You can also sign up online at www.dorchesterpub.com.

*Plus $2.00 for shipping. Offer open to residents of the U.S. and Canada only. Canadian residents please call 1.800.481.9191 for pricing information.

If under 18, a parent or guardian must sign. Terms, prices and conditions subject to change. Subscription subject to acceptance. Dorchester Publishing reserves the right to reject any order or cancel any subscription.

JOIN NOW!

Chapter Twenty

$\mathscr{I}$'m sure you realize the things one reads in the newspapers are not always the whole story," he began.

"Assuredly."

"So it is with people. Sometimes they are not what they seem. Your father, for instance."

"I fail to see what my father—"

He reached across the low chest between them and placed his fingertips on her lips. Her mouth tingled beneath his touch.

"Let me finish before you rush to judgment. The world knows Angus Dalrymple as an astute business-man who made his fortune in India." Trevelyn slowly removed his hand as if loath to sever the brief con-nection. "However, he was much more than that."

"You'll get no argument from me." She set down her teacup and looked away to regain her compo-sure. The last thing she needed was to further mud-dle the situation by giving in to the sparks that leapt between them. "Angus Dalrymple was, I mean *is*, also a wonderful father."

"No doubt," he said. "What you didn't know is that he was also an operator in the Great Game."

"What do you mean?"

"Intelligence gathering. Espionage, if you will. Dalrymple was one of the best. He ran a string of operatives that stretched from Bombay to the Punjab," Trevelyn explained. "Her Majesty's government depends upon the covert reports of men like your father to make policy in India."

"What kind of policy?"

He spread his hands before him. "We suspect Russia would like to carve up the subcontinent, and given the untender mercy the Czar shows his own people, one can only imagine how he might use the Indians."

"Of course, one might argue that we British have misused the peoples of India as well," Artemisia said. "Blessings of education and trade notwithstanding, there is a simmering resentment among the natives that even as a child I recognized. One has to wonder how we English would like it if a group of armed Hindus and Mussulmen took over the governance of our island nation, even if they claimed it was for our own good."

"I can't say I disagree with you, but we can discuss politics another time." Trevelyn's smile brought out the dimple in his left cheek. "The fact is, your father's work helped expose and end abusive practices by some of our countrymen. His contacts kept him apprised of wandering survey teams, native opinion, any covert agreements made with tribal leaders. It's vitally important work. If we can stop Russian adventurism or an Indian uprising with means short of actual combat, we will. The right information in the right hands can save countless lives."

Artemisia took this in with wonderment. She had the utmost respect for her father, but it seemed her esteem for him had been too small. She looked up at Trev.

He was much more than she'd taken him for as well. He was no bored second son who amused himself with play-acting and seducing titled widows. "And you too are involved in this Great Game somehow?"

His shoulders lifted in a self-effacing shrug.

"But how does Mr. Beddington and the key figure into all this?"

"That's the crux of the matter," Trevelyn said. "When an operative suspects he's been compromised or, in your father's case, falls ill, he sends a key. It contains the encoded names of all his contacts. You can see now why it's so important for me to retrieve it. If the list fell into unfriendly hands, the lives of your father's agents wouldn't be worth a feather's chance in a whirlwind."

She nodded gravely. "And that's why you were trying to speak with him."

"Yes," Trev said. "Mostly because I couldn't find the man to whom he sent the key. Your father's last message told us he'd given the key to Mr. Beddington. We've no agent in the corps by that name, so we've tried for years, searching out your father's known associates with no success. Once I discovered the trustee of your father's estate was a Josiah Beddington, I assumed I'd found him."

Artemisia frowned. Her father never knew she used the name as a cover for her business dealings. He was too ill by the time she took the reins of the family fortune in male guise. At any rate, he'd never given her anything she'd remotely consider a key.

"I've had the devil's own time trying to find the chap, inquiring at all the clubs a man of his stature might frequent, calling at his office, disguising myself to seek employment." He cast her a wry smile. "Even posing nude as your model, hoping you'd arrange an introduction. Not the most dignified way to serve Queen and Country, you must admit. When I finally meet the man, I have to learn how he's managed to remain so invisible. It's a trick that will stand me in good stead. Beddington's the most elusive subject I've ever tried to bag."

"And once you have the key?"

"Rumors of a Russian incursion into India have been flying fast and furious for some time, but we've no way to be sure. If the Czar is planning a venture down the Khyber Pass, Angus Dalrymple's contacts will know," Trevelyn said, barely concealed excitement in his tone. "I plan to revive your father's string of operatives and start where he left off. It's the next ship headed for Bombay for me."

Artemisia was surprised at the strange tightness in her chest at this news. Hadn't she wished him on another continent just that morning? Trev sat down opposite her and leaned forward, elbows resting on his spread knees.

"Now that you know the truth, will you help me? Once I have the key, I will see what can be done to rescue Mr. Shipwash. You have my word upon it." He reached out and took one of her hands in his. His hand was warm, but the touch sent a shiver up her arm. "Will you take me to Mr. Beddington?"

"It will do no good," she said with despair.

"How do you know till we've tried?"

"Because . . ." She paused, realizing she was about to hand him information that could sink the entire Southwycke fortune and create a scandal to rock all of London. But there was really no choice. She straightened her spine.

"I don't need to take you to him," she said. "You have already been introduced. *I* am Mr. Beddington."

He released her hand and sat back in surprise. "You?"

"I use the name Josiah H. Beddington to conduct my family's business. No one would deal with a woman. Believe me, I tried." Artemisia knotted her fingers together. "So I invented a male persona and hired Mr. Shipwash to act as my assistant. And I haven't got any dratted key." Her face fell. "I don't know what to do. If anything happens to James, I'll never forgive myself."

He sat still as stone for about a minute. Artemisia could almost see the wheels whirring in his brain as he digested this new turn of events.

"You must have it and just don't realize you do," he finally said.

"Impossible. I didn't assume the name Beddington until we returned home and I began to manage the family business. If your information is correct, my father must have sent the key from India, long before I became Beddington."

"Did your father give you anything when he fell ill? Anything at all?" His voice was edged with suppressed frustration. "He might have stashed the key inside a small chest or with a box of jewelry. Did you come across anything unusual when you unpacked your household goods?"

She closed her eyes, trying to recall anything out of the ordinary.

"No, he didn't give me anything, and you can rest assured if my mother had found something that didn't belong with her jewelry, she wouldn't have suffered in silence," she said. "You keep calling it a key, but I rather think it doesn't turn any bolts. What exactly does it look like?"

"It's a truly cunning device designed to both send

a message and provide the tool to decipher it. It's made up of a series of wooden cylinders that line up in a prescribed way to decode the list of names that is scrolled in the hollow compartment inside," he explained. "It's small. The key would fit in the palm of my hand."

Artemisia cast back in her mind but couldn't recall ever seeing an object that fit Trevelyn's description. "Would anyone be able to use it?"

"The exact sequence to bring the cylinders into alignment is tricky, but given enough time, a talented cryptographer could work out the code," he admitted. "That's why it's essential that it not fall into enemy hands. Worse yet, since someone else is also looking for Mr. Beddington, it means your father's last message must have been intercepted by whoever is holding Mr. Shipwash."

He dragged a hand over his face and stood to stare out the window. "Another dead end," he murmured.

His words lanced her heart. If Trevelyn couldn't help her, Artemisia was in dire straits.

If it would do any good, she'd go to St. Paul's herself and try to reason with the kidnappers. Somehow she must convince them that Beddington didn't have the key.

But if they believed her, they would have no incentive to release James Shipwash. They might very well do away with both of them. She could go to the authorities, but she had no great hope the constabulary would do more than blunder about St. Paul's crypt, frightening off the kidnappers and thus sealing Mr. Shipwash's fate.

The fresh face of James's young wife rose in her mind. How was she going to explain to Mrs. Shipwash that she was widowed because her husband's employer wanted to dabble in a man's world? Artemisia's thoughts flew in circles, like her cat Pollux chasing his own tail. She, who prided herself on her reasoning ability, could see no way to untie this impossible knot.

Suddenly it was all too much. Without her even being aware of them, tears began leaking from her eyes and leaving runnels down both cheeks. She made no sound, but her whole spirit wept.

"No, Larla, don't cry."

Trevelyn hurried to her side. His arms were around her and she sank against the warmth of his shoulder, letting the tears fall. When her whole body shook with a suppressed sob, he cradled her head with one hand and pressed a kiss on her crown, a curiously comforting gesture.

"Please don't cry," he repeated. "We'll figure out something."

He slipped a finger under her chin and raised her face. Looking into his eyes, she saw herself reflected in their dark depths. Beyond that image, a slow fire began to burn the gold flecks in his brown eyes.

"I won't let you down," he said softly. "Trust me."

She realized suddenly that she did. It was madness itself. Here was a man who'd presented himself under false colors, who lied with ease, whose very character was an enigma—and yet she'd trust him with her life.

And the life of Mr. Shipwash.

Artemisia reached up and pulled his head down. She kissed him. Softly. Simply. As a child might.

Then she looked once more into the depths of his eyes and felt nothing like a child.

Chapter Twenty-one

It made no sense at all, and yet she couldn't seem to stop herself. Artemisia kissed him again, parting her lips in invitation. Trevelyn rose to her challenge, claiming her mouth in a kiss that defined sweetness. Then the kiss changed, deepened, and the spark that always crackled between them burst suddenly into full flame.

His mouth moved over her lips, the hollow of her cheek and the slender curve of her throat. Chinese fireworks danced over her skin, charging her body with roaming pinpoints of pleasure.

She put both hands on his cheeks and brought his face up to hers again.

Finally she drew back to catch her breath.

"Oh, my!" she said, realizing the ungovernable power of what she'd unleashed.

"Quite." He cocked an eyebrow at her. "We're never going to be done with it, you know."

He reached up and unbuttoned the first button on her blue serge bodice. Surely he must hear her heart, pounding like a coach and six in her chest.

"This thing between us," he went on as his fingers trailed down to the next button. "Do you have any idea what it is?"

She shook her head, unwilling to trust her voice.

"Damn," he said softly. "I hoped you could explain it to me." He ran his hand through her hair, pulling out pins and loosing her curls as he went. "I've known men who become addicted to opium. It becomes an obsession for them. Now I understand their compulsion. You are my lotus blossom. From the first time I wandered into your studio, though I was initially there to find Beddington, you've been all I can think about. And when I'm with you, I can't keep from wanting to touch you."

He returned to her buttons and slid a finger in the small gap to tease the hollow between her breasts.

"You may not be happy about it, but you accomplished your goal," she said as he bent his head to deliver a string of kisses from her jaw to the hollow at the base of her throat. Her pulse jumped. "You've found Mr. Beddington."

His chuckle was a low rumble. "Yes, I suppose I have. I just didn't expect to want to take the fellow to my bed."

"That is where this is leading, isn't it?" She undid the next button herself, baring the tops of her breasts to his admiring gaze. "To your bed."

He nuzzled her ear and nipped at the tender lobe. "If there's a God in heaven . . ."

"There is," she assured him.

He kissed her again, and it was as if their previous kisses were but child's play. Their souls mingled in a shared breath, wandering together unsure which body was their natural habitation.

Both, she decided.

He continued to unfasten her tight bodice while his mouth worked its magic on hers. Her breasts ached for his touch, straining at their whalebone prison. When he raised her to her feet to remove her jacket, she helped him out of his as well. One of the buttons on his starched shirt resisted her efforts and popped off, rolling across the floor unheeded.

"Sorry," she said when he released her mouth. "I'll sew that back on for you."

He grinned at her before turning his attention to the hooks at her waist. "I would consider one lost button an acceptable casualty count for a skirmish like this."

"A skirmish, is it?" Her breath hitched as he trailed his lips down her neck and along the lace at the top of her chemise. "You make it sound as if you and I are at war."

"We are." He straightened to look down at her. "You shouldn't be surprised. Did you not christen me your god of war? This battle is as old as Eden, but it's one both sides must lose if they are both to win."

"I don't understand."

"Do you not? As a widow, I would have thought . . ." He cast her a questioning look. "No matter. It will be my great pleasure to instruct you. You see, Larla, if I cannot bring you joy in this engagement, my own is forfeit. That's why I say we both must lose in order to win."

She lifted her arms as he raised her flounced skirt and drew it over her head. She cursed fashion that required her to wear an over-petticoat, a hooped crinoline, an under-petticoat, a corset, a chemise and open-crotched bloomers. One layer down, only six to go.

"Then I wish you much success with your campaign, sir." She pushed his shirt off his shoulders and pulled it from him along with the woolen undervest. "I love winning."

"So do I." He loosened the next layer of her costume with a laugh. "But you must admit, the sari was much easier."

"Anything worth having is worth working for, my father always said."

"An extremely wise man, your father," he agreed. The last of her petticoats dropped to pool at her feet.

His smile faded as he settled to the serious work of disrobing her. She gave him her back so he could loosen her laces, then turned around to face him. He unhooked the busked front of her corset, setting her breasts free beneath her thin chemise.

With her ribs now unshackled, she drew a deep breath. The heady rush of oxygen almost made her dizzy. Artemisia watched his face as he untied the drawstring at the scooped neckline of her chemise. He pulled the opening wide so he could ease the fabric over her shoulders and down, baring her taut breasts. The muscle in one of his cheeks ticked.

"Is something wrong?" she asked.

"Why do you ask?" The strain didn't leave his jaw.

She lifted a hand to caress his cheek. "You seem . . . pained."

He covered her hand with his. "I'm having difficulty controlling myself and am afraid I may scare you."

"What about you would scare me?"

"The things you make me want to do. I've never felt like this. I want you so badly, I don't know if I can bridle myself." For a moment she thought his hand trembled on hers.

"Don't worry," she said with tartness. "If I find you scare me, I'll put the bit in your mouth for you myself."

He threw back his head and laughed. "You little minx. I believe you would." His eyes darkened with desire as he reached up to fondle her breasts, cupping them gently while his thumbs began maddening circles around her nipples. "You're so soft, Larla. I can't get enough of you." He bent his head to claim her with his mouth.

She'd started to tackle the buttons of his fly, but the sensation his mouth stirred almost made her forget to breathe. Good heavens! Was he using his teeth on her? The slight nip sent pleasure that was a knife's edge from pain streaking through her.

Then one of his hands found the slit in her bloomers and his talented fingers played a lover's serenade on her quivering flesh. With a moan of pleasure, she took a half-step to spread her legs for him. A dull ache began in her secret folds. A few more deft flicks of his fingers and she was in exquisite torment.

"Please," she begged.

"That is my very intent." He came up for air with a smug grin. "I will not rest until I have pleased you, madam."

"Then help me finish undressing you or I shall go mad," she said.

"You do have a penchant for nudes, don't you?" he teased as he unbuttoned his trouser front. "As it turns out, so do I."

He lowered her bloomers and she stepped out of them, standing in just her stockings and pointed-toed boots. He stepped back to look at her, stepping out of his own trousers. Artemisia resisted the urge to cover her sex, fig-leaf fashion, with her hands. He stood, hands fisted at his waist, his phallus fully erect, the musculature in his chest and abdomen rock hard. The god of war seemed intent on planning his campaign.

"My old elocution professor always admonished me to imagine my audience in naught but their socks so as not to feel nervous about public speaking," he said. "But I declare, I'd never be able to concentrate on speech-making with you in my audience."

Artemisia laughed, but the giggle dissolved into "Oof!" when he scooped her up and threw her over his shoulder as if she were a sack of potatoes.

"Never laugh at an Oxford don." He smacked her bare bottom once and strode with purpose toward his bedchamber. She bounced along, head and arms dangling down, and noticed that his bottom was within easy reach. She gave his tight buttocks a swat before he lowered her to the bed.

"Never mishandle a duchess," she admonished.

"Duly noted," he said. "I shall endeavor mightily not to mishandle you, Larla. But I am going to handle you." The levity left his features. "All of you."

He started with her feet. Lifting her foot high, he unhooked her boots and drew off her stockings. He rubbed the ball of her foot and ran a finger along her delicate arch. She shuddered, trying to control her giggles. She suspected Trevelyn might be the sort who enjoyed tickling, so she was determine not to let him see how his touch set her stomach jiggling.

He set her heel on his shoulder as his gaze traveled up her calf, past her knee and to her inner thigh. She was totally exposed to him, and the heat in his eyes was answered in the warm moistness of her flesh. When they'd nearly made love during the masked ball, her studio had been lit by kindly moonlight. Now she was bared to him in the stark light of day. He ran a hand along her leg, his touch setting her skin dancing.

"No, you don't," he said when she would have

brought her knees together. "I promised to have all of you and I am a man of my word."

"But . . ." How could she put into words what she felt? All her life she'd been taught that part of her was unclean somehow, not to be touched more than absolutely necessary and then only with strong soap. She feared he might not like what he found as he explored her.

"You are altogether lovely, Larla," he assured her, as if he heard her secret fears. She relaxed in the warmth of his approval and closed her eyes. He circled her triangle of curls with his thumb, seeking her deepest secrets. He touched. He teased. He lavished her with gentle insistence, and the pressure inside built steadily till she could only whimper his name.

Her aching womb contracted once, and he withdrew his blessed hand.

"No, please," she said, afraid he was stopping, but she stilled when he covered her body with his, his hips between her spread legs. "Oh, yes."

He kissed her then. His tongue slipped into her mouth and his cock invaded her slowly at the same time. She hooked her legs around his, urging him deeper, but he was taking his maddening time about it.

Then suddenly, he plunged into her, burying himself in her flesh. He raised his upper body on his elbows and looked down at her.

Neither of them was capable of speech, but their gazes locked, and Artemisia couldn't have looked away if her hope of heaven depended upon it. The wonder of holding him inside her was joy beyond speaking. It was a tight fit, but she barely managed to accept his full length.

He started to move, and she responded by raising

her hips to meet his thrusts. Artemisia's world wound down to disjointed elements. Heat. Friction. Aching.

His warm male smell filled her nostrils, and she ground herself against him, ready to receive all of him. Hungry to receive him. Her heart throbbed between her legs.

"Harder," she urged.

A ragged cry tore loose from his throat, and he pounded his rampant cock into her. From deep inside a pulse began, a convulsion that caused her to lose control of her limbs. Joy flooded her entire being.

His release followed swiftly in strong pulses as his seed flowed into her, hot and steady. For a blink, she realized they had taken no precautions against conception. Then lethargy stole over her and she found it difficult to care about anything but the sweetness of his sweat-dampened temple against her cheek.

Their hearts fell into a somnolent rhythm as she stroked the length of his spine.

He raised himself on his elbows so he could look down at her without disturbing their conjoined state. "Madam, you are magnificent."

"Thank you, Mars," she whispered. "I think you've just concluded your first successful campaign. And we both won."

Chapter Twenty-two

Artemisia drew lazy circles across his pectorals with her fingertip, just for the joy of watching his brown nipples pucker. After they'd both settled to earth, the afterglow of their lovemaking ignited a fresh fire and they took each other again, this time with deliberate slowness. Their climb was exquisite agony and their release all the more shattering for its delay. Artemisia's heart rate was finally fluttering back into normal range.

She still couldn't bring herself to care about much beyond Trevelyn's next kiss, but her conscience wouldn't let her completely block out thoughts of Mr. Shipwash and his plight. All the lovemaking in the world wouldn't change the fact that her assistant was still in danger and she was utterly lost about what to do.

"You said my father sent you word about Bedding-ton and the key." She snuggled close and laid her head on his shoulder. "What exactly did the message say?"

"It wasn't sent to me personally, you understand." Trevelyn ran a hand over her head and through the length of her hair tumbling down her back. "It came to the central office in the usual fashion. All your father said was 'Beddington holds the key.' The posts that came in after that one were frankly . . . incoherent. I'm sorry, Larla."

She sighed. "By then the illness had taken his mind."

"Why did you choose the name Beddington?" Trevelyn asked.

She snorted. "You'll laugh."

"Maybe, but tell me anyway," he said.

"Mr. Beddington was the name of my first pony," she admitted. "A Shetland with all the attributes of the breed in spades. He was a round, stubborn little thing, but I loved him dearly."

He let out a chortle, and she swatted at his chest. "I didn't promise not to laugh." He snatched up her hand and placed a lover's kiss on her palm. "A round, stubborn little thing, eh? Looks like you chose your nom de guerre well. You've more grit than most men I know, and as for the round . . ." His hand drifted up to fondle her breast. "Your round parts are exquisite, madam."

But could you love me dearly? Artemisia wondered as he kissed her once more. Then a thought struck her like a lightning bolt.

"Oh, what a dunderhead I am! Beddington! Of course!" She sat bolt upright. "Why didn't I think of this sooner?"

"What is it?"

"Beddington *holds* the key, you said. Not *has* the key. Mr. Beddington was my first artistic subject. I sculpted a little figurine of him when I was only twelve. It won all sorts of accolades and serious attention from art aficionados, but of course I'd never part with it." Her mind raced ahead, trying to poke holes in her theory.

"Is it possible your father hid the key inside the piece?"

"Not inside it. Beddington isn't hollow," she explained. "But about a month before he fell ill, he had a new base made for both Mr. Beddington and Miss Bogglesworth. The bases might be hollow."

"Dare I ask? Who is Miss Bogglesworth?"

"She was Delia's pony. Florinda was always afraid to ride. But back on point, I sculpted Miss Bogglesworth as a companion piece to the Mr. Beddington figurine. I always thought he seemed lonely by himself." One corner of her mouth turned up. "Then Father told me he'd received a request from Her Majesty. She'd heard of my artistic abilities and would be pleased to house one of my works in her own collection. Father reasoned that I could keep Miss Bogglesworth, but the Queen must have the best, the piece that won so many awards. When he put it to me like that, I gave him permission to send Mr. Beddington. Oh!" Artemisia stopped short.

If her supposition was right, the Queen's request was a ruse designed by Angus Dalrymple to spirit the precious key out of India. Her artwork was never in royal demand. The key was the only item worthy of Her Majesty's note. Mr. Beddington was merely the pack mule. Something inside Artemisia wilted.

"The Queen probably made no such request, did she?"

"I have no way to know." Trevelyn shrugged and swung his long legs over the edge of the bed. He stooped to retrieve his clothing and began to dress. "But if your father sent the key before his illness, he must have suspected he'd been compromised. Since someone else is also looking for Mr. Beddington, it seems he was right."

"But we've been home for almost three years now,"

she protested. "Surely Britain's enemies would have abandoned the search in that length of time."

"The Great Game never ends," Trev said. "Only the players change. With Mr. Beddington's business prowess recently becoming so well known, it probably set the search off again. If only you weren't so good at turning a coin, you might have masqueraded as Mr. Beddington forever." Her face must have betrayed horror, for he quickly went on, "Don't worry. Your secret is safe with me. You might want to lose a bit on the next boatload of goods, though, just to deflect interest in your alter ego."

He really knew nothing of her, she reflected, if he thought she'd lose at anything on purpose.

Trevelyn pulled on his boots. "At least we can find out if your equine Mr. Beddington is the right one. If the statue is in the Queen's collection, I can get us past the guards to test your theory. It's worth a look."

Artemisia dragged herself from the bed. The determined look on Trev's face was all business. Their shared intimacy seemed to fade like vapor, leaving her feeling strangely bereft.

Idiot! she chided herself as she pulled her chemise over her head to shield her nakedness from his casual gaze. *He's right to keep things simple. A light, uncomplicated relationship. No promises, no shackles on either side. Isn't that what you wanted?*

She mentally shook herself. "Oh, but the Queen may not have Mr. Beddington!"

"But I thought you said—"

"She did have him, but at the masked ball the Russian ambassador admired the Miss Bogglesworth statue and I made a present of it. Her Majesty said she couldn't be outdone by one of her subjects and offered to send round the companion piece." Artemisia put a hand to her lips. "Mr. Beddington may very well be in the collection of Vasiliy Kharitonov as we speak."

Trevelyn blanched at this news. "Then there's no time to lose. I'll break into the ambassador's lodgings and get Mr. Beddington tonight."

"There's no point in taking chances if the statue isn't there." Artemisia lifted her corset into place and invited him to assist her. "Seems Mr. Kharitonov has a number of interesting pieces. As it happens, I have a standing invitation to view the ambassador's collection. If we hurry, there is time enough to pay him a call before night falls."

In less than a quarter hour, Artemisia and Trevelyn made their way down the squeaky stairs and through the Golden Cockerel's common room.

"Will you and your cousin be taking supper with us this evening?" Mrs. Farthingale asked.

"I don't think so," Trev said. "Cousin Hortense so rarely makes it all the way to London, I promised to treat her to a night on the town—coffee house, theater and all."

"Mind how you go, then," the good woman said. Once they cleared the heavy oak door, Mrs. Farthingale grunted in derision. "If that little chit is his cousin, I'm the bloomin' Virgin Mary. I'd bet any amount of guineas on it."

"No takers on that one, Mrs. F.," the man seated on the tall stool said. He'd watched the couple go by behind him in the long mirror above the bar, shoulders hunched in an effort to make himself unremarkable. He turned now that it was safe to do so.

Clarence Wigglesworth, onetime writer for *The*

Tattler, plunked down tuppence to pay for the drink he'd nursed for the last two hours. He stood, hitching his breeches back up to his waist. This was too good an opportunity to pass, despite the Honorable Mr. Deveridge's threats.

Someone should probably warn Deveridge that his bed squeaks loud enough to be heard through the floorboards, Clarence thought as he prepared to follow the duchess and her escort. *Someone really should.*

But it damn well wouldn't be him.

Chapter Twenty-three

"Is lovely for you to visit my humble home, Your Grace," Vasiliy Kharitonov said as he bent to buss his lips over her gloved fingertips. "Almost I don't recognize you in dress as Englishwoman. Your beauty is—what is word?—most becoming to costume of Indian princess."

Artemisia couldn't be sure, but she almost thought she heard Trevelyn growl low in his throat.

"Thank you, Your Excellency. Allow me to introduce my companion. This is Mr. Thomas Doverspike, one of my life models," she said with sweetness. She and Trev had agreed ahead of time that it was best if she were not known to be cavorting about London with the man the *ton* believed was recently engaged to her sister. "In my Olympic series of paintings, Mr. Doverspike is destined to become my god of war."

"Oh, *da?* If paintings are fine as sculpture, them I would like to see." The ambassador raised a monocle to one eye and swept Trev's form. From his intent perusal, Artemisia wasn't wholly sure the Russian's tastes didn't lean more toward strapping young men than Indian princesses. "To what do I owe pleasure of company unexpected?"

"Why, Your Excellency, we were hoping to take

you up on your invitation to view your collection of statuary."

"Of course," he said. "Them we see right away, but first give to allow me to refresh you. Is teatime here in England, but we Russians have different time. Vodka time." He pronounced it *wodka*. "This way. You try perhaps, Your Grace?"

"Oh, no. Just tea for me, if you have it," Artemisia said as he led them up a broad staircase to the parlor. "I've heard vodka will permanently cross one's eyes, if one isn't careful."

The ambassador's belly jiggled with mirth. "*Da*, will also be good for—how you say?—'putting hair on chest'? Mr. Doverspike, how if I offer you some?"

"I'd accept, sir. Thank you," Trevelyn said. "Her Grace might appreciate the challenge of painting more hairs on my chest."

Kharitonov's laughter reverberated through the stairwell as they continued to climb. Artemisia was disappointed that the room where the ambassador's collection was housed wasn't on the easily accessible main level.

The state of relations between England and Russia wasn't cordial enough to warrant a full-blown embassy, but the ambassador's sumptuous townhouse filled the role admirably. It was a tall, narrow structure with rooms jutting off the central staircase like ribs from a spine.

Exquisitely appointed without being fussy, the second-floor parlor was obviously the ambassador's private retreat. Bookshelves lined one wall, and the room was awash in the comfortable mustiness of leather-bound volumes with a faint after-note of Fribourg and Treyer pipe tobacco.

Artemisia perched on one of the matching settees arranged facing each other before the cold fireplace while the ambassador rang for tea. She would have welcomed a small blaze but reminded herself that Russians were used to a much colder climate. The ambassador probably found soggy English days balmy by comparison.

A silent servant appeared almost instantly, bearing a tray of pumpernickel and pickled cucumber sandwiches, along with a bone china tea service. Even though the ambassador claimed not to be expecting company, his staff had obviously been ready. Kharitonov poured shots of the clear liquid for himself and Trevelyn.

The size of the drinking glasses was reassuring to Artemisia, but the sly look in the ambassador's eye was not.

"*Na Zdorovie!*" Vasiliy Kharitonov clinked his glass against the lip of Trevelyn's. "To health," he translated for them.

"*Vasha Zdorovie!*" Trevelyn countered. "*Your* health."

"You speak Russki," the ambassador said with a raised brow. "Your Grace, where you find such learned models? Most servants we must bring if wish to have conversation in tongue of Mother Russia."

Trevelyn winked at her and shrugged. "My father might have been a plain Doverspike from Wiltshire, but my mother's mother was from Odessa."

Artemisia smiled weakly at this. It only served to remind her that the man she'd taken to her bed was an accomplished liar. Thank goodness she had sense enough not to take him into her heart.

Didn't she? Her chest constricted strangely.

"*Nu.*" The ambassador inhaled deeply. Then he knocked back the contents of his glass in one swig.

He nodded to Trevelyn to follow suit as he cleared his throat with a loud *harrumph* and sent a pumpernickel and pickle chaser into his belly.

"No sipping. Sipping is for tea," the ambassador admonished. "Vodka is drink for man. Is meant to be drunk like one, *da*."

Trevelyn gamely tipped his glass and downed his entire portion in one long swallow. His chest convulsed with a suppressed cough and his eyes watered, but he managed not to disgrace the whole of English manhood with his performance. The ambassador seemed pleased and was quick to refill Trev's jigger to the rim.

"Your mother's mother from Odessa would be proud. Again, *da?*" Kharitonov gestured for Trev to toss back another round.

He did so and, after only a few sputters, stood there grinning from ear to ear. To Artemisia's horror, he held out his glass for more.

Artemisia rose and walked toward the nearest horse statuette, displayed on the butterfly grand piano in the corner. Someone had to remember why they were there. It would do Mr. Shipwash no good if Trev became thoroughly foxed before they located the Beddington statue and devised a way to retrieve it.

"This is an interesting piece," she said. The carving was done in aged ivory, mellow with time. "It has an Asiatic quality about it. Fluid lines and sparse ornamentation. Where did you acquire it, Your Excellency?"

"Island of Japans." Distracted from his role as barkeep, the ambassador waddled over to join her in perusing his collection. He showed her statues of horses from Persia and Egypt, Ukraine and Prussia, from distant Brazil and the Americas. The works were carved in jade and exotic woods. Some were ceramic, some in marble or granite, and one slightly tarnished equine was of beaten silver.

"Where are the statues you made, Your Grace?" Trevelyn finally asked when Artemisia stopped him from reaching for a rare primitive from the South Seas with a quick shake of her head. "I've heard a good deal about the one Her Majesty used to own, but I've never seen it."

Artemisia hadn't found either Mr. Beddington or Miss Bogglesworth among the ambassador's diverse collection. She fretted that he'd already discovered the hollow base and the key.

"In bedchamber," Kharitonov said. "Last thing at night and first thing in morning, they bring smile."

The ambassador refilled Trevelyn's empty glass and helped himself to another round.

"I'd admire the chance to view Her Grace's work," Trev said before he manfully dispatched his liquor.

"Of course," the ambassador said. "You wait and I bring, *da?*"

The big man waddled out and disappeared up the staircase. Trevelyn followed him to the doorway and leaned into the hall far enough to mark which level and which way Kharitonov turned to reach his chamber. Trevelyn came back toward Artemisia, swaying a bit on his feet.

"How many shots of that vile drink have you had?" Artemisia hissed. "If you're wobbling on your pins, how do you expect to help me retrieve Mr. Beddington?"

Trevelyn ignored her and made his way to the large fern in one corner. He spat out the vodka into the ceramic planter. "Two less than His Excellency has had, thank you very much. When you distracted him with the Japanese statue, I watered this poor plant the first time."

"Oh," she said weakly. She'd built up a full head of steam over his supposed foolishness. Now it was her turn to feel foolish.

"I'm hoping the vodka will help the ambassador sleep soundly this evening," he said. "Especially if he keeps Beddington in his chamber."

She nodded grudgingly. "But it will not benefit us for you to follow suit. If you keep accepting drinks, you'll be no use at all. You won't be able to kill the plant every time."

"No, but with your help diverting the ambassador's attention, I'll do my best." One corner of his mouth turned up in a wry smile. "Don't worry. I also inherited a good head for vodka from my grandmother."

"You really do have a grandmother from Odessa?"

"Of course." He cocked his head at her. "Why?"

"I thought it was another lie." Artemisia felt prickly all over, as if she was wearing scratchy wool. She didn't know what to attribute it to. "Prevarication is habitual with some. You do it quite well, you know."

He crooked a brow at her. "I would think you'd be the last person to throw stones. What was your performance as Mr. Beddington if not a colossal lie?"

"This is not the place to discuss that Mr. Beddington," she reminded him. "But since you ask, it was a matter of necessity. There was no other way for me to conduct business."

He shook his head. "No, Larla. Just like me, you enjoy the Game. You may have tried to convince yourself your motives were pure, but you liked the subterfuge as much as running the family business. Maybe more."

Trevelyn moved close enough that she could feel the heat of his body. She half expected him to take her in his arms, but he didn't. That would have been too easy. Instead he just looked down at her, his dark gaze searching.

She swallowed hard. Trev had seen her stripped bare, had taken his time to gaze on every inch of her form. Now he was doing the same with her soul, pulling back layers of self-protecting falsehoods and exposing the truth.

"We're the same, you and I," he finally said. "Your assistant is in danger and you're upset with yourself because part of you is enjoying this."

"That's ridiculous."

"Is it?" He placed his fingertips on her throat. "Your heart is hammering like a woodpecker and your cheeks are flushed crimson. Very becoming, I might add."

"Planning a burglary is more than enough cause for palpitations," she protested. "You needn't insult me over them."

"I mean no insult." He stroked her cheek with his knuckles. "It's no sin to enjoy the Game, Larla. The tingle of anticipation, the spice of danger—it lets us know we're alive. People like us need adventure like a fish needs water. We couldn't settle for ordinary if our hope of heaven depended upon it."

Artemisia was saved from a reply by the ambassador's heavy tread on the stairs. Trev brushed his lips on her forehead.

"I plan to drink our Russian friend under his mahogany table. Remember to divert his attention for me." He moved to stand by the fern on the other side of the room. "I'll need your help if I'm to *wodka* the plant."

Chapter Twenty-four

An hour later, Trevelyn had to be carried to the waiting hansom by three of Kharitonov's servants.

"Your Mr. Doverspike, he is good drinker for Englishman," Vasiliy Kharitonov said with a slur in his voice. "But vodka lays out better men than he, *da*."

The ambassador himself was unsteady on his feet when Artemisia left him, but that hoped-for outcome gave her no satisfaction. Not with Trevelyn nearly unconscious. She thanked Kharitonov's men, tucked her skirts in around her and rapped sharply on the roof of the cab to signal her readiness to depart.

She barely contained her readiness to throttle Trevelyn. His plan had backfired brilliantly. Now he was slumped beside her on the seat, head lolling back, his drunken face covered by his bowler. He was snoring softly. If it would do any good, she'd slap him silly.

"Now what do we do?" she asked the slouched form.

Then the hansom took a sharp turn around a corner. "I don't know about you," a muffled voice came from beneath the bowler, "but I intend to have a bit of a late supper and get some rest. It promises to be a long night."

To her surprise, Trevelyn sat up straight and winked at her. "Well, that was harder than I expected, but it seemed to work. The esteemed ambassador will be seeking his pillow early and settle deeply into the arms of Morpheus, just as we planned."

The urge to slap him increased exponentially. "Then you're not—"

"Drunk? No. Oh, I've a buzzing in my ears and no sensation at all in my lips, but I'll do, Larla." His eyes glittered at her with more alcoholic haze than he'd admit. "We're a good team, you and I. Every time I knocked back my glass, you pulled Kharitonov away with your interest in yet another of his little horses. I greatly fear that fern is done for." He chucked her chin. "And you, madam, are a natural at this."

"If being scared and flustered while plotting a burglary is natural." Drat the man, he actually seemed to be enjoying himself. "Do you think the ambassador will take the Beddington statue back to his room or leave it on the piano?"

"I won't know until I break back in tonight," he said cheerfully.

"You mean when *we* break back in," she corrected.

All cheer drained from his features. "When I said we were a good team, I only meant you were helpful with the ambassador. I don't intend to involve you in the actual theft of Mr. Beddington. It's too dangerous."

"But not too dangerous for you?"

"Larla, I've been trained for this type of activity. You haven't."

"Her Majesty's Intelligence officers stoop to burglary often, then?

"Oftener than you might think," he admitted. His stern expression made her realize that even more grievous acts might be required of Trevelyn in the Queen's service. For a moment, she wondered if he'd been forced to kill to protect the Crown's interests.

She decided not to ask.

"Still, you need me with you," she insisted, "if for no other reason than to help you find the right statue."

"I got a pretty good look at it."

"Really? Describe it for me." The rhythm of the cab wheels over the cobbled streets jostled her closer to him with every bounce.

"It's a Shetland pony, rearing on his hind legs, his fat little belly bulging," he said. "A ridiculous pose for the breed but cleverly done. I can see why it caught the Crown's attention."

"Do you realize that description fits either Mr. Beddington or Miss Bogglesworth?" She tried to ignore the solid plane of his thigh against hers. "The statues are very similar, as like as two peas. You won't be able to tell which you have in your hand. But I will."

"I'll burgle them both," he said.

"And burden yourself unnecessarily at a time when you may need a free hand," she argued. "The statues themselves aren't too heavy, but the new bases are."

"Then I'll put them both into a sack so as to have a free hand," he countered.

Artemisia gasped in indignation and edged away from him, pressing herself against the side of the compartment. "And risk damaging them?"

"My apologies. I thought we were chiefly interested in the saving of Mr. Shipwash, not the preservation of clay horses," Trevelyn said darkly. "Besides, you sculpted them. Can't you make them again?"

She shook her head. "The twelve-year-old who made those statues for the sheer joy of it is gone. Once my work started winning competitions, the expectations began to press down on me. I've never been as free in my creations as I was when I had no artistic reputation to live up to."

With that flash of insight, she realized why she'd been so mercilessly particular with her art, so obsessed with perfection. It was draining all the joy from not only her work but her life as well. And only she could free herself from the crushing weight of the pursuit of the perfect.

"Of course, you are right. Do what you must with the statues," she said. "Retrieving the key to free Mr. Shipwash is the most important thing. But I do insist on accompanying you whether you will it or no. If you refuse to take me, I shall simply follow you. And who knows what trouble that could lead to?"

"I shudder to think." He leaned toward her and took both her hands in his. "Why, Larla? Why must you come?"

Because you are going into danger and I can't bear the thought of you risking yourself for me and not being there to help.

But she knew she couldn't say that. It would be admitting that she cared more than a little for him when he'd not spoken a word of love to her. Their relationship was complicated enough without becoming entangled in the sticky web of sentiment.

"Because Mr. Shipwash is in my employ. I'm responsible for him," she said truthfully. "One way or another, I will see this through to its end."

"You are stubborn as a rock." Trevelyn gave her a grudging smile and reached up his warm hand to cup her cheek. "And softer than silk." He leaned forward and kissed her, the sting of the ambassador's vodka still flavoring his lips. "And sweeter than brandy."

"Careful," she said when he finally drew back. "One shouldn't mix drinks."

"I'll risk it." He jerked the cab's curtains closed, thrusting them into semidarkness, and pulled her onto his lap.

She surprised herself by going willingly. His vodka-tinged kiss lit a fire in her belly. A fire that could only be extinguished by more of him. "Trevelyn Deveridge, you are turning me into the most brazen wanton."

His mouth was on her neck, sending delicious shivers of pleasure over her. When he began to unbutton her bodice, she made no move to stop him. Artemisia watched in fascination as he loosened her buttons one by one.

"You've already proven I can't make you anything other than what you are. But you're no wanton," he said. "You're a desirable woman with needs she's not afraid to acknowledge. When you first told me you required a lover, I said to myself, 'There's a rare find.' Most women I've known haven't a clue what they really want or how to go about getting it."

"There's where you're wrong. Most women want marriage," she said as his fingers slid in to toy with the hollow between her breasts. "And they have definite ideas about how to get it."

His hand stilled beneath the hollow at the base of her throat and he met her gaze squarely. "And is

this your idea of how to snare a husband? Because
if it is—"

"Gracious, no! The last thing I need is a husband."
Artemisia forced a laugh. Why had she even brought
up the subject? He'd think she was trying to trap him
into marriage. "I enjoy my freedom. But I do still
have plenty to learn about what passes between a
man and a woman. The gravity of our situation could
hardly be more dire, and yet your mere presence
makes my toes curl, sir. Why is that?"

"Danger is a powerful aphrodisiac," he explained.
"It's like spice for the sauce. Flirting with danger sets
the body's juices flowing."

Even though she wore her many layers of petticoats, she felt the length of him hard beneath her
skirts. The answering warmth between her own legs
started a low pulse beat of longing. "So I see."

"Gives a man a terrible cockstand."

"Oh, dear." She kissed his ear and nipped at the
lobe. He groaned softly and plunged his hand down
the front of her bodice to knead her breast. "What
can we do about that?"

"A resourceful pair like us, we'll think of something," he assured her. When he bent his head to
sample the exposed tops of her breasts, she arched
her back, thrusting the aching mounds up to him.

"No sensation at all in your lips, eh?"

"It's starting to come back to me," he said with a
wicked grin. His hand crept under her voluminous
skirts and found the slit in her bloomers. He sepa-
rated her delicate folds and ran his finger the length
of her wetness. A jolt of desire sent her blood singing
through her veins. "It's a long trip back to Tydburn
Street, thank God."

She closed her eyes and let him take her to that dark, hot place, waiting to burst into light.

"Amen," she whispered fervently. "Amen."

"Stop the presses!" Clarence Wigglesworth shouted as the door to *The Tattler* office banged behind him. "I've got your front page right here."

Mr. Upton, the editor, looked up from his clanking press and shoved his spectacles back up to the bridge of his nose. "Hold your noise, Wigglesworth. I've no time for your nonsense."

"This is no nonsense, and if you don't buy this story, I'll sell it to your competitor. Old Farsinglass over at *Bon Mots* will probably pay double, no questions asked." Clarence waved the ink-blotched paper under his employer's nose. "In fact, I've half a mind to do just that."

Upton snatched the paper from him and ran his gaze over it, his lips moving wordlessly as he read.

"You're right, for once," the editor said. "Help me reset the page then. This will curdle the *ton*'s milk, and no mistake."

Several hours later, Clarence sat down among the stacks of the print run and read his career-making piece. No doubt about it, this story was his finest hour as a journalist.

A Troth Betrayed

The Honorable Mr. Trevelyn Deveridge only recently announced his engagement to Miss Florinda Dalrymple but seemed to have forgotten that obligation this evening.

Lord Warre's second-born son and an ostensible "cousin" of the female variety enjoyed a se-

*cret "tête-à-tête" in a decidedly seedy establish-
ment in a less than fashionable London neigh-
borhood. This reporter can attest to the fact that
there was little conversation going on during
the meeting, which lasted several hours. Nothing was heard from the Honorable (and we use
the term with extreme looseness) Mr. Deveridge's room, unless one counted the com-
plaints of his creaky bedstead.*

*Then Mr. Deveridge flaunted his "cousin" in
a lark about London in a hired hansom. Upon
their return to the aforementioned seedy estab-
lishment, when said hansom came to a halt, the
cab continued to rock rhythmically for about a
minute before the pair emerged, disheveled and
windblown from their exertions.*

*The cabby, a Mr. Winthrop Hornby from
Chelsea, was most impressed with Mr. Deveridge's performance. He commented to this reporter that he'd have said the gentleman was
incapable of carnal knowledge of a woman due
to extreme intoxication. Apparently, the Earl of
Warre's second son had to be carried bodily from
an undisclosed location and deposited in the
hansom with his unnamed "cousin" for the return trip to their illicit love nest. One is filled with
admiration for Deveridge's recuperative powers,
if not his morals.*

*One hopes the hapless Miss Florinda Dalrym-
ple will have friends kind enough to warn her
of her future husband's proclivities before it is
everlastingly too late.*

"Proclivities," Clarence repeated. "Good word,
that." After a few more well-deserved moments of

self-congratulation, he gathered his payment and shoved it in his pocket. The stack of coins was still on the low side of paltry, but markedly better than he'd done in recent days.

Deveridge will have no kick coming, he reasoned as he stepped into the dark, empty street. *Write anything you like about me, he says. So b'Gad, I did. And I didn't mention the duchess by name once. No, by thunder, not once.*

Chapter Twenty-five

"Well, Larla, I think we've broken some kind of record." Trevelyn lay back on his pillow, spent and gasping. Each time he thought there was nothing more in him, but at the slightest provocation—a smoldering look, her sultry voice, the smooth whiteness of her bare skin—his cock was primed and ready for another round. The woman might well be the death of him, but he'd die smiling. He laced his fingers behind his head. "But we've not gotten a smidge of rest."

Larla raised up on one elbow to look down at him, her long dark hair tumbling over her shoulders. He'd never think of her as Her Grace or even plain Artemisia ever again. She'd always be his Larla, even though he still had no idea what her secret name meant. Her rosy nipple was tantalizingly near, but he was satisfied for the moment just to look. It puckered tight and was undoubtedly aching under his scrutiny.

"No rest, eh? Is that a complaint?" she asked.

"Never."

He decided seeing wasn't quite as good as tasting after all and took her delightful berry in his mouth once more. He suckled till she made that noise again, the low growl of contentment with an edge of desire, before he released her nipple. Then he pulled her close to him, snugged up against his side.

As close as Adam and his Rib, he thought drowsily. He peered over his cheekbones at the top of her tousled head, now resting in the crook of his arm. *Surely Eve was no more glorious than this woman. Though I'd wager a good deal less stubborn.*

"What are you thinking?" her voice floated up to him, small and surprisingly timid after the abandon of their lovemaking.

He ran his hand down the length of her spine and stayed to dally with the dimple above her round bottom. "Actually, given our most recent occupation and current situation, my thoughts are surprisingly ecclesiastical."

"How do you mean?"

"It's foolish really," he said.

"Foolish or not, you can tell me."

"Being here naked like this makes me wonder how Adam and Eve felt. I mean, there Adam was, with none but the animals for company, all alone in an empty world, and then suddenly he sees someone he recognizes without being introduced."

"I suspect the Almighty provided the introductions," she said with the practicality he'd come to admire.

"No, I'm inclined to think Adam saw Eve and knew right away who she was. Blood of my blood and bone of my bone and all that. Something in him called to her and she answered." Trev dropped a kiss on the crown of her head. "And then, even in an empty world, suddenly he wasn't alone anymore. I was just wondering if it felt . . . well, something like this."

She was still for a few moments. Then she wrapped her arms around him and squeezed. "I think it must have felt exactly like this."

Trevelyn breathed deeply and realized, against all

odds, that he was happy. It was totally illogical. After all, his father, whom he'd never been able to please, had now disowned him. He was planning a burglary with naught but a duchess for assistance. And then a rescue that even with supreme good luck stood little chance of success, but he couldn't stop his mouth from turning up into an idiot's grin. He was happier than he'd ever been in his entire life.

"You know," she said, teasing the hairs whorled around one of his nipples, "even given, as you put it, our previous occupation and current situation, I don't think it's at all strange that your thoughts should turn spiritual. I mean, the way we lift each other out of ourselves, the giving and receiving of pleasure, is no small thing. When we're joined, it does almost seem supernatural. What we've shared has something of the Divine Spark about it."

His grin grew even wider and definitely more wicked. "Maybe that's why you kept saying 'Oh, God!'"

She snatched her pillow and pummeled him with it. At first he could only raise his hands in self-protection, he was laughing so hard. Then he found his own pillow and made a good bout of it, whacking her delicious bottom. Finally one, or maybe both, of the pillows burst open. A flurry of white feathers fluttered around them, coming to rest on their bare bodies, tickling their skin and catching in their hair.

Trevelyn threw down the empty casing and grabbed Larla around the waist. They collapsed together on the bed in a giggling heap.

He loved her laugh. It was no girlish twitter. It was the sound of a woman completely pleased with the world. He realized, with a great sense of accomplishment, that he was responsible for it. When he first met her, he'd have been satisfied just to make her smile. Now she was laughing like a fool and he loved it.

They rolled together on the bed and, as luck and superior strength would have it, Trevelyn managed to end up on top. His hips rested between her splayed legs. He took his weight on his elbows and looked down at her.

She was flushed with pleasure and the green depths of her eyes sparkled. Her little pointed tongue flicked over her top lip and she blew away a stray feather, her belly quivering beneath him.

Trevelyn stopped laughing. He could watch this woman for the rest of his life, he realized with a start.

"What is it?" she asked, obviously sensing his change of mood.

He lowered his lips to hers and took his time about kissing her. All the while his tongue made love to her mouth, his mind churned furiously.

This cannot be good, he told himself with sternness. *You're needed as soon as possible on the Indian subcontinent. A whole string of operatives is waiting, looking for some direction from London. There's no permanent place for a woman in your life just now, old son. A romp, yes. A romance, emphatically no.*

And yet the kiss went on, deepening and draining. He felt his soul pouring itself into her, seeking her secrets and loving all of them.

Love? Where in the name of perdition did that come from?

He pulled back from her sharply.

"Larla, I—" Trev caught himself before the words spilled out of his mouth. Suddenly, he knew what Larla meant, at least to him. *Beloved.* He laid his head between her breasts, too much a coward to meet her gaze.

He loved her and he shouldn't have her. The life ahead of him in India was too uncertain, too full of potential danger to include a wife. It wouldn't be fair. And maybe he couldn't have her even if he offered. Hadn't she proclaimed in no uncertain terms that she'd never marry again?

"Oh, God," he said.

This time, Trev figured, the words counted as a prayer.

The night was more than half-spent when Artemisia and Trevelyn reluctantly left his well-used bed. They dressed in near silence in the moon-washed room. Trevelyn assisted her with her laces without being asked, and she helped him tie his cravat in a fashionable knot.

Just like an old married couple, she thought absently. *But most old married couples don't lark about breaking and entering, do they?*

"I counted at least six servants in the ambassador's townhouse. It won't be easy to slip past them unnoticed." She adjusted her bonnet over her hastily swept-up hair. "Have you thought about how we'll do it?"

"Not to worry, madam." He cavalierly offered his arm. "A Deveridge always has a plan. Do you still ride?"

"Not nearly often enough, but yes." She switched to a whisper as they entered the hall. The common room below was empty, but she reasoned they might as well begin as they meant to continue this night. Stealth was the watchword. "Remember, Mr. Beddington started out as my pony."

"So he did." He chuckled softly as they made their way down the stairs. He helped her avoid the third step from the bottom.

"Squeaks abominably," he whispered. "I keep a horse in the stable out back. We'll have to ride double. It may be hard on the nag, but frankly, there's nothing I'd rather have between my knees than your well-rounded bottom."

His words sent a rush of remembered pleasure over her. With a sigh, she pushed the sensation aside. The time for love games was done. Now they played for keeps.

Trevelyn saddled the sturdy-looking cob, mounted him in a fluid motion and held a hand down to Artemisia. She used his booted foot in the stirrups as a step and sidesaddled herself before him. He wrapped an arm about her waist and snugged her in tightly before chirruping to the gelding to urge him into a brisk trot.

Artemisia leaned back into Trev's chest. He planted a quick kiss on her neck as they rounded a gaslit corner. She'd had very little sleep the night before and only a few snatches amid their lovemaking this night, but she was too excited to be tired.

Every fiber in her body hummed with well-being and the afterglow of pleasure. Surrounded now by his strong arms and sharp male scent, Artemisia wished the ride to the ambassador's townhouse was much longer.

After all, if they were successful tonight, if they recovered Mr. Beddington and used him to free Mr. Shipwash, then Trevelyn would be off to India at the first opportunity. Her chest ached. She wondered if he'd miss her, even a little, but she couldn't ask him.

"You realize that we can't actually give the key to the ruffians holding Mr. Shipwash," Trevelyn said as their destination came into view. "We'd be signing the death warrants of all your father's contacts."

"Then what is your plan?"

"We retrieve the key and substitute it with a decoy. Chances are the kidnappers don't know exactly what the key is. They only know it was important enough for your father to send it to safety."

Artemisia nodded. Her father would counsel the same, she was sure. She just wished she didn't feel so responsible for her assistant's abduction. If she'd never masqueraded as Beddington, none of this would have happened.

"But we will still free James," she said emphatically.

"Of course," Trev said. "We'll have all day tomorrow to come up with a substitute, and I will make the exchange for you at St. Paul's tomorrow night."

"But Felix said I was to come alone. I mustn't call in the authorities, they said."

"No, *Beddington* is to come alone. And since no one but we knows who Beddington really is, there's no reason I can't be him for the exchange. They're expecting a man, after all."

Trev reined in the horse and guided him down the narrow alleyway behind the ambassador's row of townhouses.

"But this is my responsibility," she said.

"We'll discuss it later." He slid from the saddle and then lifted her down lightly. "Other matters are more pressing at present. Come."

Instead of approaching the rear of the ambassador's home, Trevelyn led her to the adjoining townhouse. He tried the door, which was locked, and then worked to jimmy open a window.

"You are aware this is the wrong house," she whispered.

"Yes, but it works to our advantage. This whole row

of townhouses is built just like my father's pied-à-terre. There's a little-known design flaw about them."

A strained look passed over Trevelyn's face that had nothing to do with his exertions. It occurred to her that Trev had never mentioned his father or mother. She knew very little about his home life, save that he was the second-born of twins. She supposed that made him as expendable in the currency of progeny as a first-born daughter when one is hoping for a son. Not that her father ever said so in so many words, but the fact that he had raised her as if she were a boy spoke volumes about his secret hopes.

And his disappointments.

"These residences share a common attic." Trevelyn winced as the window frame budged only fractionally. "We can enter here, make our way to the attic and then into the ambassador's residence from the garret."

"What if the people who live here catch us?" Artemisia asked.

"Take a peek in the window."

In the pale moonlight, Artemisia saw only ghostly shapes dotting the room. The furniture was all draped in white muslin to protect it against the sooty London air, a sure sign the owners were not in residence.

"I noticed this house was closed down when we were here earlier." Trev ran his penknife's blade around the edge of the window casing to free it from the coat of paint that held it closed. "But we'll have to be quiet, just in case."

He drew a deep breath and gave the sticky window another shove. This time it gave, rising with a creak of wood on wood. Trevelyn disappeared into the opening and waggled his fingers for Artemisia to follow.

Well, he is trained in this sort of thing, she reasoned. She hitched up her skirt and followed him through the dark portal.

Chapter Twenty-six

"Careful," he whispered as her feet touched the floor. "We still need to move quietly. If there are any servants left, they'll most likely be in the rooms off the cellar kitchen."

"Not in the garret?"

"My father's servants who live in the highest rooms of his townhouse suffer with cold or bake with heat depending on the season, but the ones housed near the kitchen are comfortable year-round," Trev explained. "The earl and I battled over this several times, but he refuses to do anything about it." He shook his head, as if to clear his mind of thoughts of his sire. "If you had your choice of a cold garret or a cozy kitchen fire, which would you pick?"

"I see your point." Her manor house was arranged differently from the earl's townhouse. Her home had a multitude of fireplaces and windows, even in the topmost story. Surely Cuthbert would have spoken up if there was a problem. The stiff-lipped butler certainly never restrained himself when he thought her behavior required comment. But just in case, she made a mental note to see to the condition of her own servants' rooms as soon as possible.

Trev bent to unbuckle his boots. Then, in his stocking feet, he picked Artemisia up and sat her down on the broad, flat top of a grand piano. The strings inside the casing vibrated softly in a cluster of tones as air currents soughed over them.

"Oh!" Artemisia felt Trevelyn's hand on her ankle. He started to remove her slipper. A fizz of excitement shot up her leg and stayed to simmer in her feminine core. Part of it was his casual familiarity, the way his fingers lingered over her instep in a caress. But part of her prickling skin was the excitement of the forbidden. Cuthbert had chided her for scandalous behavior often enough. This was the first time she could rightly be accused of something criminal.

Trevelyn was right: Danger was exciting. The fact that breaking and entering set her pulse dancing might trouble her if she examined it long enough, so she shoved the thought aside.

"Come." Trev lifted her from her perch and set her back on her feet. He dropped a quick kiss on her forehead and then took her hand to lead her through the stark landscape of gray shadows and white muslin, ghostly in the moonlight.

They slipped wraithlike between the lumps of covered furniture toward the base of the stairs. Just like the ambassador's residence, this house was organized around the central staircase. Artemisia placed a hand on the smooth brass rail and followed Trevelyn up the curving stairway.

A round window at each landing lit their way. They climbed past the parlor that was the mirror image of the ambassador's and past the floor that held the bedrooms. Their trek came to a dead end at a locked door.

"Oh, dear! Will we have to break it down?"

"Not as long as we have the right tools." Trev produced a slender pick to work in the keyhole. The lock proved only a minor deterrent. Trevelyn Deveridge indeed had skills that didn't become a gentleman, but his bow as he held the door open for her would have done credit to a prince.

"Ordinarily I'd defer to a lady, but in this instance perhaps you'll allow me to go first," Trevelyn said with a lighthearted attempt at gallantry.

Artemisia appreciated the effort. Staring into the gaping blackness, she dimly made out a set of ladderlike steps disappearing into the rafters. She wondered if there might be bats. With a shudder, she waggled her fingers toward the entrance. "No, by all means, please lead the way."

Trevelyn lit the candle in the tin stand that had been left at the base of the steps and then climbed into the void. The small flame sent shadows dancing into the rough timbers under the eaves. Trevelyn disappeared from her view for a moment, and then the light stopped wavering when he'd obviously set the candle down. His shadowed face appeared in the opening, backlit by the guttering flame. He reached down a hand to her. "Coming? Or have you changed your mind?"

As an artist, she was a creature of light. She even preferred to sleep with a low fire or a lamp burning should she wake in the night. Strange dark places always made her uneasy. And dark places that might house flying rodents were even worse.

"No, of course I haven't," she snapped, more brusque than she'd intended. She tried to disguise the tightness in her chest as pique rather than fear. "You need me."

"Yes, I do," she thought she heard him mutter softly before raising his voice in a stage whisper. "Give me your hand and don't mind the cobwebs, then."

He grasped her wrist and neatly lifted her up with him in a single motion so that her feet barely grazed the steep stairs. A sticky strand tickled across her cheek. Definitely cobwebs, but nothing with wings that she could detect. For as far as the meager light of the candle shined, she saw only odds and ends of household goods—a dressmaker's dummy propped against a rafter, a canting spinning wheel and countless dusty chests.

"Careful, now." Trev retrieved the candlestick and took her hand. "Watch your step. There's no flooring here, just open joists. Try not to slip between them. There's no guarantee you won't go right through the ceiling plaster."

His hand was a warm anchor. Toes curling to grip each step, she moved from timber to timber behind Trev as he led the way down the long, dark space toward the ambassador's residence. At one point he stopped and swept the candle behind him, indicating with a jerk of his head that she should look downward. Thin cracks of light were visible in the plastered space between the timbers.

A gas lamp was burning below them. Someone was still awake in Kharitonov's home.

Trev put a finger to his lips and settled into a crouch, cocking his head to listen. Artemisia lowered herself to sit on a chest balanced on two timbers. She strained to hear.

At first there was only the creaking groans of settling lathe and plaster common to all houses. Then came small skittering noises of tiny claws scurrying away from their source of light. A mouse she could stand, though she didn't want to be surprised by one. The dust cloud she raised from sitting on the chest tickled her nostrils. She brought a scented hanky to her nose and successfully fought back a sneeze, but only by intense concentration.

Then she heard the voices. They were muffled, but one of the speakers became agitated and the tone increased appreciably. She followed the conversation beneath her feet with horrified fascination.

"I tell you, there's no point in torture. Shipwash either doesn't know or can't be broke," a voice she thought she recognized was saying. "There are some who can't, I guess. If you want my advice—"

A vicious smack stopped the speaker. Artemisia flinched at the sound.

"When we need *adwice* from traitor, we tell you," Kharitonov said, no longer the charming diplomat. "If Lubov and Oranskiy force information from Beddington's man, I will not make—how you say?—fuss over how."

"But the duchess might not make the trade if you've abused him." The speaker sniffed loudly. "She's on good terms with the Queen on account of her art. She'll make trouble for you once she learns you're behind this."

"And how shall she know? You will tell her?" the ambassador demanded. His tone was very different from that of the genial host who'd plied Trev with vodka only a few hours earlier. Clearly, Artemisia could take no one at face value anymore.

"No, no, of course not." Fear sent the voice straying into another octave. "But Beddington will know, and he won't keep mum, you can be sure of that. Whatever he knows, she'll know."

"Then Mr. Beddington we kill same as Shipwash when time comes," Kharitonov said icily. "Perhaps, we do favor and send troublemaking stepmother to fishes with them, *da?*"

Artemisia's hand went involuntarily to her chest. Trev's grip on her other one tightened. She'd hoped her ears were playing tricks on her, but that hope died with the ambassador's deadly offer. The other speaker really was Felix after all.

"What? No need for such drastic measures, I'm sure," Felix said. "I'll handle the duchess. Forget I mentioned it."

Artemisia could almost smell his fear. It was clear her stepson had fallen in with the worst of companions and now had no clue how to extricate himself. At least he hadn't entirely thrown her to the wolves—or, in this case, to the fishes—but he'd placed her in a deucedly difficult spot. Whether he realized it or not, in bartering for the key, Felix was hip-deep in the traffic of national secrets.

Men had been tried for treason and hanged for less.

Artemisia was so afraid for him, she was seized by the urge to give him a good shake. His father, the old duke, would have been mortified by Felix's actions.

While she stewed over her stepson, the dust she and Trev had stirred in the attic began to make her nose twitch. She tried to suppress it again, but when a body wants to sneeze, it's almost impossible to gainsay it a second time. She managed to cover her nose and mouth, but the sneeze erupted in an imploded squeak.

The voices beneath them fell silent. A booted tread clicked across the floor and stopped directly beneath her. She didn't dare draw another breath. Trevelyn squeezed her hand, pleading for silence. Her heart hammered so loudly, she was sure the men below her would hear it.

"A flymouse. Or rat maybe," a different voice finally

said. "Whole city crawling with rats. Tomorrow, I lay out poison."

"*Nyet,*" Kharitonov said. "Once we have key, back we go to St. Petersburg. Already I have dismiss English servants. Couldn't cook anyway. First thing I do back in Mother Russia is have real food. Give me to eat stroganoff and borscht and you can keep kidney pie and stewed eels."

Artemisia heard a thumping sound and imagined the ambassador pounding Felix's back with mock affability.

"These pale Englishmen—any slimy thing between two pieces of bread they call sandwich and they eat, eh, Lubov?"

Felix giggled nervously at this slur on his national cuisine and excused himself.

Once he was gone, silence reigned for about a minute. Then the voice Artemisia didn't know spoke again.

"Before we leave for St. Petersburg, you want me tie up loose end?"

"To kill Felix is waste of time," the ambassador said dismissively. "Someone will do for us. The boy cheats at cards. Besides, him we own. A duke, bought and paid for, is like hog. We goad him now to do our will. Later, we make bacon."

The ambassador laughed at his own wit, then groaned. Artemisia heard the creak of a chair.

"You are ill?" Lubov asked.

"No, too much wodka. The Englishman this afternoon nearly bested me, but him I sent out feet first." A smile crept into his voice, followed by another groan. "His head I hope is worse than mine. Feels like peasant with pickax."

Trevelyn grinned wickedly at the ambassador's discomfort.

"You need sleep, Excellency. Here, I have laudanum. Keeps Shipwash quiet when workers are about," Lubov said. "Is good, *da?*"

Trevelyn nodded, his excitement at this development clear. They needed the house quiet and the occupants somnolent before they could attempt the burglary. Artemisia had hoped to learn that Mr. Shipwash was held somewhere here in the residence, but Lubov's words dispelled that notion. Workers being present sounded more like a factory of some sort.

The Russians talked a few more minutes about Mr. Shipwash, but Lubov finally took his leave without giving any other clue as to his hostage's whereabouts. Then the light from the cracks winked out.

Trevelyn blew out their candle, plunging them into total blackness.

"Trev—"

His hand found her and traveled up her body to clamp over her mouth. Suddenly his lips were beside her ear.

"If we could see their light, the ambassador might see ours now that his is out," he whispered, so close his breath tickled the small hairs that escaped her chignon. He must have felt her tremble, for he moved onto the chest beside her and took her in his arms. "Hush now, there's my brave girl."

Darkness enveloped her like a suffocating shroud. She couldn't see anything. Not the rafters above her. Not the hand she waved before her face. Not the man who held her to keep her from crying out. Panic rose like gorge in her throat, but she swallowed it back.

Artemisia heard the heavy tread of the ambassador and his servant leaving the room below them, but

Trev didn't relight the candle. She knew they needed to give the ambassador time to go to sleep, but the knowledge was small comfort there in the dark.

Trevelyn rocked her slowly, and gradually she let her head settle on his shoulder, her breathing slow and even. She closed her eyes. There was no point in leaving them open, after all. The tremors drained from her body as time stopped around her. She had no idea how long they sat there together in the darkness.

"That's better," he said softly. "I'm sorry. I didn't realize you were afraid of the dark. After all, I found you in your dark studio the night of the masquerade."

"There was still moonlight coming through the window. Ever since I was a little girl, dark places give me nightmares," she admitted, burrowing deeper into his shoulder, drawing comfort from his solid presence in the black void. "I couldn't have been more than five or six."

"What happened?"

"There was an uprising. A unit of sepoys rebelled and went rampaging through the district, killing and looting. We hid in a dark root cellar while Rania and Naresh told the raiders we had fled to the hills. They destroyed the residence and moved on. But we didn't dare come out of hiding for fear they'd return. Finally, the military routed them."

"How long were you there?"

"I don't know. Days. To a child, it seemed like an eternity, but the thing I remember most is that my father was afraid as we huddled in the dark. That scared me more than anything."

"He was afraid for you," Trev said. "That's why it makes more sense for a player in the Great Game to be a confirmed bachelor."

Like you, she almost said. She put a hand to her forehead. She couldn't think about him leaving for India yet.

"Now the dark always calls that terror back for me," she whispered. "I'm sorry. I feel so foolish."

"Don't. Only the foolish fear nothing."

"So what are you afraid of?" she asked.

"Losing y—" He stopped himself.

She wished she could see his face so she could read on his expressive features what he'd decided not to voice.

"I know you're no fool." Artemisia brought up a hand to caress his jaw. "So by your own words, you must have some fear."

"I used to fear never being able to please my father," he admitted. "Now I know pleasing him is impossible, so I've stopped trying."

"You must love your father greatly if it meant so much to you to win his approval."

He snorted softly. "Love is not a word my family is accustomed to using. But the truth is, my father is a miserable person. My brother Theobald trots after him like a basset hoping for a scrap. But even bootlicking isn't enough. No one is worthy, you see. I have to live with the fact that I haven't ever . . ."

"Ever what?"

Artemisia felt him struggle to find the right words. When his muscles went slack, she thought he'd abandoned the search.

"I haven't ever given him reason to be proud of me," he finally said.

Her heart constricted for him.

"He'll die someday." His voice held the flat monotone of a prophetic utterance. "And word will come to me and there will be this unspoken conversation hanging over us, never resolved. But I fear by then I won't care."

She felt his body shudder.

"I fear I'll be just like him."

Chapter Twenty-seven

Trev gave himself a brisk shake. "Well, that's about as maudlin as I've ever been in my entire life." He rose to his feet and retrieved the candle. "Must be the aftereffects of too much vodka, though I'm not suffering from a bad head like the ambassador fortunately is. Surely it's been long enough for that laudanum to send him to oblivion."

He struck a match. The amber circle of light illuminated his face, and Artemisia's spirits rose considerably. Not just for the way the shadows retreated around them, either. Trev had bared far more of himself there in the dark than he ever had when his body was unclothed in her studio. He'd allowed her a glimpse of his soul.

Whatever his faults—and she suspected they were many—she was convinced that soul was a good one. Whatever became of them, she was glad she knew him.

"Now what?" she asked.

"We look for the trapdoor. There must be a set of stairs leading down into the ambassador's residence."

They tiptoed from beam to beam, searching in earnest. Finally Artemisia found the framed opening hidden beneath an ancient trunk plastered with travel notices from the four corners of the globe. When

Trevelyn eased the door open, they discovered no narrow stairwell at all. Instead, the candlelight illuminated an upstairs maid's linen closet, about four feet square. The shelves were filled to bursting with muslin sheets and pillowcases and velvet draperies no longer in use, but too good to be thrown to the ragpicker. The musty smell of old linen and dusty velvet mingled with the stale, vaguely mousy air of the garret.

"Gentlemen first," Artemisia said hopefully.

"No help for it, I'm afraid." He braced his arms on either side of the opening and lowered himself down. He found his footing on one of the shelves and eased his way to the floor without a sound. "Right, then. Can you hand down the candle?"

It would leave her in darkness again. She hesitated.

"If it's too hard, just leave it. We'll muddle through," Trev whispered.

"No, we may need it," she said, determined to be a help instead of a hindrance. She dropped to her knees, balancing on the beams, and stretched her arm down, leaning her ear to the frame of the opening.

"Got it."

She sat back up, grateful that the candlelight still shot up through the trapdoor at least. Then it dimmed as Trevelyn pushed the linen aside and placed the candle on one of the shelves.

"Now, for you, Larla," he said. "Feet first."

She swung her legs over the opening and tucked her skirt through so it wouldn't catch on anything. Even with her layers of petticoats, if she didn't keep her knees together, he'd have a clear view of the slit crotch in her bloomers. A naughty tingle of sudden warmth shot to the area in question.

"This arrangement provides quite an indecent sight for you, sir," she whispered down to him.

"Why do you think I insisted on going first?" He grinned wolfishly, raising his arms in invitation.

"A gentleman would close his eyes."

"And yet mine will remain wide open."

"Swine," she said.

"How well you know me, sweeting," he whispered up to her. He grasped her dangling ankle and gave it a tug. "Easy there. No, not on my head. Put your foot on my shoulder. That's good. Now, if you can just—oh!"

She lost her grip on the edge of the frame and fell. Her skirts billowed over him and she landed with one thigh on either shoulder. His face was hidden beneath the many layers of her petticoats. He swayed slightly and she grasped his head to steady herself, pushing his face even more firmly between her legs.

"Don't drop me," she hissed as they tottered dangerously.

"Furthest thing from my mind," came the muffled reply. He spread his stance and braced his feet, grasping her buttocks to steady her. Artemisia's wobbling ceased. She felt his breath hot on her delicate folds. The feeling was delicious.

"Larla," his voice floated up to her through the many layers. "Any fellow who tells you this isn't a man's dearest dream is lying, but perhaps we could choose a more appropriate time and place."

She pulled up her skirt and petticoats and looked down into his face. Here they were, breaking and entering, preparing to burgle, and Trevelyn could still set her pulse dancing.

"Perhaps we could," she conceded. "I don't suppose you have a linen closet back at the Golden Cockerel."

"No, but I'm inspired to have one built." He waggled his eyebrows at her naughtily.

Swallowing a giggle, she eased her thighs off his

shoulders and slid down his body till her toes touched the floor. She loved his hard, broad planes. He slipped a finger under her chin and tipped up her face. His brows now furrowed together.

"It will probably be dark in the ambassador's chambers," Trevelyn said in a whisper. "You said the statues are very like."

"They are. The poses are virtually identical," she admitted. "But I can tell them apart by feel."

"How?"

"Perhaps you didn't notice this afternoon, but Mr. Beddington has . . . well, I tried to make him realistic, you see," she said.

"From the brief glimpse I caught of your work between drinking the ambassador's vodka and killing his fern, I'm sure both your statues are true to life."

"Yes, but Mr. Beddington has a . . . well . . . it's really quite understated, but I always aimed for realism, even as a child." She rolled her eyes at him. "Mr. Beddington is definitely a male."

She felt his belly quiver with a suppressed laugh. "You mean to say he's got a tallywhacker."

"An exceptionally small tallywhacker. In fact, you might miss it if you didn't know it was there."

"You do seem bent on making them smaller than usual. How old did you say you were when you sculpted him?"

"Twelve," she said primly. "I wonder if that's why my art was considered precocious."

"Without doubt." His lips curved into a lopsided grin. "A kiss for luck, my precocious one." He covered her mouth briefly and then released her. The smile disappeared. "If something goes awry—"

"It won't."

"If it does, I will detain whoever is interfering with

us and I want you to take the statue and run. Do not
look back. Take the horse and do not stop until
you're safe in your own home." He lifted the candle
from the shelf and put a hand on the ivory doorknob.
"Promise me, Larla."

She swallowed hard. No matter how enthusiastic
Trevelyn was about the Great Game, clearly this was
no child's play. "I promise."

"And even if you must destroy it, the key must not
fall into the wrong hands."

And if it comes into Trev's hands, she reminded
herself with a catch in her breath, *he'll be gone with
the next ship.* With great effort, she thrust that thought
away. The peril to Mr. Shipwash and the fate of her father's operatives back in India were surely of more
import than her personal loss.

It just didn't feel that way right then.

She nodded, and he turned the knob. The latch
gave with a soft click and they tiptoed into the hall-
way. There were three doors leading from it besides
the linen closet.

"Which one?" she asked in the barest of whispers.
It still sounded like a shout to her ears. It really was
most fortunate the ambassador had dismissed his extra servants. She wondered if the gruff-voiced Lubov
was still somewhere in residence, perhaps sleeping
behind one of the closed doors.

Trevelyn pointed to the dark portal at the end of
the hall. No light showed on the polished hardwood
through the crack at the base of the ambassador's
chamber. Artemisia followed Trev down the narrow
corridor. They took care to move slowly, feeling their
way to avoid any creaky boards.

He stopped when they reached the door and
tossed her a wink. It eased her nerves no end. They

might be in a precarious position, but Trevelyn's light manner kept her from panic. She smiled back at him and wished they'd had more time—no, she couldn't let her mind travel that road. She must focus on retrieving Mr. Beddington, not on whether this would be their one and only great adventure together.

Trevelyn blew out the candle and set it down outside the threshold of Ambassador Kharitonov's room. The scent of old wax and burnt wick rose around them. He eased the door open by inches while Artemisia prayed someone had oiled the hinges recently.

One of the ambassador's windows had been left open, the dark curtains billowing. The room was much too cold for sleeping by English standards, but the stentorian snores coming from behind the bed curtains proved Kharitonov was unaffected by the brisk breeze. Fortunately, moonlight followed the fresh night through the open window, washing the room in shades of silver and gray. There was light enough to see her way as Artemisia crept toward the shelving in the corner that held the ambassador's collection.

She hadn't feigned interest in the statues; they were fascinating. After a glance at the ones he kept in his chamber, clearly the others weren't even his finest pieces. Here was an Arabian stallion of worked gold with carbuncles for eyes, an onyx and ivory zebra, a small marble piece obviously the work of an ancient Greek—it was all Artemisia could do to keep her hands from straying to explore the exquisite pieces.

But where was Mr. Beddington?

Finally, she spied him on the topmost shelf, far beyond her reach.

"Up there," she mouthed to Trevelyn.

He stretched, but even his long arms were unequal to the task.

She pointed to the overstuffed chair before the cold fireplace and lifted her shoulders in a questioning shrug.

It was a massive piece of furniture with gigantic wings protruding on each side. She suspected Trevelyn and she could fit snuggly together in the deep seat. The ambassador was a large individual. He obviously chose his furnishings with an eye to his scale.

Trevelyn tried to heft the unwieldy chair, but as Artemisia feared, it would take two men and a boy to lift it. And when Trev dragged it, the scuffing sound on the hardwood forced him to stop.

Behind the bed curtains, the rhythmic snoring ceased and the ambassador snorted loudly. Artemisia and Trev froze. Kharitonov smacked his lips twice, loosed a prodigious rolling fart and fell back into his deep wheeze.

Artemisia released her pent-up breath.

Trevelyn moved, light-footed as a cat, to her side and pantomimed lifting her to reach the statue.

She nodded and placed her hands on his shoulders. He bent and wrapped his arms just beneath her hips, then lifted her in a clean motion. Unlike in the linen closet, when the tower they created together had tilted drunkenly, now Trevelyn had a firm grip on her and she held her back rigid to help him balance.

He's much steadier without his face between my legs, she mused. A little thrill of power coursed through her with the thought that she seemed to be able to weaken his knees.

He edged closer to the shelves, backing toward

them so Artemisia could face forward. When his tight buttocks came within inches of the lower shelves, Artemisia dug her thumbs into his shoulders to signal him to stop.

She patted his cheek by way of thanks, then raised one arm toward the top shelf. The fitted bodice of her ensemble had extremely tight sleeves that limited her arm movement. She was only able to brush the base of Mr. Beddington with one fingertip.

Bother and confusticate those French dressmakers!

She strained toward the statue and felt the seams of her garment pop under the pressure. She managed to poke two fingers at Mr. Beddington, but only succeeded in pushing him farther away.

Artemisia looked down at Trevelyn in frustration. She motioned for him to lift her higher. He grimaced back at her and grasped one of her feet to give her a boost. She shifted her weight and leaned a knee on his shoulder. He was surely suffocating under the press of her many layers of skirt and petticoats. If she could only stretch high enough, she'd be down again in three shakes of a lamb's tail. As she reached again, she heard a tiny ripping noise when her shoulder seam gave way. She leaned farther. Just another couple of inches and she'd—

Got him!

She clutched Mr. Beddington to her chest with one hand and leaned her other one on Trevelyn's head, hoping he'd realize she needed to descend. He took the cue and let her slide down slowly through his grip, her skirts bunching around her waist.

In that moment, she realized why Trevelyn was so drawn to the Great Game. All her senses were on full alert. Her ears pricked to such sharpness, she suspected she'd hear an ant treading on the windowsill.

Every item in the ambassador's chamber was doubled with a sharp-edged moonlit shadow. She was surrounded to the point of intoxication by Trev's sandalwood scent and the pounding drum of his heartbeat as he lowered her. Even through their clothing, she felt the hard length of him pressing against her belly.

She was shiveringly alive. Outlandish erotic thoughts danced in her head and spread warmly down her body. She wished suddenly that Trevelyn would push her against the wall and have his very thorough way with her.

But, of course, there was no time for even the quickest of couplings, however much her aching groin demanded one. With effort, she stepped back from the circle of his arms and turned toward the door. Trevelyn followed closely behind her and pulled the door shut with a gentle click of the latch.

Artemisia continued down the hall, the statue still pressed against her breasts. Her relief at slipping in and out of the ambassador's chamber undetected left her feeling almost giddy. Her fingers slid over the smooth glazed clay, then stopped.

"No, it can't be," she whispered.

"What?"

She ran her hand over the statue's belly again. The small horse had no tallywhacker at all.

"This is not Mr. Beddington."

Chapter Twenty-eight

*A*re you sure?"

"Positive," she whispered with a sigh. "The statue was so far out of reach, I just assumed it must be the one we wanted. I should have realized something was wrong when we didn't find both Mr. Beddington and Miss Bogglesworth together. Do you suppose Mr. Kharitonov has discovered Beddington's secret already?"

Trevelyn shook his head. "If he knew he had the key, he'd be on his way out of the country with it by now. Beddington must still be in his room. I'll have to go back."

"No, Trev. We go together."

"There's no need. Since you so kindly removed the look-alike, I'm not likely to mistake the statue this time." His quick smile absolved her niggling guilt over her mistake.

"But two sets of eyes are better than one," she insisted. "Other than the bed and the chair before the fire—oh, and a monstrous wardrobe opposite the statuary—I don't recall seeing any other furniture in the room. If it's not on the display shelves, do you suppose he's hidden Mr. Beddington in the wardrobe?"

"No point in having art if you're not going to display it." Trevelyn dragged a hand over his face. Then his eyes lit with sudden discovery. "Didn't he say something about seeing it last thing at night and first thing in the morning?"

She nodded.

"There must be some kind of shelf on his bedstead," Trev reasoned. "I've seen the like before."

For a waspish moment, she wondered how many bedchambers Trevelyn had been in and out of. He certainly knew his way around the mysteries of the female body with the assurance of an adept. Then she forcefully banished the thought. She had no claim to him, no right to feel possession of either his past or future. She only had him now.

"Which is why I insist on accompanying you," she said as though she'd voiced her thoughts and was completing them aloud. "I mean, you may need my help in ways you can't envision now."

He hesitated only a moment, then took her hand and led her back to the ambassador's door. His lips brushed against her temple before he turned the knob.

"Remember your promise, Larla."

"I always keep my word," she said testily. Then, because she needed to lighten the tension that banded her chest, she crossed her eyes and stuck out her tongue at him. "Like a craven coward, I will bolt at the first hint of trouble and leave you to twist in the wind."

"I'm serious."

Her false smile faded. "So am I."

"Good girl."

He pushed open the door and they tiptoed back into the chamber. The ambassador's snore continued to cleave the night with the rhythm of a two-man saw. Moving with stealth, Artemisia followed Trevelyn to the bedside nearest the open window.

Good thinking. The moonlight will show us what is on the other side of the ambassador's bed curtains. It was nice to know that along with being clever and exceptionally fine to look upon, Trev was also practical.

He fingered the heavy velvet drapes and found the opening. As he parted the curtains by finger-widths, Artemisia leaned to peer around him. Stale vodka fumes laced with sickly sweet opiate and a cheesy male tang floated toward them. Artemisia raised her scented hanky to her nose to disguise the ambassador's odor, but only succeeded in adding faint rosewater to the miasma.

Trev parted the curtains farther, careful to shield the ambassador's face from the encroaching moonlight with his own shadow. Artemisia ducked and peered under Trev's upraised arm. Then she saw them.

Lined like a small boy's toy soldiers, a string of five statuettes were propped on the rail that ran along the head of the bedstead. And there was Mr. Beddington, perched not a foot from the ambassador's slack lips.

Artemisia saw immediately that Trev couldn't reach for the statue without leaning across the entire bed. And he'd need to release the curtains, which would plunge him into darkness, making it difficult to choose the right statue or keep from knocking the wrong ones off their narrow ledge. Or else she could hold the curtains back and risk the moonlight waking the ambassador, since she wasn't tall enough to block it out like Trev.

Or . . . she could tiptoe around the bed and fetch the statue from the side on which the ambassador was sleeping.

Clutching Miss Bogglesworth to her bosom, she

was halfway around the bed before her hands began to shake.

This is ridiculous, she scolded herself. *You're far too strong-minded to let a little thing like larceny reduce you to a quivering mass of pudding.*

She groped for the parting in the curtains and drew them aside. Across the ambassador's bed, Trevelyn grinned at her and nodded encouragement. The snoring continued in a steady cadence. She let the curtain fall behind her and edged toward the head of the bed, her gaze never leaving Kharitonov's quivering jowls.

Once he snorted and stopped breathing briefly. Artemisia froze until the ambassador resumed his wheezing. Her hand was surprisingly steady as she set Miss Bogglesworth on the rail beside her mate. Intent on her goal, she lifted the Beddington statue slowly.

The ambassador rolled over and his meaty hand grasped one of her breasts. A soft squeak escaped her lips before she realized he was still asleep. She forced herself to remain motionless. Even so, the way his fingers mauled her nipple made her stomach roil.

Trevelyn looked as though he could spit tacks, but he stood resolutely at his post, shielding the ambassador's face from the moonlight. He jerked his head toward the door, telling her that she needed to extricate herself from the sleeping Russian's lascivious attentions.

As if I didn't know, she thought at him with upraised brows.

But how to do it without waking the ambassador? That was an exceedingly sticky wicket.

She eased away slowly, leaving Kharitonov's fingers grasping at thin air. When his hand drooped back to his side, she released her pent-up breath.

He mumbled something indecipherable.

Then, suddenly, Kharitonov reached out and grasped her by the waist. He pulled her down into the bed with him, pressing her face against his rising and falling chest.

Artemisia had heard of sleepwalkers. They took unremembered jaunts about their home, carried on lucid conversations and did all manner of things that normally required one to be conscious.

But she'd never heard of someone being ravished by one.

She only needed to disentangle herself and the ambassador would drift back into what were obviously becoming exceedingly naughty dreams. She managed to free one arm and tried to hand Mr. Beddington to Trevelyn. He wasn't looking at her. Trev's gaze was riveted on the ambassador's roving hand. Kharitonov had found her skirt and was pulling her hemline northward, baring her legs to the knee. The Russian mumbled again, his voice thick as he patted her on the rump.

"No way in bloody hell," exploded from Trevelyn's lips, and the ambassador's eyes snapped open.

Trev leaped onto the bed and pried Artemisia from the ambassador's arms. Kharitonov rolled Trevelyn into a bear hug in her place.

"Lubov!" Kharitonov bellowed.

"Trev!" she demanded. "I had the matter perfectly well in hand—"

"No, the ambassador was the one with something in his hand," Trev snarled as he tried to free his arms from Kharitonov's grip.

"Lubov!" the Russian roared, all traces of too much alcohol and opiate gone from his enraged face.

Artemisia thought about bashing the ambassador

with Mr. Beddington, but if the base shattered and the key was exposed here, their situation would be even more grim. She settled for grasping one of His Excellency's fingers and bending it back as far as she could.

Kharitonov yelped and growled a Russian curse at her but didn't lessen his hold on Trev.

"If you'd only waited," she said to Trevelyn, "I'd have—"

"If you think I'd stand here and watch him molest you, you're daft. Now run," he yelled to her as he grappled with the ambassador. "Run, damn it!"

So she ran.

Out the door and down the corridor, not pausing before the linen closet. There was no possible way she could hoist herself into the garret and no time for a candle to light her way in the dark. She skidded to the head of the stairs.

The heavy tread of someone pounding up the steps made her stop. She could still hear Trev and Kharitonov, their voices growling, the crash of heavy objects shattering on the hardwood—the collection of statuettes being destroyed, she realized—and the dull thuds of fists hammering flesh. She was sure Trev could acquit himself admirably in a match of fisticuffs, but the ambassador was a very large man. Artemisia hoped Trevelyn wasn't on the receiving end of the blows she heard ringing down the hall. Obviously he was trying to buy time enough for her to make good her escape.

She wanted to turn back, to help him if she could.

But she'd promised Trev she would run at his command, and she knew he wouldn't thank her for breaking her word.

"What we have here?" Lubov's voice rose to her

from the lower landing. His pale eyes raked her form in a deliberate invasion. He ran a thick tongue over his lower lip. "English miss have fun with Lubov, *da*."

She shuddered with revulsion. She'd scolded Trev for interfering in the ambassador's chamber. Now she wished he were here with her to trounce this fellow as well.

Artemisia couldn't make it past the hulking Lubov on the stairs. There was no exit for her through the garret alone. At best she and Trev might leap from the ambassador's window, but it was a three-story drop and no friendly gorse bushes below to break their fall.

Lubov flashed her an evil smile and began to advance up the steps.

There was nothing else for it. She threw her leg over the brass stair railing and slid down, sailing right past the stunned Russian. She had to hitch herself around the turn at the landing, but she managed to stay ahead of Lubov as he pounded after her.

When she reached the main floor, she resisted the urge to fly out the front. Instead, she dashed toward the rear of the townhouse, hoping to locate the back door into the alley where Trevelyn's horse waited. She barked her shins on several pieces of furniture as she stumbled through one room after another before finding the exit.

She pushed through the door, Lubov almost upon her. Trevelyn's horse's head was down, cropping a few late mums sprouting near the house. She grasped the saddle and hurled herself onto his back, blessing her father for insisting she learn to ride like a boy.

"Not so fast, English miss." Lubov grabbed the horse's bridle, but Artemisia threw out her right foot and drove her heel into his eye socket. He released her mount and clutched his face.

"Yah!" she screamed like a savage. The startled horse bolted down the cobbled alley like the hounds of Hell were on his tail.

Artemisia did nothing but hang on as the gelding fled for the safety of his own stable. She wouldn't allow herself to feel anything. It would hurt too much to dwell upon how she'd abandoned Trev when he needed her most.

Chapter Twenty-nine

"Madam, we were not expecting you." Cuthbert knotted the sash at the waist of his dressing gown with characteristic fussiness. "Master Felix told us you were visiting friends from Bath who'd invited you to a house party—" He stopped abruptly when he turned up the gas lamp. "Oh, my word. Your Grace, what has befallen you? Are you injured?"

"No, I'm not hurt," she said as she pulled off her ruined gloves. At least Felix's artless lie had kept her family from worrying over her absence. Freshly mud-spattered from her wild ride through the London night, her hair frizzled out in all directions, her sleeve ripped at the shoulder, Artemisia knew she looked a fright. It was why she'd tried to sneak into the manor house without attracting anyone's notice. She should have known Cuthbert was part blood-hound.

"Here, Your Grace. Please do sit." He pulled out one of the kitchen chairs for her, then rebuilt the fire to heat water. "I daresay you'll feel better after a nice cup of tea."

"Thank you, Cuthbert," she said shakily, laying the Beddington statue in her lap. "Of course, tea. Father always said it was the sovereign remedy for all ills."

But there was nothing steeping in the china teapot

that would fix her ills. She folded her arms on the sturdy table and laid her head down, wishing this was all just a horrible dream from which she'd momentarily awaken.

To his credit, Cuthbert remained silent till she raised her head.

"Does Madam wish one to call for a physician?"

She must look worse than she thought.

His old eyes drooped with concern. It occurred to her that he actually did resemble an aging bloodhound in this light. "One can send someone straightaway."

"No, no, I'm quite well." She pulled a hankie from her reticule and blew her nose like a trumpet. That attic was crammed with years of dust. "I will take tea when it's ready."

A steaming cup appeared before her.

"You are a wonder, Cuthbert," she said.

"One does what one can," he said with pompous humility. "If there's nothing further, I'll wake the chambermaid to see to your bath."

She sighed. "There is something more. Please sit."

"Madam, that would be highly inappropriate—"

"Please, Cuthbert, no more lectures on what's done and not done. I can't bear it right now. Just sit." She looked up at him. "Please."

He pasted an uneasy smile on his face and perched on one of the other chairs.

"I need help," she began. "And I need someone I can trust."

"You may rely upon me, madam, on both counts," he said automatically.

"Thank you, but I want you to wait till you've heard what I have to say before you commit yourself." She stared at the wisps of steam rising from her cup. "Though truth to tell, if you won't help me, I don't know what I'll do."

Cuthbert gave an injured sniff. "Madam, how can you doubt me? My father would be spinning in his grave if ever I turned my back on Southwycke."

"Very well," she said. Then she proceeded to tell him everything, starting with her father's work in the Great Game in India, her masquerade as Mr. Beddington, Trevelyn's covert attempts to locate the key and Mr. Shipwash's abduction, and ending with their disastrous raid on the ambassador's home. She left out only the heart-stopping affair that had flamed between herself and Trev. In truth, she could hardly bear to speak his name, lest fear for him render her incoherent. "So you see why I need your help."

"We must alert the authorities immediately." Cuthbert rose to his feet.

"No, that's the one thing we may not do," she said with dull certainty. "It would eliminate our one advantage. If we contact the constabulary, the Queen's agents will almost assuredly confiscate this."

She set Mr. Beddington on the table before her.

"A statue?" Cuthbert's wary look spoke volumes. He obviously feared for her mind.

"No, Cuthbert, not the statue. What's inside it. Mr. Beddington holds the key. The key to my father's contacts in India and the key to two men's lives here. It is our only bargaining chip." She drew a fingertip from the end of Beddington's muzzle to the statue's base. "I just have to figure out which lock to open with it."

The door to Artemisia's darkened chamber was thrown open with force. She jerked to full wakefulness to see her mother storming across the room and drawing back the drapes to let in the full light of midday.

"Artemisia, I cannot believe you can sleep after all that's happened," Constance began. "And to cap everything, your Mr. Beddington is gone."

Gone? Artemisia struggled to sit up. In a flash of panic, her gaze flew to the wardrobe in the corner. The statue was still prancing on top of the massive piece of furniture. She breathed a sigh of relief. Her mother must mean the other Mr. Beddington.

Her.

She knuckled her eyes. She wasn't thinking clearly at all, and small wonder. Cuthbert had insisted on rousing her abigail so she could bathe, even though she felt she could sleep on her feet. But once she was clean and snug in her own bed, sleep fled from her like shadows from a candle.

Where was Trevelyn? Had he been harmed? How was she going to free him and Mr. Shipwash and still keep her promise not to let the key fall into the wrong hands? Her mind circled in unresolved questions until she dropped off from utter exhaustion just before dawn.

"Mr. Beddington is gone?" she echoed her mother.

"Vanished into thin air and taken his assistant Shipwash with him. And just when I'd like to give him a piece of my mind." Constance sank onto the foot of Artemisia's bed. "How could he have led us so far astray?"

"Mother, what are you talking about?"

"Th-this." Florinda was standing at the open doorway holding a bit of newsprint by two fingers. She kept the offending paper so far from her body that Artemisia wondered if it was contaminated with plague. "Here, sister. Read it."

Artemisia skimmed *The Tattler*'s lead story. In stark black and white, a scurrilous description of her tryst with Trevelyn at the Golden Cockerel was blasted across the page for the *ton* to snicker over. The reporter, one Clarence Wigglesworth, made their loving seem so tawdry, so common.

But it hadn't been anything like that.

Her affair with Trevelyn Deveridge was the finest, purest thing she'd ever experienced. Even though she wasn't named in the article—for which she thanked Trev's threats to Mr. Wigglesworth, rather than any delicacy on the reporter's part—it hurt her heart to see Trevelyn's character maligned in so public a fashion. He wasn't the whoremonger depicted in *The Tattler*. He was a good man, and a brave one. But she was probably the only soul in London who knew the truth about Trevelyn Deveridge.

"This is dreadful," she murmured. Trev's father would probably read this article as well. If he didn't see it on his own, surely a helpful busybody would make certain it came to his attention. "And so unfair."

"Precisely," Constance said. "It makes poor Florinda seem such a duped ninny. Not to mention the rest of us."

Artemisia cast a glance at her mother from under lowered lashes. "As in, you."

"It's all that Mr. Beddington's fault," Constance complained. "He didn't do his job properly. Why did he not uncover the flaws in Mr. Deveridge's character before we linked Florinda's name with his?"

"As I recall, you were told Mr. Deveridge's pursuits were those of a healthy young man," Artemisia said. "If you cared not to read the subtext of Mr. Beddington's report, that's hardly his fault. Besides, it was foolhardy to betroth Florinda to a man—any man—to whom she has scarcely spoken two words." She turned to her sister and held out a hand. "This slander is no reflection on you. I hope your heart is not injured by this."

"Th-that would be difficult since my heart was never in the match in the f-first place," Florinda said, giving Artemisia's hand a squeeze.

Constance sputtered. "But I so wanted her connected with the house of Warre. Now people will expect her to cry off."

"That is what you wish to do, isn't it?" Artemisia asked her sister. She'd planned to extricate Trevelyn from his engagement to Florinda in any case. This seemed a tailor-made solution.

"Mr. Deveridge seemed a pleasant f-fellow," Florinda said. "But Mother is always telling me to watch what I say, so I was afraid to t-talk to him much. Now I suppose I will have to renounce our engagement, w-won't I?"

"Not if we find some way to salvage this," Constance said. "Bother that Mr. Beddington! What's the point in having a factor if he disappears just when he might have been useful? I was so counting on a connection to Lord Warre. It's too annoying not to see this match through."

"Mother, we are not going to marry Florinda to a fellow just because not to do so would inconvenience you," Artemisia said firmly.

When their mother turned away to pace the room like a caged tigress, Florinda mouthed, "I need to talk to you." Her brows nearly met over the bridge of her pert nose.

"Mother, I wonder if you would please speak with Cook. I find I haven't the energy to decide on our menus today and I know it is something you enjoy."

"But what are we to do about—"

"These things have a way of settling themselves. Gossip can only flare white-hot for a short time before it burns itself out." Artemisia tossed her mother a pointed look. "I will handle Florinda's connection to Mr. Deveridge."

Constance adopted an injured expression and flounced out of the room, slamming the door behind her.

"Thank you." Florinda heaved a small sigh. Then she settled on the foot of the bed. "Now she'll be on even more of a r-rant."

"No matter," Artemisia said. "A rant now and then is good for her. No one needs to get their way all the time. It's not healthy."

Florinda giggled. "No, but it's healthier for me if sh-she does."

Artemisia leaned forward and patted her shoulder. "Now's the time for you to declare your independence. She can't order your life unless you allow it."

"No," Florinda said. "But I'm not like you. If Mother's upset with you, you don't give a f-fig. It frets me dreadfully when she's cross. Besides, it's not as if I have so m-many choices."

"Of course you do," Artemisia said. "You can stay with me as long as you like. You don't have to marry if you don't wish."

"You did."

"You're right." Artemisia bit her lip. "I was doing it for Father, but I've come to realize one can't make such important choices just to please someone else. Marriage isn't right for everyone."

"M-mother would be most upset to hear you say so."

"But that doesn't make it less true," Artemisia said.

"When a woman marries, Florinda, she surrenders all rights to her husband. The duke was a good man, but even so, my liberty was strictly curtailed when he was alive. Do you think I could pursue my art if I were still a married woman?"

"I sneaked into your studio and p-peeked at your work." Florinda's eyes took on a sly gleam. "I'd have to say you're right. The paintings are wonderful, but I expect a husband would take a d-dim view of your art."

Unless he was my model. She gave herself a mental shake. She couldn't think about Trev that way now. Not when there were more important matters at stake.

"B-but don't you think if you had the right husband, you'd be content to let him make the decisions for you?" Florinda fiddled with the fringe on one of the bolsters.

"Why do you ask?" Artemisia tried to ignore the flutter in her belly. She'd never been much for praying, but if she were to begin negotiations with the Almighty, she'd be willing to barter away her freedom for Trevelyn's safe return. "Have you set your cap for someone?"

"Yes." Florinda dimpled prettily; then her face crumpled. "But I can't have him with Mother's b-blessing."

"Why not?"

"Because . . . because it's Hector."

"Hector?" Artemisia couldn't remember meeting any gentleman of the *ton* by that name.

"Hector Longbotham."

Artemisia was still in the dark.

"Our f-footman," Florinda said.

"Oh, *that* Hector." He was a gangling youth from Staffordshire, with carrot red hair that stuck up at all angles. Artemisia always thought he resembled a startled hedgehog. Still, if her sister wanted him . . . "And does Hector return your feelings?"

Florinda's face glowed like a sunrise. "You're not shocked?"

Artemisia smiled wryly. "I paint nude young men. Do I seem the type to be easily shocked?"

Florinda hugged her with exuberance. And the whole tale spilled out. Hector accompanied Florinda and Delia on their daily rides around Hyde Park, and it was during those outings that the fellow from Staffordshire had drawn out Florinda in shy conversation.

"Hector's uncle has arranged a post for him on a small estate in Staffordshire as a man-of-all-work. It won't be much money, but there's a cottage provided," Florinda said, her words tumbling out so quickly, she forgot to stammer. "I'll be ever so much happier with Hector in the country than here in the city with people snickering at my stutter."

"Are you sure?"

"I'm not beautiful like Delia or talented like you," Florinda said. "I never w-was cut out to be a great lady, but Hector makes me feel like the queen of May. I love him with all my heart."

Wistfulness pierced Artemisia's chest. She'd always pitied shy, stammering Florinda and tried to insulate her from cruel jabs. Now she envied her. Florinda knew exactly what she wanted. Artemisia couldn't say the same. Even if she managed to secure Trev's release, he was bound for India and she wasn't ready to surrender the freedom of widowhood.

Even if they somehow made it through this mess, there was no future for them. The realization made it difficult for her to draw breath.

"What do you think I should do?" Florinda's voice pulled her back from her dark musings.

"I think you should pack a satchel and help yourself to my jewelry box. You're going to need some portable wealth. Write a short note if you like for Mother and Father and take the barouche," Artemisia said with assurance. Here at least was one problem she could fix. "You and Hector are off for Gretna Green."

Chapter Thirty

$\mathscr{A}$rtemisia paced her studio, trying to decide what to do. She rarely was at such a loss. Whether it came to business or her artwork or even helping Florinda decide to elope with the footman, she usually knew the best course of action.

But now she hovered in indecision.

She set the Beddington statue down on the table that held her model's props. There was the Greco-Roman helmet. She fingered its crest, a half-smile on her face as she remembered the first time she crowned Trevelyn with it.

Back when he was Thomas Doverspike. Of course, even then he'd set her fidgeting in her drawers.

She wandered among her shrouded canvases, pulling off the protective sheets and examining each one. They were good, she decided.

But not terribly important.

She stopped at last before Mars, her hand hesitant when she reached to remove the drape. Difficult or not, she must see him. She yanked the sheet and let it fall to the floor. Her gaze traversed the canvas, noting the graces and insufficiencies of the work. Of course, she needed to redo his genitals. She was ashamed that spite had led her to depict Trev with such pint-sized attributes. Besides, after their heart-stopping tryst, she had a much rosier view of that part of his anatomy.

In truth, she loved every part of him.

She looked at his face, drawn with anguish on the canvas. Why had she ever thought he was the god of war when so clearly he was crafted for love?

She loved him.

Oh, God! She *loved* him. The realization hit her with the force of a boot to the stomach. Then it galvanized her will as a bucket of cold water tempers steel.

She ran back to the Beddington statue and picked it up. It was the first evidence of her artistic ability, and possibly the last to ever garner the honor of royal and critical praise. In a swift motion, so she wouldn't have time to change her mind, she raised it over her head and threw it to the floor with all the force she could muster. The statue shattered into thousands of shards of fired clay, and the base cracked neatly in two.

"Your Grace, is anything amiss? I heard . . . oh!" Cuthbert burst into the studio with Naresh at his heels. They skidded to a stop before the remains of Mr. Beddington.

The two of them must have been huddled by the door waiting for her summons. Artemisia thanked God she had such faithful retainers. She was going to need them.

"Everything is fine," she said to Cuthbert as she knelt to sift through the ruins of her early masterpiece. She found the cylindrical device Trevelyn had described nestled in the hollow of the statue's base. She lifted it gingerly.

" 'Beddington holds the key,' " she whispered.

"Oh, yes, of course," Naresh said with a puzzled frown. "Did you not know it was there?"

She turned to Naresh sharply, regarding him with fresh eyes. "You did, it would seem."

The old Indian nodded. "The master, your father, he told me to put the key in the base and send it to the great Queen over the water. Just in case, he said. Then, when the sickness fell over him, I sent the message as he bid." A pained expression stole over his brown features. "I did not know you were looking for it, Larla, or I would have told you, yes."

"So you did much more for my father when we lived in your country than starch his shirts and brew his tea," Artemisia said as she stood. "You were a player in the Great Game."

Naresh straightened his back. "Oh, yes. The master and I had many excellent times on the Grand Trunk Road together. Up and down all of Hind, we gathered the news that no paper will print and few will ever know. When your father heard of an injustice by the English, he saw to it there was change. When I caught wind of rebellion, I warned him. Between us, we hoped to make an India fit for both our peoples."

"Then you know the names that are encoded in this key?"

"Not all of them," Naresh admitted. "But if you pluck a single thread, will a cloth not unravel?"

Artemisia rolled the cylinder between her palms, knowing it represented countless men and women who were trying to continue the work her father began and Trev was pledged to bring to fruition. A plan began to take shape in her mind to protect those unknown Players, much as Naresh and Rania had shielded her family during the dark days of the sepoy mutiny. A plan that would hopefully see Trev and Mr. Shipwash freed as well.

"I know a man who wants to pluck that thread and

pick up where Father left off," she said. "But I fear he's in terrible trouble and I need your help, both of you."

Then she laid out the rough idea that had just come to her. Cuthbert and Naresh listened without comment until she was finished.

"Will you help me?"

Naresh smiled at her. "Even though you were not a child of my body, since I first dandled you on my knee, you have been the child of my heart. It pains me that you must ask if I will help you."

She stood on tiptoe to place a kiss on his sunken cheek. Then she turned to Cuthbert.

He didn't say anything.

"Cuthbert?" His hesitation surprised her.

"Madam, I greatly fear that once I confess to you my activities of late, you will require neither my help nor my continued service in this house." Cuthbert stood ramrod straight and unblinking, but a muscle ticked in his jaw, the only outward sign of his inner agitation. "My motives were of the highest order, you understand, but I now realize I have done you a grave disservice through my actions."

With a queasy belly, Artemisia sank onto her straight-backed chair. "What have you done?"

"I have served Southwycke since I could walk, and it has ever been my aim—nay, my chief goal in life—to see the reputation of this house held in highest esteem," Cuthbert said, unable to meet her eyes. "When you chose to flout convention with your choice of artistic subject, I thought perhaps the weight of public opinion might sway you to pursuits more appropriate to your station."

"And you didn't consider that sitting in judgment

of my behavior was inappropriate to *your* station?" she said archly.

He nodded miserably. "Indeed, Your Grace, the thought crossed my mind more than once, but as I said, I felt I was acting for your greater good."

"Very well, we have established that your intentions were pure and noble," Artemisia allowed, unable to remain upset with him when he was so clearly unhappy. "What have you done for my own good?"

He looked her squarely in the eye and held her gaze, something she couldn't ever remember him doing for more than the flicker of an eyelash.

"Madam, I deemed you flighty and undependable and in grave need of public reprimand, which of course it is not my place to deliver."

"No, of course not. Especially since you are so good at *private* reprimands." Her tone dripped sarcasm.

"Nevertheless, I was approached by a certain member of the press who assured me that he would do all he could to amend the unfavorable opinion Polite Society had conceived for you. He encouraged me to believe that a glowing article about you would lessen the negative gossip. So I gave him information that to my sorrow he used for very different ends," Cuthbert said without flinching. Then his face crumpled in misery. "Yet this past night, you risked your own person in the interests of England and now destroyed a masterpiece that was dear to you in order to save others." His pale eyes glistened. "I am unworthy to serve so gracious a mistress, but I do crave your pardon before I leave."

"You mean you conspired with *The Tattler?*"

He shook his head, his expression sadder than a Bassett hound's. "I would never see you shamed."

A giggle made her belly quiver before it fought its way out of her throat. Soon she was laughing with near hysteria.

"Madam, I am overcome with remorse. Pray, do not take leave of your senses," Cuthbert pleaded. "It would be more than one could bear."

This statement only served to increase her hilarity.

"I will summon a physician at once." He turned sharply on his heel and headed toward the studio door.

"No, no!" Artemisia finally managed to subdue her laughter and recover her power of speech. "I'm not destined for Bedlam just yet, Cuthbert, though I daresay there are those who might argue the point."

"Then why do you laugh when this is no laughing matter?"

"Because the things that used to seem so terribly important are so clearly not," she said, the last of her giggles gone. "The *ton* may deride me all it wishes and welcome. I care not at all, if only I can see Mr. Shipwash freed and Trev—"

Her voice broke with suppressed emotion. She didn't dare contemplate what had happened to him. He must be all right. If not . . .

"You're right. In the eyes of society, I am flighty and undependable and in need of reprimand. I was all that you say. I still am. Since your opinion of me was but the truth as you saw it, there is nothing to forgive, Cuthbert," Artemisia said. "Unless you still intend on quitting my service, in which case, I will never forgive you."

A quick smile flitted across his thin lips. "One is gratified," he said, his somber demeanor firmly back in place. "How may one serve you this night?"

A new idea struck her, one that might grant them

all a thin layer of protection. It was no thicker than a sheaf of newsprint, but it was better than nothing.

"For starters, you can contact Mr. Wigglesworth again," she said. "He doesn't deserve it, but he's about to be handed the story of a lifetime."

Trevelyn wasn't sure which sound stirred him to full consciousness—the steady drip of condensed moisture or the skittering of rat claws on ancient rock. He became dimly aware that he was lying facedown on an uneven surface, his cheek pressed against grainy stone. He tried to open his eyes, but only managed one since the other seemed to be swollen shut. A sleek, fat rodent was nosing along the floor of his cell, trying to work up the courage to nibble on Trevelyn's outstretched fingertips.

"Bah! Get away." Trev scrambled into a sitting position. The rat disappeared down a drain in the center of the small space. Trev's quick movement cost him a streak of pain that arced from the base of his skull down the length of his spine.

He brought a hand to the back of his head. A goose egg swelled beneath blood-matted hair. The last thing he remembered was straddling the ambassador's chest with his fingers wrapped around Kharitonov's neck. But for the life of him, he couldn't remember why. A sudden burst of pain, a flash of light had splayed across his vision, then darkness. Someone must have clubbed him from behind with a pistol butt.

He supposed he should be grateful they didn't pump a lead ball into him instead. But the ambassador's residence was on a fashionable London street. The neighbors might take exception to the report of a pistol and send a constable round to investigate.

Trev rose to his feet, swaying with nausea, the aftereffect of the blow to his head. He was certainly far from the fashionable district now. In the dimness, he made out a few details of his cell—the rough ocher walls, the tally marks gouged into the sandstone by previous occupants, the pervading stench of ancient misery leeching from the very rocks around him. A narrow corridor disappeared in either direction outside the bars of his cell, leading to the foot of a stone staircase to the left and down into deeper darkness to his right.

A brisk wind whipped up from the blackness, making him shiver. A strong scent came with it, a fishy, tarry smell that could only mean he was being held close to the Thames. If he strained his ears, he thought he could hear the steady lapping of an incoming tide.

Trevelyn tried the iron bars that formed the front of his cell. He strained at each one, hoping for signs of weakness, but finally gave up, collapsing in a loud groan.

"It's no use," a voice said. "I've tried till my fingers bleed, but the bars still hold."

Trev cast his one-eyed gaze to the cell across the narrow corridor. A man lay on his side on the bare stone floor, one arm tucked to pillow his head. He'd been so still, Trev hadn't even noticed he was there.

"Shipwash. James Shipwash?" he asked, not sure why the name suddenly leaped into his brain.

The man sat up. "Yes. How did you know?"

"Because I'm working with the duchess." Trev's memory came back in shattered fragments, like a stained-glass window reassembled by a blind artisan. He prayed Artemisia had been able to escape the ambassador's house in the confusion. Why had he allowed her to accompany him there? He fingered his swollen eye and winced. "I think we're trying to free you."

James shot him a mirthless grin. "Not having much success with that, I'd say."

"Where are we?"

"As near as I can figure, we're in the Tower, the part that hasn't seen service for a couple hundred years," Shipwash said. "I'd heard rumors that there were secret cells accessible from the Thames by way of the Traitor's Gate and deep under the rest of the Tower. Guess that's where we are. They dose me with laudanum during the day, but sometimes I hear things. Or maybe I'm dreaming I hear things," he admitted, hanging his head. "But I was sure I heard the guard shouting out the changing of Queen Elizabeth's keys."

The key, Trevelyn thought sluggishly. Perhaps he'd been drugged as well. There was something important, he was sure, about a key. Suddenly the whole tale rushed back into him in a blur that left him lightheaded. Surely Artemisia had Beddington's key safe now.

If *she* was safe now.

He'd never know if he stayed here. Trev eyed the heavy lock that held his cell closed. It was much more of an obstacle than the simple door locks he'd successfully picked before, but he'd lose nothing by trying. He reached into his boot for the jimmy he'd been taught to use.

It was gone.

He looked around the cell for a shim of metal. Surely the previous residents hadn't gouged the walls with nothing but their bare hands.

"What are you looking for?" Shipwash asked.

"Something I can use to pick the lock. A thin piece of metal—a knife blade, a file . . ."

"All I have is a spoon," Shipwash said.

"And I have nothing," Trev concluded after an exhaustive search.

"I suppose that means our captors don't intend to feed you. Tough luck, old son," Shipwash said in an attempt at gallows humor. "In truth, the gruel they serve is worse than hunger."

"Or we aren't going to be here long enough for me to need to be fed," Trev guessed. "Give me your spoon."

"Why?"

"I may be able to use the handle. It's worth a try." He leaned against the bars and stretched his arm across the void. "Come, man. If it doesn't work, I'll give it back."

Shipwash dragged himself to his feet and handed Trev the spoon. The man flashed Trev a quick smile, revealing a missing front tooth; their captors obviously weren't above mistreating them. At least most of the damage done to Trevelyn had been while he was unconscious.

Trev nodded his thanks and went to work on the lock. He had to wedge himself between the bars as far as he could to find the proper angle to insert the spoon handle. The lock was an ancient piece, the tumblers stiff with rust. Trev was soon sweating with exertion, trying to make the delicate mechanism turn in the correct order. Tongue clamped firmly between his teeth in concentration, he finally felt the last notch give and the lock fell open.

"Now for yours," he said as he swung open the heavy gate.

He'd only inserted the spoon handle into Mr. Shipwash's lock when he heard the tramp of booted feet.

"Someone's coming," James said.

"If we are near the Tower, maybe it's the guard you thought you heard earlier." Trev bit his lower lip as he worked the spoon back and forth in the lock.

"No, the sound's too close for that. It's them—the Russians. They've come back," James said with a tremor in his voice. "You need to go."

"Not without you."

"It's no good if they take you again."

Shipwash reached between the bars and gripped Trev's wrist.

"The water's that way." He jerked his head toward the darkened end of the corridor. "They'll be here any moment. You haven't time to free me."

Trev shook off Shipwash's hand. "Not if you keep interrupting me."

"The duchess may need you."

That stopped him cold.

"Go," James said.

Trev looked down at the slightly built clerk and saw only his lion-sized heart. Courage came in all sizes, he decided.

The footsteps were nearer now. A flare of torch-light danced down the stairwell.

"I will see you free," Trev promised and reluctantly turned away. He bolted down the corridor toward the smell of the Thames.

Chapter Thirty-one

The night air was thick with the green miasma that drifted up from the Thames each year with the turning of the leaves. Slogging from one sickly yellow pool of gaslight to the next, Artemisia and Naresh made their way toward the dome of St. Paul.

When they reached the top of the steps at the cathedral's west entrance, Artemisia turned to her companion and stopped him with a hand to his forearm.

"Wait here, Naresh," she said. "If I don't return within a quarter hour, you know what to do."

The tall Indian frowned at her. "I do not like this plan, Larla. It is too full of many dangers. Why do you not allow me to go into the crypt in your stead?"

"Because they are expecting Mr. Beddington," she said, putting up a braver front than she felt. "Whether they like it or not, I am he. Besides, our time is nearly up. I must go or they will harm Mr. Shipwash." She gave his arm a squeeze. "Please, Naresh, don't make this more difficult than it already is."

He gave a grudging nod and took his station, fierce determination creasing his usually placid brow.

The Banger, the biggest bell in the West Tower, chimed midnight in deep, mellow tones. At the twelfth strike of its monumental clapper, Artemisia slipped into the cathedral through the tall western door.

The long nave was lit only by a few tapers and silver shafts of moonlight filtering in through the high stained glass. She saw no late-night worshippers, but someone had pulled the heavy rope to sound midnight. It gave her comfort to know the sexton must be someplace within the echoing vault. But as she traversed the open space, the only set of footsteps she heard clicking down the central aisle were her own.

The gigantic dome that crowned the center of the cross-shaped structure receded upward in shadowed concentric circles. Before Artemisia reached the quire, she turned aside to make her way down the curving staircase to the crypt beneath the cathedral.

The air belowground was stale and thick. Artemisia shuddered. She fancied she could scent the moldering corpses of those luminaries interred beneath St. Paul's dome. Did the ghost of Christopher Wren, the small genius who had designed the great cathedral, sometimes haunt its empty halls? Or would the spirit of Horatio Nelson, hero of Trafalgar, rise from his brandy-soaked inner coffin to roam the labyrinth of his crypt?

"Dinna fash yerself, Larla," she suddenly heard her father's voice in her head, his Scottish brogue thick and warm as boiled parritch. *" 'Tis not the dead ones ye need be worrit about. 'Tis the live ones."*

A smile teased the corner of her mouth, and she straightened her spine. The daughter of Angus Dalrymple had some surprises in store for the live ones waiting for her in the crypt this night. She hoped it would be enough.

Lantern light shown against the whitewashed walls on the far side of Nelson's black sarcophagus. She heard the faint sibilance of a whispered conversation. The abductors were here, then. She cast a silent prayer upward, and walked around Nelson's tomb into the light. The Russian ambassador turned to her.

Trevelyn had done some damage while he covered her escape. A bruise purpled the ambassador's jaw, and the bridge of his nose was swollen and slightly askew. Artemisia smiled in satisfaction.

"Your Grace," Kharitonov said with a frown. "What do you do here?"

"I've come to negotiate the release of Mr. Beddington's assistant," she said in a voice that was surprisingly even. So far her prayer seemed to have been efficacious. Mr. Shipwash was there, after all. She'd feared they might have left him in his hidden location. Behind the ambassador's bulk, her clerk was propped up by a man she recognized as the burly Lubov. But there was no sign of Trevelyn, and her heart sank. She swallowed hard and forced a polite nod. "How are you faring, Mr. Shipwash?"

"Tolerably well, madam," he said gamely, despite a missing tooth and a swelling cheek. His mistreatment sickened her, but nothing would be gained by hysterics. She arched a brow at the ambassador and adopted her most imperious tone.

"I hold you personally responsible for his deplorable condition, sir."

Kharitonov scratched his thick thatch of graying hair, obviously still confused by her presence. "Where is Beddington? Him you were to send."

"Did my stepson tell you that?" she asked, trying to rattle them with her knowledge of their business dealings. "If so, you were woefully misinformed. Mr. Beddington is . . . indisposed at present. I am acting in his capacity in this matter."

"Are there no men left in England that they send woman?" Kharitonov muttered. "Go home to painting, Your Grace. With woman, I cannot deal."

She'd hoped to throw him off balance just so. "Nevertheless, I am all you will get. Let us proceed to business," she said. "You are on British soil. It is unlawful for you to hold an Englishman against his will. I demand you release Mr. Shipwash and—" here her voice faltered for a heartbeat "—and a certain other gentlemen I have reason to believe you hold as well, at once."

The ambassador folded his beefy arms over his chest. "Give me Mr. Beddington's key and he go free." He jerked a thumb toward Mr. Shipwash. "No one else we hold."

Her vision tunneled briefly, but she forced herself to draw a slow deep breath. "There was a man at your residence last night—"

"There was *thief* at my home, *da*. With him, he had woman, but she ran. Was dark. Her we do not know for certain." Kharitonov narrowed his eyes in speculation, then shrugged. "The thief, he not so fast. In Mother Russia, we know how to treat criminals. With him we have already dealt."

"No, madam, he—" Mr. Shipwash began, but was silenced by a clout to his head from Lubov.

Artemisia flinched at the vicious blow, but a small flicker of hope grew in her chest at her assistant's words. Had Trev won free somehow? But if so, why had he not contacted her? Her small candle of hope guttered.

"If you act for Beddington, you must have key, *da?*" The ambassador's gaze turned crafty. "Give me to help you and I release your friend."

"The key is not with me, but rest assured, I know where it is," Artemisia said as she flipped her brooch watch up to check the time. "And unless Mr. Shipwash and I leave here together within the next few minutes, another friend of mine will send word that the key is to be destroyed. It's your choice."

She crossed her arms over her chest and glared at the ambassador, willing herself not to blink. Brinksmanship was not a game she relished, but her hand was so weak. She was obliged to make up for it with bravado.

The tramp of heavy boots echoed in the limewashed crypt. Another Russian, even bigger than Lubov, rounded the corner to join them. He was carrying something over one shoulder. In the dimness, Artemisia couldn't make it out. Once he reached the lantern's light, the man deposited his burden on the stone floor. An inert body flopped bonelessly between her and Kharitonov.

Naresh.

Artemisia's stomach flipped with sick foreboding. Then again with relief, when she saw his chest rise and fall. Only unconscious then.

"Good work, Oranskiy," Kharitonov said to the newcomer, before turning an evil smile on Artemisia. "This was friend who will send for key to be destroyed, *da?* Better friends you must choose in future, Your Grace."

"Or less vile enemies," she spat.

Kharitonov snorted at this. "High marks I give you for courage, madam, but you are—how you English say?—out of your depth. Come. We go now to get key."

"No, Your Grace. Don't give it to them," Mr. Shipwash said. His captor shook him like a rag doll.

"Stop this instant," she ordered Lubov. "Your Excellency, I must protest. I thought better of you. As a diplomat, you must realize your country's reputation is in severe jeopardy through your actions. There's no honor in abusing the defenseless."

Artemisia doubted her appeal to the ambassador's sense of decency would be effective. To her surprise, he raised a hand to restrain his lackey.

"Enough, Lubov. Time there will be to play later if Her Grace does not give key," he said before turning back to her with lowering brows. "Honor is small matter to diplomat. I am man under orders and not dare disobey. We do what we must do."

Artemisia detected a smidge of remorse in the sigh that followed, but then the ambassador's face hardened and he took a step toward her.

"You must give key. Or you force me hurt your friends."

She bit her lip. The key must not fall into the wrong hands. She owed Trev that. But Kharitonov was right: She was out of her depth. She didn't have it in her to make this choice. She never should have tried to do this. How could she let Mr. Shipwash and dear Naresh pay for her failing?

"Very well," she said. "After you have helped Mr. Shipwash and me move Naresh into my hansom, I give you my word I will shout out the location of the key to you as we drive away."

The ambassador threw his head back and laughed unpleasantly. "*Nyet.* I will have key now."

Artemisia knotted her fingers together. She was running out of cards to play.

Kharitonov made a low growl in the back of his throat, impatient at her delay. "Kill Hindoo."

"No!" Artemisia fell to her knees, trying to shield Naresh with her own body. "I will take you to the key, but you must not hurt him."

"Very good, Your Grace." The ambassador extended a beefy hand to her. "Wise choice. We go now, *da?* Bring prisoner," he barked to Lubov.

"What of him?" Oranskiy pointed to Naresh's prone figure.

"Tie him and leave him," Kharitonov said. "Him, no one find till morning. By then, we out of England and back to land of borscht and stroganoff. Not too soon either." He laughed mirthlessly and grasped Artemisia's arm. "Come, madam."

He didn't wait for a reply, but dragged her up the stairs and back through the silent nave. She heard the shuffling of Mr. Shipwash being propelled behind her by Lubov and Oranskiy. For a moment she thought one of the statues on the right side of the narthex moved. She decided it was only a quirk of moonlight as Kharitonov hurried her through the darkened central aisle.

Just before they reached the tall western doors, he broke the silence. "Where we go, Your Grace?" he asked, as if he were offering her a pleasure ride in his barouche.

"Westminster Bridge." She swallowed back the knot in her throat. It had seemed a good idea at the time. With Cuthbert positioned dead center on the aging structure, he could see an advancing party from any direction. At her word, he was fully prepared to throw the key into the Thames and devil take the hindermost. "But I must warn you, Ambassador, if Mr. Shipwash and I do not present ourselves there unharmed by a certain hour, the key will be destroyed regardless."

"Then haste we must make, *da?*"

If only Naresh hadn't been taken, she might have been able to bluff her way through and see Mr. Shipwash free right there in the crypt. She'd made the mistake of thinking of Kharitonov as the slightly bumbling functionary she'd met at her masquerade. Now that notion had been crushed like a bug.

At least part of her plan was still intact. Cuthbert was waiting for them, ready to act at her command.

She just didn't know now if she could give it.

As soon as the door closed behind the duchess and the rabble that held her, the statue broke his pose and headed for the crypt at a run. Trevelyn thanked the stars for his training as Larla's figure model. He doubted he'd have been able to hold himself motionless like that without it.

He'd tried to arrive at St. Paul's in time to stop Artemisia from going into the crypt. It had taken him longer than he anticipated to liberate a horse from his father's stable. He was slipping silently through the church's side yard when Naresh succumbed to the big Russian's superior size and strength. Trev considered engaging the man in hand-to-hand combat, but he was more interested in Larla's whereabouts, so Trev followed him and the unconscious Naresh into the cathedral. Thanks to a trick of acoustics, he was able to listen to the conversation in the crypt from the top of the steps.

It took every ounce of his will not to vault down the stone stairs to come to Artemisia's aid. He would have happily shaken her till her teeth rattled for going down there alone, but the odds were three against one, and he couldn't be sure he could extricate her without endangering her further.

Such action violated all his intelligence training. If he followed his instinct and tried to save her from this predicament, he jeopardized his mission to retrieve the key.

What a perfectly vicious little cycle.

His gut churned. So this was why the Service recommended men involved in the Great Game remain bachelors. It was too hard to choose between personal and state interests. If push came to shove, he had no doubt Queen and Country would fall a distant second to the Duchess of Southwycke.

"Westminster Bridge," he repeated under his breath. On horseback, he could beat the ambassador and his captives there by taking a few judicious shortcuts. But he needed reinforcements now that he knew where to send them.

He found Naresh struggling against his bonds. With a few slashes of his penknife, he cut the man free. "Are you well enough to run for help?"

Naresh nodded. "Where shall this help be coming from then?"

"Take this." He pulled off his signet ring. "Show it to Ezekiel Rakestraw at the Blind Dog on Beacon Street. Tell him Mr. Doverspike is in need of assistance on Westminster Bridge. Tell him the key is in play. He'll know what to do."

Naresh rose to his feet. "There is no code phrase? Always when I took a turn at the Great Game with Angus—"

"The ring will serve. There's no time," Trev said, suddenly impatient with the cloak-and-dagger nonsense surrounding his clandestine activities. Once it had all seemed so romantic and exciting. Now that Larla was caught in the middle of the Game, it had lost its allure. "Tell him not to dally. Send as many as he can. Tell them to come quietly and wait for my signal."

Then he and Naresh ran up the stairs, through the nave and into the deepening night.

Chapter Thirty-two

Trevelyn waited in the dark alley, listening for the clatter of the ambassador's coach. His horse's withers were lathered and the beast heaved beneath him. He regretted the necessity of pushing his mount so, but he had to cut Kharitonov off on the way to Westminster Bridge. They were sure to come along this street from St. Paul's. Trev only hoped he'd beaten them to this point.

The gelding he'd taken from his father's stable was unshod in preparation for the coming ice of winter. Even so, the horse had delivered every ounce of speed Trev had required. He'd ask more of the gelding before the night was over.

"One more push, old boy," he whispered as he leaned down to pat the horse's quivering neck. "Then so help me God, I'll see you're sent out to the country estate with nothing but soft grass underfoot for the rest of your life."

The gelding snorted a horsy laugh, as if he'd heard that promise before.

Then the ambassador's coach rumbled past, its running lanterns swaying. One of Kharitonov's henchmen was lashing the pair of matched bays into a canter. The other stood on the rear rail, clinging for dear life.

Trev smiled. *A chance to even the odds.*

He dug his heels into the gelding's sides and the horse leaped into a gallop, head down, ears laid back, surging after the coach. With all the rattle and clatter the ambassador's vehicle made, Trev hoped the Russian perched on the rear rail wouldn't hear the pounding tattoo of his approach until it was too late.

He leaned over his horse's neck, crooning soft encouragements, as they gained on the coach with each stride. He was almost close enough to reach out and grab the man's flying coattails when the carriage made a sharp turn. The Russian must have seen Trev from the corner of his eye, for he gave a startled shout to his companion. The driver tossed a look over one shoulder and whipped the bays into a gallop.

The coach inched away from Trevelyn as his horse tired by the moment.

"Yah!" Trev exclaimed as he whacked the gelding on the rump. The startled horse erupted in a fresh burst of speed and brought him even with the rear wheels of the coach.

Trev grasped the brass rail that topped the vehicle, hauling himself out of the saddle. As he dangled there, fighting for a toehold, his horse fell swiftly astern, like a punting boat in the wake of a royal barge.

A Russian fist came flying at Trevelyn's head, and he managed to dodge the blow by releasing one hand to swing away from it. Then Lubov brought his hammerlike fist down on Trev's knuckles, trying to break his hold on the brass rail. He clenched his fingers all the tighter and swung his other hand back up.

Trev knew he couldn't match the larger Russian blow for blow, so he lashed out with his feet. He knocked Lubov's boots off the coach rail and his weight and gravity did the rest. The big man lost his hold and cartwheeled to the pavement.

Trev scrambled to secure his own footing on the rail and then turned to look over his shoulder. Lubov rolled to a stop in a tangled heap, his limbs splayed in unnatural angles. The big Russian would trouble no one else this night.

One down, two to go. Wonder if that driver has a blunderbuss under his seat?

As it always did, the intoxication of the Great Game sent blood screaming through his veins. But the Game had taken a deadly turn and Larla was still in the middle of it. He shoved the thought aside. If he let himself dwell on her danger, it would paralyze him, and he needed to act to save her.

Now.

From inside the swaying coach, Artemisia heard the shouts but couldn't understand the Russian words. The ambassador fidgeted in his seat and craned out the window, trying to see what disturbed his subordinates.

"What is it?" she asked.

"Nothing," the ambassador snarled.

Several loud thumps sounded overhead, as if someone were on top of the coach. Before Artemisia had time to wonder what it meant, the vehicle swerved wildly, knocking her from one side of the seat into poor Mr. Shipwash's already battered form and back again. Then there was another cry, and the coach bounced into the air as first the front wheels, then the back lurched over a large bump in the road. Artemisia knew the condition of many London streets was deplorable, but surely not so bad as that.

Her breath hissed over her teeth. Had someone

fallen beneath their carriage? If someone was trying to interfere with their progress, it could only be Trevelyn. The thought of him lying broken along the cobblestone street almost caused her to be sick on the spot.

The coach continued to rumble into the night, and she heard the deep tolling of Big Ben's chimes sounding three-quarters past the hour. The ambassador settled back in his seat, satisfied that his men had dealt with the problem. If Trevelyn had intercepted them somehow, surely they wouldn't still be clattering toward Westminster.

Tears pricked at her eyes, but she refused to give the ambassador the pleasure of seeing her weep.

"We are near bridge." Kharitonov reached into his jacket pocket and drew out a derringer. "Do not to try my patience, Your Grace."

The coach rolled to a stop at the west end of the bridge.

"Out," the ambassador said to Mr. Shipwash. "And do not run, or I have to shoot you. That would give to me pain."

"Heaven forefend we should cause you pain," Artemisia observed tartly. She climbed out of the coach after her assistant, relieved that he was able to stand on his own. In the waning moonlight, a lone figure stood at midspan on the dark bridge. Faithful Cuthbert was there with the key in hand. At the far end of the bridge, a carriage waited to bear them all away.

"Call to come here your man." Kharitonov hauled his bulk out of the coach.

"He is under orders to remain where he is no matter what. The only thing he will do now is toss the key into the Thames at my command," Artemisia said. "Cuthbert has given me his word of honor that he will not respond if I countermand my previous directive under duress. Believe me, the gentleman has a will of iron. If you want the key, you must release us. Once we are settled in the far coach, I will direct Cuthbert to leave the key on the stone railing."

"Clever, Your Grace, but I more clever," Kharitonov said, one bushy eyebrow cocked. He brandished the derringer in her direction. "Come. To him we go." Without taking his gaze from her, he barked an order to his driver. "Stay with coach, Oranskiy. Lubov, come."

"Sorry to disappoint you, Ambassador, but Mr. Oranskiy left the coach some blocks back," a cool-sounding voice came from the driver's perch. "Along with the unfortunate Mr. Lubov."

Artemisia looked up to see the face she wished most to see in all the world. Trev grinned down at them, despite having one eye nearly swollen shut. A blunderbuss rested comfortably on one knee, the barrel cocked and ready to fire at the ambassador. Relief flooded her at finding Trevelyn well and whole—barring the shiner, of course—and, most especially, firmly in possession of a wicked-looking firearm.

"You, sir, will kindly allow the lady and her friend to leave unmolested," Trev said, his tone even, almost cordial, but there was a glint of steel in his eyes as he glared down at the ambassador.

"*Nyet.* Shipwash can go, but I keep duchess." Kharitonov grabbed Artemisia and yanked her in front of him. She felt the cold circle of the derringer's barrel at her temple. Her blood pounded against the steel. "Don't move, Your Grace. This trigger, very—what is word?—touchy. For to go off by accident I would hate."

"I'm sure none of us want that. Please, Your Excellency, I'm not really large enough to make do as a shield. We're rational adults here. Surely we can come to an agreement we can all live with," she chattered, knowing she did so but unable to keep her mouth from rattling on.

"Here is agreement Her Grace can live with," Kharitonov said to Trevelyn with menace. "You blunderbuss to put down and I bullet do not to put in her brain."

"If you harm the duchess, you'll never leave this bridge alive." Trevelyn was unmoving as granite.

"In game of chance, man who cares least wins. Who cares least, I wonder, whether this lovely woman alive tomorrow? I give to count of three. One . . . two . . ."

"Stop," Trev said with an upraised hand. "I agree to your terms. Now I'm going to move very slowly and stow the weapon under the seat."

"*Da,* that will do."

Without taking his eyes off Kharitonov, Trevelyn uncocked the blunderbuss and slid it back into its niche. Then his gaze flitted to Artemisia.

In that split second, she read his frustration, his fear and his love for her. She also saw that every muscle in his body was tense as a watch spring.

"Better," the ambassador said.

Artemisia felt the derringer ease away from her skin, still perilously close, but no longer touching.

"Now what?" Trev asked the ambassador.

"Now, Mr. Thief." Kharitonov turned the derringer

on Trevelyn. The gray muzzle glinted in the moon-light. "Is your turn to die."

"Not if I have anything to say about it." Artemisia cupped her mouth to shout. "Cuthbert! Toss the key!"

As time expanded and contracted around her, Artemisia was acutely aware of a multitude of things at once. She turned to see her butler heave a small weighted packet into the sludgy water with the force of a cricket pitch.

"*Nyet!*" Kharitonov screamed in fury.

Trev leaped onto him, and they rolled together to the pavement, fists flying. The pop of the derringer was followed by a man's groan. Then, from the darkness on the far side of the bridge, there was a flash of light, followed by the stench of sulfur and a gray cloud.

Another flash and cloud burst closer to them. Then another. She was robbed of her night sight by the brief brilliance. Westminster Bridge came alive with tiny explosions, followed by expletives about burned fingers. Artemisia distinctly heard a voice ask, "Did you get the picture?"

It was Mr. Wigglesworth and his fellow members of the press slinking belatedly from their places of concealment to capture the story. Artemisia had hoped the journalists would show themselves in sufficient numbers to warn Kharitonov off from his plans, but they had cowered overlong in the darkness, waiting till the opportune moment had passed.

She waved away the choking smoke. Trevelyn and the ambassador lay in a heap, neither of them moving. She ran to them and found the big Russian's inert form on top of Trev.

"Trevelyn, are you hurt?"

There was no answer.

She tried to push the ambassador off but couldn't budge him. However, her hand did come into contact with something wet and warm and sticky. A coppery tang filled her nostrils.

Blood.

And she had no way to tell whose it was.

Chapter Thirty-three

A soft rap on the guest room door roused Artemisia from lightly skimming the surface of sleep. She rubbed her eyes and rose from the chair next to the bed.

"Come," she said softly, massaging the crick in her neck with both hands.

Cuthbert poked in his head. "Has Mr. Deveridge wakened yet, madam?"

Artemisia looked back at the still form under the clean linens and shook her head. She waved the butler in without a word. Cuthbert bore a silver tray heaping with buttered scones and a fresh pot of chocolate, which he set on the desk by the shuttered window. He pulled back the drawn drapes and let the full light of midmorning wash the room.

"The doctor did say he thought Mr. Deveridge would wake naturally, did he not?" Cuthbert said, his voice unusually bright, as if he were putting the best face on a grim situation.

"Yes, but he made no promise of when." Artemisia took the offered cup of chocolate and sipped slowly, lest she burn her tongue.

Last night—had it only been last night?—she'd been on her knees, trying to separate Trevelyn and the ambassador, when she was set upon by half a dozen armed men, led by none other than Naresh.

"Friends of Mr. Doverspike," the Indian explained.

Trev's reinforcements from the Blind Dog had arrived only in time to lift the ambassador's body from his. To her relief, it turned out to be the ambassador's blood on the cobbles on the bridge. Kharitonov had been rushed to the hospital but was not expected to recover from the round he'd taken from his own gun.

Trevelyn, however, was far from unscathed. In his scuffle with the big Russian, his head had been knocked against the stone of Westminster Bridge. Cuthbert had sent for a physician, who pulled back Trev's eyelids to examine the pinpoints of his pupils.

"It appears he's taken more than one blow to the head. If only Your Grace would allow me to bleed the patient, perhaps that might speed the recovery," the doctor had suggested.

Artemisia took a look at the stained condition of his lancet and bowl and ordered Cuthbert to show the good doctor out. She only hoped he was a better prognosticator than his medical equipment might indicate.

"Does Madam wish to send word to the Earl of Warre?" Cuthbert pressed a plate of scones into her hand.

She nodded, almost too tired to speak. Surely under these circumstances the earl would shelve his differences with Trev.

"Might one suggest we also send this?" Cuthbert handed Artemisia a neatly pressed edition of *The Tattler*.

She ran her gaze over the copy beneath the blurry image of a woman kneeling beside a man's prone form. She knew it was a picture of her and Trevelyn, but no one else would be able to guess their identities from the shadowy daguerreotype. The prose was execrable, but to Mr. Wigglesworth's credit, the facts were essentially correct. The article detailed the exploits of a certain unnamed aristocrat and an intrepid son of a prominent member of the House of Lords in their quest to preserve national secrets from grasping foreign spies. The Russian menace on the Indian subcontinent, a favorite subject of warmongers in the Empire, was discussed with strong invective, if few facts.

Then the reporter went on to praise his own invention, a method of using ignited gunpowder to illuminate an object to facilitate photography by night. The process still needed refining, Mr. Wigglesworth admitted, but with the proper financial backing . . . Artemisia let the paper slip through her fingers.

"The earl might wish to know that his son is a man of valor," Cuthbert said approvingly.

"Yes, please do send word." She sank back into the chair. Trevelyn was a hero. She hoped the earl would take note of his second son before it was too late.

"Then perhaps Madam would wish one to take over her vigil. If one may be forgiven for saying so, Your Grace looks fair done in." Cuthbert's eyes were ringed with dark circles as well, but his offer was genuine.

"No, Cuthbert, I'll stay," she said. "I want to be here when he wakes."

"Very good, madam." He inclined his head in deference. "Please ring if you require anything. Anything at all."

"Thank you." She took a last sip of chocolate and turned her attention back to Trevelyn, smoothing back the errant lock of hair that insisted upon hanging down on his forehead.

Cuthbert stopped at the door and cleared his throat.

"Is there something else?" she asked.

"Only this, madam," he said, his old back ramrod straight. "One has served Southwycke all one's life, with not unwarranted pride, one might add. However, one has never been prouder to serve this house than one is at this moment, Your Grace. Your actions of late have been brilliant and courageous in the best traditions of English womanhood, if—ahem!—not strictly traditional, you understand."

"Thank you, Cuthbert," she said, deeply touched by his slightly qualified praise. It was rarely given and therefore precious.

He bowed once more and closed the door softly behind him.

Artemisia looked back at Trev's sleeping face, the strong bones beneath the planes of his cheeks and beard-stubbled chin. His chest rose and fell in a comforting rhythm. She moved the chair closer and laid a hand on him, just to feel the warmth of his skin. His bruised eye was still swollen, but beneath the thin skin of his other eyelid, she thought she detected slight movement.

The eye opened and looked at her. A smile curved his lips.

"I like Cuthbert well enough," Trev said. "But is the old windbag always so pompous and condescending?"

"No, sometimes he's worse. Oh! Oh, Trevelyn, you're awake." She hugged him and found her feet leaving the floor as he swept her onto the bed with him. "Careful, you've been injured."

"It'll injure me more to let you go, Larla."

His lips brushed hers and then, as if a fire rose up

in him, he claimed her mouth in a searing kiss. Her lips softened and she yielded to his thrusting tongue. When she did a little exploring of her own, he groaned into her. Despite her exhaustion, his kiss sent new vigor flooding her limbs. His hand stroked the length of her back.

Even though her skin screamed out for more of his touch, she settled beside him, pressing the length of her body against his, and rested her head in the crook of his shoulder. She ordered her rioting insides to be satisfied that Trev was on the mend. The last thing he needed now was a midmorning romp with a woman who couldn't control the twitch in her own knickers.

"How do you feel?" She drew circles around his bare nipples. How thoughtful of Cuthbert to have undressed Trev before tucking him into bed. "You've taken a nasty knock on the head."

He winced as he sat up to explore the swelling lump on the back of his skull. "Well, that explains the railway gang pounding away in my brain."

"You really should be resting, you know." She eased him back into the eiderdown pillows.

"I will, if you will," he promised.

"Agreed," she said.

He slipped a finger under her chin and tipped up her face to his. "One of us is not dressed for bed, Your Grace. Guess which one?"

She sat up. "Are you suggesting, sir, that I strip out of my clothes in broad daylight and climb naked under the covers with you?"

"I can think of nothing that will speed my recovery more," he assured her as he fingered the buttons that ran down the front of her bodice.

"If you've a pounding headache, how can you think of lovemaking?"

"It's not my head doing the thinking just now, Larla. You and I have had a splendid adventure and now we're safe. It's only right we should celebrate by refusing to be celibate."

He narrowed his gaze at her, noting the smudges of blue beneath her eyes, no doubt. "You've been up all night, haven't you?"

She nodded, smothering a yawn with her hand.

"Where are we?" he asked.

"A guest room in my home," she said.

He frowned. "Then you wouldn't want to be found under the sheets with me here, would you?"

There was no place else she'd rather be, but after Cuthbert had just praised her stellar behavior, she did hate to chance losing his hard-won approval so quickly. "It would be considered shocking."

"It's all right, Larla." He starting a teasing assault on her row of buttons once more. "If Cuthbert comes back, tell him I grabbed you in my sleep and wouldn't let you go."

"And you somehow managed to undress me while in a state of unconsciousness?"

"What can I say? I am a man of many talents." He waggled a brow at her. "Care for a demonstration?"

She laughed. "You really did take a blow, didn't you? It seems to have removed all sense of propriety from your mind. Has it escaped you that if we were found nude in bed—"

"Naked," he corrected as he pulled her close and delivered a string of feathery kisses down her neck.

"If we . . ."

Her eyes drifted shut when he took her earlobe between her teeth and bit down softly. Stars burst behind her closed lids.

"You were saying?" He transferred his attention to

pulling the pins from her hair and running his fingers through the length of her tresses.

"If we are discovered . . ."

Somehow he managed to part the front of her bodice, and his clever hands teased the tops of her breasts and made her bound nipples ache. One touch, just one flick of his fingertips, and she might shatter altogether. The power of speech deserted her.

"Yes?" he prompted unhelpfully.

"If you and I are found naked in bed together, we'd have to . . ."

His kiss saved her. She wasn't usually unable to finish a coherent sentence. One of his hands busily gathered up the yards of material in her skirt. Now he unbound her garters and pushed down her stockings. Then his hand moved up her leg, pausing to linger on the curve of her calf and dally in the dimple behind her knee.

"We'd have to what?" he asked.

"Well, propriety would dictate that . . ."

Her bloomers were an impediment, but even so, the warmth of his hand burned through the thin cotton on her thighs.

"If we are found in flagrante . . ."

His hand discovered the slit in her bloomers and exploited the breech in devastating fashion.

"Delicto," he finished for her.

"Delicto," she repeated, as shudders of pleasure rolled over her. Her world narrowed to primal elements.

Heat. Pressure. Need.

She felt herself near that exquisite little death when he pulled his hand away.

"No," she moaned. Every fiber of her body cried out in dismay. "Why did you stop?"

"Hush, Larla." His hands slid up and down her inner thighs. "I won't leave you like this. But you're right. We shouldn't be found naked together. You offered me the position of your lover some time back." His smile defined wickedness. "I've a mind to take up the post right now by showing you how inventive lovers get around little details like clothing."

Chapter Thirty-four

*S*he wanted to point out that if they were discovered, the pressure to marry would hammer them from all sides. Even though she loved Trevelyn, how could she submit to the semichildlike state allotted to a married woman? She meant to explain it to him, but his hand was playing that maddeningly sinful game with the slit in her bloomers again.

Artemisia couldn't form a complete thought to save her immortal soul.

"I mean to have you, Larla." His voice was a husky whisper. "You may as well relax and enjoy it."

She let her head fall back and surrendered to the waves of sensation. While he drove her to an aching fury with one hand, his other was on her hip, moving her into position so slowly she wasn't even aware of what he was doing until he withdrew his hand and the tip of him entered her through the slit in her bloomers in a long, slow thrust.

"There you go," he said huskily. "As you requested, we're not naked together. In fact, you're dressed well enough for a tea party in the garden."

"I don't feel like a tea party," she managed to stammer.

"Neither do I."

He pressed her hips down and she hugged him

inside her with tiny muscles she hadn't realized she possessed before. His eyes glazed over and he groaned. A thrill of power washed over her because she was able to so sweetly subdue him. Then he pulled her down for a kiss and they slid into the madness of their joining.

She'd been so near that hot, dark place she knew as her ultimate destination, it didn't take many of his deep thrusts to send her over the edge. Those same small muscles that she had tormented him with moments before now contracted in a frenzy that cost her control of her limbs. Then, just as her release subsided, Trev stiffened under her, pulsing into her, hot and deep.

She looked down at him. His eyes were still unfocused with pure animal pleasure. But then he seemed to return to himself, for he reached up a hand to stroke her cheek.

"I'd never have thought it," he said softly.

"Thought what?"

"That I could lose myself so completely and never want to be found."

"Ah, but it's too late to hide, sir, for I have found you."

"So you have, madam," he said with a lazy grin. "And what do you intend to do with me? Now that the key is irretrievably gone, there's no pressing need to go to India. I'll talk to my commander and see about an assignment that will keep me here in London. If I have my way, I intend to spend my days making Father wish I was on another continent and my nights loving you. And perhaps I should warn you that I'm very set on having my way."

The blasted key. She hadn't had a chance to tell him.

"But if you had the key, you'd still leave?"

"I'd jolly well have to." He stroked the length of her arm with his fingertips. "Lucky for me old Cuthbert tossed it in the Thames." A frown creased his brow. "Just not so lucky for England."

Artemisia bit her lip. There was nothing else for it. He had to know. She started to pull away.

"Where do you think you're going?" He gripped her tighter.

"There's something I must show you."

"Not interested. I like what I'm seeing right now just fine," he said with a wicked grin.

"Please, Trev. It's hard enough for me to leave you. Don't make it worse."

"All right, love." He let his arms fall to his sides. "But hurry back."

She climbed off him, tucked the covers across his chest and smoothed his hair from his forehead.

"Why, thank you, Mummy," he said.

"Cheeky devil." She gave him a playful swat on the shoulder. Then she crossed to the dressing table and picked up the fussily decorated bandbox. She opened the box and pulled out the small, intricate mechanism. "England's luck is still intact. You didn't really think I'd let Cuthbert throw something as important as Beddington's key into the Thames, did you?"

Trev sat bolt upright. "You're joking."

"Not a bit," she admitted. "You told me to make certain it didn't fall into unfriendly hands. The only way I could think of to do that was to make a decoy, as you had suggested. If it came to choosing between you and the real key . . . well, I knew I couldn't put the Crown's interest before my own." With a growing heaviness in her chest, she handed the cylinder to him. "So there it is."

Tears pricked at her eyes and she turned away lest he see. "And there you go," she whispered.

"No." He caught her hand in his. "There *we* go."

She looked back at him.

"I know this isn't the way such things are normally done, Larla," he said. "I should speak to your father, then arrange to be on bended knee in your wild garden with a ring in my hand, but the truth is, I don't think I can wait." He rose from the bed and stood before her, as heedless of his nakedness as Adam before the Fall. "I have no title or lands to offer you, Larla. There's only myself, and if I'm to play the Great Game in Hind, there may be little enough of that. But I do love you as I never thought to love anybody. And I hope that you love me." He brought her palm to his lips and planted a soft kiss in the center. "Be my wife and come with me."

Joy leapt inside her. She'd never wanted to be a bride the first time. But now she was offered the chance at life with a man she loved beyond all expectation.

She threw her arms around his neck and hugged him fiercely. "Yes, yes, I'll marry you."

Trev kissed her deeply. Then he scooped her up and twirled her around, her long skirt draping around them like a banner wrapped around a flagpole. She laughed for pure joy, too caught up in the moment to care if anyone heard her through the closed door.

"There's just one thing," she said, slightly dizzy from the twirling. "Well, two actually."

"Name them, my heart."

"Mr. Shipwash has learned a great deal, but he still needs some guidance. You won't mind if I continue to be Mr. Beddington from time to time, will you?"

"You don't intend to grow a beard and mutton-chop sideburns, do you?"

"Of course not," she said.

"Then I'll be pleased to have Mr. Beddington in my bed as long as you wish to play him."

She stroked his jaw, dark with the stubble of his heavy beard. "I'll send Cuthbert in to shave you. Of the two of us, you're the only one in danger of sprouting muttonchops at the moment."

"Point taken." He grinned. "What else do I need to agree to if I'm to become the luckiest man in the British Empire?"

"It's so silly of me to worry about this. You'll laugh when you hear." Her heart fluttered in her chest like a caged bird. "You won't have any objection if I continue painting?"

"I think you're a splendid artist, Larla. Of course you must keep painting."

"Oh, I'm so glad." She hugged his neck again. "I was afraid you might not understand how important it is to finish my work."

"I've enjoyed posing for you so far. I can manage for a while longer, I suppose."

"Good. You have such a natural bent for this sort of thing. After we're finished with Mars, perhaps you could help me find the right model for Eros."

His smile flattened. "You mean you intend to keep on painting *other* naked men?"

"Not naked. Nude. There's a difference."

"Damned if I can see it." He set her back on her feet and crossed his arms over his chest. His scowl would have frightened most men, but it only served to stiffen Artemisia's spine.

"Trevelyn, all major artists have used the human figure as subject matter for their greatest pieces. Our own Queen is having a bacchanalia painted on the walls of her boudoir. You can bet Pan and his nymphs will be scantily clad. Good heavens, even the Vatican is filled with nudes," she said heatedly. "There's no cause for you to use rough language."

"Let me understand you. After we're married, you still intend to spend hours and hours with strange men. Naked strange men, and you don't think it cause for rough language. By God, madam, rough language is the least of your worries. You'll be lucky if I don't take you over my knee and—"

She took a step backward. "You would not."

"Try me." Mayhem glinted in his dark eyes. "No man in his right mind would allow his wife to do such a thing."

Artemisia lifted her chin. "Then it is my great good fortune to be no man's wife." She turned and strode to the door, head high, heart drooping to her ankles. "I will send Cuthbert to you directly. Then if you are feeling quite recovered, I ask you to leave this house."

Her voice caught in her throat and she couldn't bear to look at him. Her resolve might crumble if she did.

"Larla, wait—"

"Good-bye, Trevelyn," she whispered before she slipped out of the room. The latch caught behind her with a soft click. The door that closed in her heart nearly deafened her with its resounding thud.

How could he profess to love her and yet understand so little about her? She needed to paint, needed to create as other women needed children. The pull of her art left a yawning ache if she was forced to abandon it for even a few days.

As she fled down the long corridor to the top of

the stairs, she realized an even larger gap had formed in her chest. Her heart was missing the piece that Trevelyn still had in his keeping.

It would never be whole again.

Chapter Thirty-five

Trevelyn stormed down the cobbled street, his long-legged strides eating up London's uneven and twisting blocks. His head still pounded, but he refused to hail a hansom to take him back to the Golden Cockerel. He needed to move. Needed to hit something.

Preferably his head against a brick wall.

The angry words had spilled out of his mouth before he thought better of them. His jealous rage had cost him the most infuriating, most disturbing, most wonderful woman he'd ever known. She was the only one he'd ever considered spending his life with.

Now she wanted nothing to do with him.

If only he'd exercised restraint, remembered his training and taken a conciliatory tone, she might have been brought to a more reasonable frame of mind with time. He could be persuasive when the occasion called for it. He'd been recruited for his ability to charm and disarm, hadn't he? Artemisia was an intelligent woman. Surely she'd understand his position. How would she like it if he spent his time in the company of naked women?

Nude, he heard her voice correcting in his mind.

Was there really a difference? Could she somehow disconnect that part of her nature and view a male body as merely a collection of lines and angles? God knew the sight of her stirred him to aching lust even when she was fully clothed. Could it be that different for women?

Even if it wasn't, he realized now it didn't matter. None of it mattered except for the part when she said good-bye.

He had only himself to blame. Good God, he'd threatened to paddle her as if she were a naughty child. He could still picture it—Artemisia draped across his knee, her skirt hiked around her waist, her luscious, heart-shaped bottom rosy and warm and his palm stinging. He was ashamed to admit that thought stirred his blood. What was wrong with him?

A great deal, evidently.

Now his thoughts chased each other furiously around his brain, trying to see a way past this obstacle of his own making. He was so intent; he didn't even notice the gilded barouche with the Warre crest emblazoned on the door. It slowed to match his pace.

"Trevelyn, a word with you."

The earl opened the door and beckoned Trev to join him with an imperious gesture. The top was down, all the better for the occupants to see and be seen. Apparently, his father felt the need to humiliate him publicly.

His misery was complete. Not only had the woman he loved rejected him—with reason, he added crossly. Now his father was here to torment him further.

No less than I deserve, he decided ruefully.

He climbed into the barouche and settled opposite the earl.

"Sir," he said tersely.

"Well, what have you to say for yourself?"

"About what?" Trev silently added *this time*. When-

ever his father had administered a dressing down, he
started with the same preamble. Occasionally, Trev
had no idea how he'd offended the earl. More often,
he wasn't sure which of his indiscretions his father re-
ferred to, so the safest course was feigned ignorance.

"About maintaining a double life. About engaging
in dangerous activities without my knowledge," the
earl said as he handed him a copy of *The Tattler*.
"About securing the Crown's interests at great personal risk."

"Sir, my involvement in this matter has been exag-
gerated beyond recognition."

"Horse feathers," his father said with uncharacteristic inelegance. "As a member of the House of Lords, I
have access to information that exceeds that of the
yellow press. Yet only this morning was I made aware
that my son is not the lay-about I took him for."

"Sorry to disappoint you."

"Don't be insolent. It doesn't become a Deveridge."

"No insolence. Very well," Trev said woodenly. He
was far past any pain his father might be able to in-
flict upon him. "I shall add that to the long list of be-
haviors unbecoming to a Deveridge."

"I was informed you were injured—a blow to the
head, I believe."

"I'll mend."

"I'm gratified to hear it," the earl said stiffly. Then
he turned his gaze to the members of the *ton* strut-
ting through St. James Park, the better to be seen by
their peers.

The barouche bounced through the fashionable district, and the earl took time to nod at those he deemed
worthy of his notice. As they neared Westminster
Bridge, his father turned his attention back to him.

"Trevelyn, in the past you've given me ample cause

for grief, Lord knows," the earl said, his lips tight with suppressed emotion. "But in this instance I must say I can feel only . . . hearty approval for your actions and . . ." he paused to tear the words from his throat, "genuine pride for your heroics."

There it was. Finally. All his life, Trev had longed for some hint of approbation from the earl, the slightest crumb of affection from this most emotionally constipated of men. And now that the moment was here, it lay in his belly like a lump of underdone mutton.

"Thank you," Trev said, more to break the silence that stretched between them than from any sense of gratitude. All he could feel at present was self-loathing.

He'd lost the love of his life. And nothing else would fill the void.

"Of course, the world isn't privy to your identity as the unnamed hero in this article, but I will see that those who have need to know—men of power, you understand—" the earl laid a sly finger alongside his nose—"will be made aware of the full facts of the matter."

"I'd rather you didn't."

"Nonsense, son," the earl said. "False modesty is also not—"

"Becoming to a Deveridge," Trev finished for him. The blood pounding at the base of his skull made him light-headed. But the weight of Beddington's key in his waistcoat pocket anchored him firmly to the earth. He placed a protective hand over it now.

"I haven't the least bit of modesty, sir, false or otherwise." He'd certainly proved that when he made the irretrievable error of posing as Artemisia's model. "But if I am to continue my work, anonymity is essential."

"Perhaps you're called to work of a more public nature."

"I think not."

"Sometimes we cannot make those choices for ourselves. Some things are thrust upon us." The earl adjusted the monocle in his left eye and skewered Trev with an assessing stare. "Your birth, for example, compels certain things of you."

Trev had never envied his brother the title. He knew as soon as he could toddle that one day he'd have to make his own way in the world. Theobald would stand in their father's shadow, waiting to step into the earl's shoes once he vacated them. Theobald was still waiting, but it was time for Trevelyn to move on.

"Which is why I shall shortly be departing for India to continue my work in Her Majesty's intelligence corps," Trevelyn said. "There will be little opportunity to send personal correspondence." Particularly since he'd almost certainly be living under one of his aliases. "However, in the event of my death, I'm sure you would be advised."

The earl cleared his throat loudly. "That is out of the question. We cannot chance your untimely demise."

A small flicker of warmth grew in his chest. Appearances to the contrary, perhaps his father did care for him after all.

"Nevertheless, my path is set," Trev said. "I shall take a berth on the next available ship for Bombay."

"I cannot allow it."

"You have nothing to say about it."

"The devil I don't," the earl said. "Doesn't a man have the right to protect his heir?"

Trevelyn frowned. Was it possible his father was experiencing some sort of apoplexy? Theobald was the elder. There was never any question of succession.

"It's time you knew the truth," the earl said. "The pertinent facts are all documented, sworn statements by those in attendance, in a sealed file in our solicitor's office. You are the firstborn, Trevelyn, not Theobald."

"My entire childhood was a lie?"

His father's lips turned up in a smug smile. "It's rare for a man to have the opportunity to select his heir, the right of primogeniture being what it is. How often does one see a firstborn who's an absolute ass and a deserving second son who hasn't a prayer short of fratricide of inheriting? When we were blessed with twins, I saw a chance to change that."

"What have you done, Father?" Trev's gut churned.

"By giving your place to your brother, I was assured the opportunity to name the most worthy of the two of you to succeed me. Given your past performance, it appeared I had made a wise choice. Then you surprise me with this unlooked-for display of heroism. It seems the perfect time to reveal your true destiny." The earl spread his hands in a gesture that proclaimed the matter already accomplished. "Trevelyn Deveridge, you will be the ninth Earl of Warre."

Trev let that astounding idea wash over him for a moment. As a peer, he'd have more power than he'd ever dreamed. He could influence policy in the House of Lords. He might spare the Empire far more needless wars as a Member of Parliament than he ever could as a procurer of information on the Indian subcontinent. He might somehow win back Artemisia's affection if . . .

His brother's face rose in his mind.

"I've had my entire life to reconcile myself to the lot of a second son," Trevelyn said. "What of Theo?"

"What of him?" The earl steepled his fingers. "His only accomplishment thus far has been siring a gaggle of daughters. Now, if he'd managed to father a son, one who showed promise—"

"You mean one who was willing to be molded to your liking."

"Exactly," his father said with raised brows. "How quickly you've grasped the subtleties of my position. It further reinforces that I am correct in naming you my heir."

"Well, I refuse to be so named. Stop the barouche," Trevelyn ordered the driver. The clacking wheels rolled to a halt. "You cannot manipulate people, least of all your own sons, in such a cavalier manner."

"Of all people you should understand the irony in that. Your work in Her Majesty's secret service requires you to manipulate and—yes, I'll say it—lie to everyone around you at all times. However, as your father, I have the right to raise you and your brother in whatever manner I see fit. My 'manipulation,' as you call it, has made you a man with far more spine than Theobald." The earl's dark brows lowered. "It is my wish to reveal you as my heir and I will have it so."

Trevelyn climbed out of the barouche. "Then you will be disappointed, Father, because I have no intention of complying with your wishes any longer. Be satisfied with Theo. He lives to please you in ways I never would."

He slammed the door closed. "You can't remake people to conform to your notions of what they should be. You can't slice them up and reassemble them to suit yourself."

"I'll not stand such insolence." The earl's face turned deep purple.

"Yes, you will, but I promise it will be the last time. You shall not see me again, Father."

"You ungrateful puppy."

"Guilty as charged but unrepentant," Trevelyn agreed. "However, I will offer you some parting advice. If you continue to try to change the people you should love without conditions, one day you will die as you have lived—alone."

Trevelyn turned and strode away. How had he come to it so late? He'd tried to change the woman he loved.

And he'd just pronounced his own punishment.

Chapter Thirty-six

"Madam, please. You must stop to take nourishment or you'll fall down in a faint." Cuthbert's face was creased with concern as he poured out a steaming cup of tea and laced it liberally with thick cream and two lumps of sugar.

"It's almost finished." Artemisia mixed a dollop of umber and brown on her palette. The studio was even untidier than usual, with trial sketches and experimental elements of her work scattered about. She'd forbidden Cuthbert to move anything. There was no discernible system to the disarray, but she knew where every scrap of it was. "Just a bit more here."

"So you've said for days, Your Grace." Cuthbert thrust the teacup before her. "Please, madam. Stop for only a moment to refresh yourself. One fears for your health if you continue thus."

The tea sent an aromatic summons that could not be denied. She put down her palette knife long enough to take a sip. The warm, sweet infusion of spices and cream slid down her throat. Perhaps she could do with a respite, after all.

"Thank you, Cuthbert. It seems you are right." She lifted her cup and her brow at him. "As usual."

"One does one's best," he said with modesty.

Artemisia sank onto the settee, cradling her cup in both paint-stained hands. Pollux leaped onto her lap as if to add his weight to Cuthbert's desire that she be anchored to the seat for a few minutes. His warmth and rumbling purr leeched out all need for frenetic activity, and she relaxed for the first time in days.

After Trevelyn had left her home, she hadn't had time to mourn his absence, though she felt it keenly. The rest of her life clamored for her attention.

Felix had appeared before her, sober and genuinely contrite for his part in the whole sordid business. He was even willing to confess to the authorities and accept whatever punishment was required, but Artemisia decided it was enough if he allowed her to tie up the estate until his thirtieth birthday. Felix agreed with gratitude and hadn't given her a moment's regret since.

Her mother was beside herself, because Artemisia had been involved in such a scandalous business as espionage. Even if the matter remained undiscovered by the precious *ton,* it was horrible of Artemisia to have put them all at risk of such sordid doings coming to light. It wouldn't do to jeopardize Delia's match with another unsavory episode. The shame of Florinda running away to Gretna Green with one of the stable lads had already sent Constance into a severe attack of the vapors. She'd only been revived when promised carte blanche in arranging for Delia's grand wedding.

Angus was delighted when he heard Florinda was going to settle in the country with Hector Longbotham, but then Angus was delighted by most everything these days.

Her father's mind was still stripped down to the barest flashes of normalcy, but his heart was always merry. Artemisia decided that such was truly the measure of a person. If in the end, one was left with only the ability to feel happy with life, perhaps that was no bad thing.

She, however, did everything in her power not to feel anything at all. She pushed herself beyond normal limits trying to finish Mars. She took advantage of every moment of natural light to do detailed brushstrokes on the central figure of the piece in the foreground and toiled by lamplight on the shadowy background. Now that she had a moment to step back and really look at it, she realized suddenly that Mars was done. Even one more dab of paint would diminish, not add, to the effect.

Whether it was any good or not, she couldn't decide. It was too dear to her to make that sort of judgment. More than any other piece she'd ever produced, she'd poured her soul onto this canvas. She was an empty cup, drained to the last dregs. It would take far more than Cuthbert's remarkable tea to revive her.

As if he sensed her thoughts, her butler pressed a plate of biscuits into her hand and then turned to look at the canvas. He took two steps forward and stopped.

"Well, what do you think?" she asked before nibbling half heartedly on the crusty pastry.

"Ordinarily, one is of no opinion—"

"On the subject of art, yes, I know," she finished for him dryly. "But what do you *feel* when you look at it?"

He stared in silence at the canvas.

"Honestly, madam?"

"I wouldn't have it otherwise."

"Hopeless," he finally said.

"Oh, good. I was afraid I was projecting my own sentiments onto the piece. Very well." She brought the cup to her lips again. "That was the point, after all. Art is about what it makes you feel. It seems I got it right this time."

Cuthbert tugged his waistcoat down in front and fiddled with the watch fob dangling from his pocket, checking the time with uncharacteristic preoccupation.

"You're nervous as a cat. What is it?" Artemisia asked.

"Madam, he's back again."

"Is he?" Her chest constricted.

"He refuses to take no for an answer. In fact, if I don't admit him in precisely two minutes, Mr. Deveridge has threatened to break down the studio door." Cuthbert adjusted his neck stock. "If one may be so bold as to suggest, one thinks, no, one *feels* Your Grace should see him."

"Sometimes I think he's all I do see," Artemisia murmured. Nothing had changed. She had hoped driving herself to finish the painting, emptying herself on the canvas, would clear her soul of the desire to continue with her art. Even though she was exhausted, she knew it hadn't worked. After a brief spell of recuperation, she'd be ready to create again. She'd *need* to create again.

She loved Trevelyn, but he didn't love her if he thought to change this most intrinsic part of her. If she saw him, she feared her will would crumple and she'd give in to his demand to stop her work. It might seem like a fair trade now, when she craved him more than sunlight. But what if in the years to come, her love was tainted by resentment for the sacrifice he required? She hadn't insisted he stop *his* work, had she? The Great Game was infinitely more dangerous than painting nudes.

She set her cup on the windowsill. "If Mr. Deveridge is coming in whether I will it or no, we haven't much time to prepare then, have we?"

"Artemisia, I know you're in there." Trev pounded on the English oak till the door threatened to come off its hinges. "Please, I must see you. How can I apologize properly through a closed door?"

He raised his fist to hammer the portal again, but it opened before he could deliver another blow. Cuthbert waved him into her studio.

Evidence of her recent presence was everywhere, from the still wet paintbrushes congealing on the palette to the cooling teacup on the windowsill. The faint scent of oleander still lingered in the air. But Artemisia was nowhere to be seen.

"Where is she?"

Cuthbert gave a discreet shrug and lifted one hand toward the open window.

Trev could see it clearly in his mind. The little minx must have hoisted herself up and over the sill and disappeared into her overgrown garden to avoid him.

"So she ran rather than face me." Trevelyn leaned on the windowsill and peered out, disappointment sagging his shoulders. If she was that determined not to see him, his case was truly hopeless.

The orange tabby sunning itself on the back of the settee laid its ears flat and hissed at him.

"Thank you very much," he said to the cat. "Your mistress made her point most eloquently without your help. I'll not trouble her again."

Trevelyn turned to go but stopped when he caught

a glimpse of the canvas Artemisia had been working on. "Mars in Defeat" was emblazoned in gilt lettering across the bottom of the work.

It gave him an odd sense of detachment, viewing his own nude form. His image strained in a prone gesture of despair. His gut clenched in remembrance of the cramps he'd endured to produce the contorted figure for her.

The canvas seethed with emotion. It was all there, just as they'd discussed—the misery, the needless death and destruction, the ultimate failure of war— etched on the same face he shaved each morning.

He noted that she'd made quite a few changes since he'd seen it last. His genitals were rendered in careful detail, and thankfully in correct proportion this time. A rueful smile curved his lips.

"Well, perhaps she's forgiven me a few things at least," he murmured.

"It's not one's place to say," Cuthbert began and went on to say, nevertheless, "but one suspects one's mistress does not hold you in any but the highest regard."

Trev cast him a sideways glance. "Since she refuses to see me, I seriously doubt that."

"No, it's true," Cuthbert said. "She is most particular about her art, as you well know, and yet she—" He stopped himself abruptly.

"What?"

"Perhaps one is speaking out of turn," Cuthbert said.

"Pray continue. I'm embarking on a journey to India on the *Tiberius*. We make sail with the tide, so there's no need to concern yourself about the tale spreading further. What did you almost say?"

"Just that for your sake, Her Grace didn't hesitate

to shatter the Beddington statue. It was utterly destroyed and all she could think of was your welfare."

So the Beddington statue that started the whole tangled affair was gone. Artemisia had sacrificed it for him. He hadn't even thought to ask how she'd removed the key from her prized artwork.

"What an ass I've been." He studied the paint spatters on the hardwood between his feet.

Cuthbert refrained from comment.

"At least the world will not be deprived of the future works your mistress will create." Trevelyn looked at the Mars canvas once more. "She truly is brilliant, isn't she, Cuthbert?"

"Indeed, sir, she is that."

"There's so much I wanted to tell her," he said softly. "And yet only one thing really." He shoved his hands into his pockets and trudged toward the doorway.

"Is there a message you wish to leave, sir?" Cuthbert asked as he swept before Trevelyn to hold the door for him.

"Tell her . . ."

Where to begin? That he was sorry. That he could barely breathe for wanting to hold her. That contemplating the long march of days ahead without her made him go numb inside.

That he'd love her until he was dust.

None of it was a message he could leave with Cuthbert.

"Tell her I like the painting."

Chapter Thirty-seven

He likes the painting," Artemisia repeated. "You specifically asked if he had a message for me and all he said was he likes the painting?"

"Those were his precise words, madam."

"You and he spoke together for some time. I was watching through a crack in the dressing room door, but I couldn't hear well enough to make anything out. He must have said something else."

Cuthbert's eyes darted up and to the right, obviously searching his memory. "I believe he did say you were brilliant."

"Brilliant." The word fell flat as a paving stone on her tongue. "For pity's sake, Cuthbert, men say cricket players are brilliant."

"If it gives Your Grace any consolation, Mr. Deveridge took solace from viewing the painting. There was something about it which seemed to indicate that you'd granted him absolution for some offense."

"He noticed I lengthened his willie, no doubt," Artemisia said irritably. She ran a hand through her hair, heedless of the cerulean streaks her fingers left in their wake. "Do all men believe the sun rises and sets in their own groin?"

Cuthbert blinked at her owlishly.

"Never mind. The question was purely rhetorical,"

she said. "Honestly, there must have been something else."

Cuthbert's lips formed a cut across his face like a spade mark on an old potato. "Well, Mr. Deveridge did mention that he's due to sail to India with the tide."

"Today?" Artemisia's heart dropped to her ankles. It was one thing to stubbornly refuse to see him while part of her heart secretly hoped he'd try again. It was quite another to realize he was giving up on her entirely and fleeing to a far corner of the world. She'd not see Trevelyn again in this life.

Her knees gave way and she collapsed onto the settee.

"Madam, are you quite well?" Cuthbert hovered about her, anxious as a bee over a drooping flower.

She realized that she'd stopped breathing. Artemisia forced herself to inhale. "No, I may never be well again."

It will not end like this, she told herself. The daughter of Angus Dalrymple didn't let a little setback like a passage to India get in the way of her future happiness. She rose to her feet and tore out of her paint smock. She wished there was time to change into something grander than her simple day dress, but there was no help for it.

"On what ship does he sail?" she asked.

Cuthbert tapped his temple with his knuckles for a moment. "The *Tiberius.*"

Artemisia surprised the stiff-backed gentleman by giving him a quick hug. "You are a treasure, Cuthbert. Bring the barouche around, and quickly now. Mr. Deveridge only thinks he's gotten away easily. He and I are not finished with our disagreement yet."

One corner of Cuthbert's mouth lifted in a knowing half-smile. "Indeed, Your Grace, one suspects there may be enough points of conflict to keep the pair of you fully engaged for at least the next fifty years or so."

"Let us hope," she agreed. "But time is of the essence."

"Very good, Your Grace." Her butler dispensed with his customary bow and nearly sprinted out of the studio.

Her noble intentions of sacrificing her happiness on the altar of her art evaporated like morning mist. Much as she loved her work, she realized she lived for Trev. The two-dimensional men she created were a poor substitute for the real one. Artemisia was determined not to let him go without a fight. She took a last look at the Mars canvas.

"And if in the end, I have to give up painting . . . so be it."

The London wharf was an anthill of industry. Sweat-slick men rolled barrels and pushed handcarts along the docks to the accompaniment of piped commands and profuse swearing. This noisy, malodorous place was the commercial hub of the Empire. Goods from a thousand ports intersected and changed hands several times, often even before being off-loaded. It was chaos in motion.

And a deucedly difficult place to find one specific ship in a hurry.

Finally Artemisia gave up trying to read the faded ships' names as the barouche fought its way down the crowded street. She ordered a halt.

"You there, boy," she called to a scruffy-looking lad. Cast off or run away, London's many street urchins either found a way to survive on the lowest rung of the demimonde or perished anonymously as they lived.

The boy turned his thin face up to her.

"I'll give you a guinea if can you tell me where the *Tiberius* is berthed," she promised.

The lad shrugged. "Coin first, milady."

"Cuthbert, pay the lad, and quickly."

Her butler fished out the appropriate mintage and tossed it to the boy.

A sly grin split the youth's face. "The *Tiberius* already slipped 'er cables, guv. If you 'urry, you can just see 'er sails rounding the bend in the river." The boy took to his heels lest he be forced to surrender the guinea.

The coin was the furthest thing from Artemisia's mind. She didn't wait for Cuthbert to open the barouche's door. She clamored down unaided and ran as fast as her legs would carry her to the end of the nearest pier.

Canvas flying in the distance, the heavy-laden merchantman was making its way down the Thames and out to the Channel with the receding tide. A dozen punts bobbed in its wake. Artemisia's first thought was to hail a small craft to overtake the *Tiberius*, but after seeing the way the larger vessel pulled away from the river boats, that hope sank like an anchor.

Her breath caught in her throat. Perhaps she could arrange passage on the next ship bound for Bombay and overtake him at one of the ports of call.

Compose yourself, she ordered fiercely. *There's no need to chase a man who obviously doesn't want to be caught.*

Tears pressed behind her eyes, but she tried to hold them back. If he was content to leave her forever, she must accept the idea. In time she might even come to bless him for it. A dedicated operative in Her Majesty's intelligence service had no need of a wife to encumber him. And hadn't she only grudg-ingly accepted the idea of placing herself under the thumb of a husband once again?

Surely it was for the best.

Then why did her chest feel as if a lodestone had replaced her beating heart?

She covered her face with both hands and wept. What a fool she'd been. She'd demanded more of Trevelyn than he was able to give. Unlike the gods on her canvases, he wasn't made for her to mold into the image that most suited her. If he couldn't abide for her to continue painting nudes, she should have accepted him for who he was. Her damnable pursuit of perfection had driven away the one man who might at least have given her slices of the ideal.

She felt a warm masculine hand rest on her shud-dering shoulder. *Dear Cuthbert.* Heaven only knew what it cost that most reticent of men to demonstrate his sympathy with the simple gesture.

"Oh, Cuthbert, he's gone," she sobbed. "And I have only myself to blame."

The floodgates opened afresh, and her tears flowed unabated. A handkerchief dangled before her and she grasped it like a drowning woman latches on to a lifeline.

"I should have . . ." Words failed to form in the back of her closed throat. A lifetime of quiet despair rose before her eyes and she dissolved into incoher-ent sobs. Finally she managed to stammer, "Now what am I to do?"

Long arms came around her and drew her into a surprising embrace. Shock stopped her tears.

"Really, Cuthbert, I appreciate the sentiment, but this display is wholly inappropriate."

"Madam, if I were Cuthbert, I'd totally agree with you."

She whirled in his arms. "Trevelyn! What are you—"

He stopped her with a kiss that warmed her to her toes. Finally he released her mouth but still held her tightly against him. She wouldn't have left his embrace willingly for the world.

"I couldn't go without you," he said simply. "I was late in coming round to it, but now I know I haven't the right to demand that you give up something so important to you. Conditional love is no love at all. And I do love you, Larla. Slap as many nude men on your canvases as it takes to make you happy. I don't care so long as I'm the only one you slap in your bed."

She tapped his cheek with her fingertips. "Careful, sir, or you may find yourself slapped in my bed posthaste."

"Promises, promises," he said with a sinful smile. Then his expression turned sober. "Seriously, now. For my past behavior, I own myself an ass. But I mean to make amends."

"And how long do you think that will take?" she asked.

"The rest of our lives, I expect," he said with a laugh. "I want to be your husband, but I wonder if you have the patience for it."

"I greatly fear you'll be the one who needs patience," she admitted. "But yes, Trev, of course I'll be your wife. I love you more than my next breath. The very thought of living without you knocked all the fight out of me."

"Well, if that's all it takes . . ."

She swatted his shoulder.

He covered her with kisses.

"Hold there, mate," one of the passing sailors called to them. "That's like pouring out water before a parched man. Don't be making love to the lady on the wharf. Not when there's rooms to let over at the Tipsy Dutchman."

Artemisia's chuckle stopped his kisses. Trevelyn let her come up for air. Then he scooped her up and swung her in a dizzying circle.

"I can hardly believe you've consented," he said breathlessly. "You've made me the happiest man in Britain."

"Only Britain? I think we can do better than that," she said with a smile full of promise. "Let's go see about a room at the Tipsy Dutchman."

Epilogue

From *The Tattler*

NUPTIALS AMONG THE BEAU MONDE

By Clarence Wigglesworth, Esq.

All the crème de la crème of London Society was present at the grand wedding of Miss Delia Dalrymple and Lord Shrewsbury the younger on Saturday last. In pomp and spectacle, it was easily the most lavishly garish event of the Season and almost makes up for the not-quite-hushed-up scandal of the bride's sister's elopement to Gretna Green with a mere stableband.

But only a select few were present at the private ceremony uniting the Duchess of Southwycke with the Honorable Mr. Trevelyn Deveridge. Held in a tiny chapel in Wiltshire, the marriage service was simplicity itself. The bride's sister Florinda (she of the Gretna Green debacle) served as matron of honor while the brother of the groom, Theobald Deveridge, the future Earl of Warre, served as best man. The Duchess's parents, her stepson Felix Pelham-Smythe, the Duke of Southwyck (upright and sober and sorely missed at various gaming hells of late) and an unlikely collection of servants (notably Her

Grace's butler and an East Indian couple in full barbaric dress) were the only other guests.

Conspicuous by his absence was the groom's father, Lord Warre. However, as the happy couple left the chapel, the earl made a tardy appearance. He approached the newlyweds and, after a few moments' conversation, kissed the bride's cheek and shook the groom's hand. Upon this evidence of noble approval, the bride's mother had an attack of the vapors and swooned. The earl and the bride's father attempted to carry the lady back into the chapel, but she revived suddenly and began shrieking to be put down. Pandemonium ensued, and the bridal couple escaped in the confusion.

Truly, such goings-on make this reporter sad that Constance and Angus Dalrymple have run out of daughters to be wed. And with the former Duchess of Southwycke, now Mrs. Trevelyn Deveridge, making her home in faraway Bombay, one wonders if scandal will take a holiday in London.

However, Mr. Deveridge assured this reporter that since his wife will continue to paint, London has not seen the last of the duchess and her infamous art.

One lives in hope.

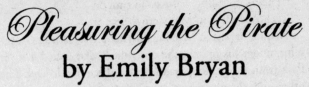

Pleasuring the Pirate
by Emily Bryan

Coming August 2008.
Read ahead for a sneak peak.

The next time I decide to kill a man, Jacqueline thought, *I really need to find better help.*

She struggled toward consciousness, but pain blocked her way. She sank back with dreamlike slowness, as though it wasn't her body lying on the dusty Cornish road. She lightly skimmed the surface of blackness, ready to plunge downward again, when the voices above her began to make sense.

"No more than a whelp," a deep baritone said with disgust.

"Dead?" another voice asked, the tone reedy and unabashedly cheerful.

Work-roughened fingers searched for the pulse point below her jawline. "Not yet."

Jacqueline hardly dared breathe.

"No blood so far as I can tell, but he took a wallop. Look at that goose egg. Still, we may get some answers from him." A booted foot nudged her hip. "Wake up, lad."

Lad. At least her disguise still held. Her eyes rolled in their sockets before she forced her lids open. A stab of sunlight made her squeeze them closed again. Her head pounded in tandem with her heart.

"Rum, Meri," the deep voice ordered, punctuated by the commanding snap of his fingers.

"There's no call to waste good rum on—"

"Whose rum is it, Mr. Meriwether?"

Jacqueline peered from beneath her brown lashes. Grumbling under his breath, the one called Meri fished a silver flask from the gelding's saddlebag and handed it over. The other one, the one whose strong arms forced her to sit up, the one she loathed with every fiber of her being, held the drink to her lips.

"Steady now. Not too fast," he urged. "This rum's raw enough to put hair on your chest."

The spirits burned down her gullet. When she choked and sputtered, he pulled the flask away. She didn't dare look up at him.

He was coming to destroy her life and the lives of all she held dear. She didn't want to see his face.

Not until she had a sword in her hand.

"Well, lookee there, Cap'n. He's still in the land of the living, after all. Must have just had the breath knocked from him, I warrant. Good. I like me boy's liver fresh." Meriwether flashed a wolfish grin. "Pity we've no onions to fry up with it."

She'd been warned the new lord and his minions were heartless and utterly without conscience, but Meri's threat was beyond the pale. Even so, the blood drained from her face. She was probably blanching white as a fish belly.

Damn her weakness! Why hadn't she been born a man?

"You aren't really going to eat my liver." She tried to sound sure about it, but her voice broke with a squeak.

"I won't," he promised. "But Mr. Meriwether spent longer in the Caribbee than I. He has peculiar tastes. But if you tell me what I want to know, I'll make sure your liver stays where it is. Now what's your name?"

She needed time to gather her wits. Keeping her eyes

downcast, she wobbled to her feet. A sword lay a bare five feet away, the hilt toward her.

"J-Jack," she stammered as she edged toward the weapon. "I'm called Jack."

"Very well," he said. "You may have been with that lot that tried to waylay us, but perhaps you can make amends."

With them? She'd tried to *lead* them, but her last fuzzy memory was one of the oafs clobbering her senseless with his sharp elbow as he drew his sword. The wretches professed to be experienced assassins and the royal seal they flashed about gave their claims the ring of truth. They must have grown wings since their initial assault failed. There was no sign of them now.

"I'm willing to believe you fell in with bad company sort of accidental like," the captain went on.

"Aye, 'tis easy enough to fall in with villains, bad company being so much more pleasurable than good company as a general rule," Meriwether chimed in. "And who should know that better'n you, Cap'n?"

"In any case, I've done you a good turn for an evil one," he said. "Will you help me then, Jack?"

She crossed her arms over her chest, pulling the ill-fitting smock-shirt tight around her form, trying to seem as if she were weighing her options. She glanced at Meri, who was now picking rocks from his horse's hooves, totally disinterested in her since it appeared his captain wasn't going to let him cook her liver.

This might be her only chance.

"Aye, I'll help you." She dove for the sword and by some miracle came up with the hilt in her hand. "I'll help you on your way to hell." Remembering her training with Dragon Caern's old master-at-arms, she brought the blade up in a glittering arc, trusting to surprise for success.

She only managed to catch a corner of his hat and knock it off his head.

Quick as an adder, his sword was out and facing her down. He was much bigger than she expected. He stood a hand's width more than six feet and carried fifteen stone in weight, most of it in work-hardened muscle.

Jacqueline swallowed hard. The folk of Dragon Caern depended on her to make good decisions. Clearly this was not one of her finest.

She'd imagined the new lord would be whey-faced, powdered and perfumed, slightly effeminate in the manner of most courtly folk. But this man's face was bronzed the color of oiled cedar and there was nothing the least soft about him. Something inside her rebelled at the injustice. He had no right to such a strong-boned handsome face. Not with as black a heart as he must possess. She felt a surge of triumph when a trio of red drops appeared on his smooth-shaven chin. He wiped them off and gave her a mocking bow.

"First blood to you then, Jack."

Meri chuckled. "And I was afeared life as a landsman would be dull."

Circling, the captain retrieved his fallen hat. The tip of his sword never dipped as he slapped the tricorne against his thigh, sending small clouds of dust puffing. The cockade and plume were decidedly worse for the wear but he cocked the hat on his head at a rakish angle.

"I don't think you want to do this, boy," he warned.

The fine brocade frock coat and velvet breeches bespoke him a gentleman, but his dark eyes glinted beneath his darker brows, feral and cold as a dragon.

The dragon that would devour her world, the note with the royal seal had promised. She clenched her teeth and gripped the hilt of her sword all the tighter. "Oh, yes, I do."

"Me thanks to ye, Jackie-boy. Cap'n Gabriel swore anyone who wished him bodily harm was still sailing the Spanish Main." Meri settled on a rock to watch the combatants in comfort. "I recollect he wagered fifty sovereigns on the matter."

A wry grin lifted one corner of Gabriel's mouth.

"Apparently, I lose." The smile faded. "But I must warn you, Jack. I don't make a habit of it."

"Don't worry," Jacqueline said with more bravado than she felt. "I don't intend for you to live long enough to get used to losing."

She lunged, swinging her blade with all the spite she possessed.

LAURA DREWRY

GIVING THE DEVIL HIS DUDE

Shoveling sulfur and brimstone could really get a girl down.
When her dad offered freedom from the fiery depths in
exchange for one simple soul-snatching, Lucy Firr jumped
at the chance. With her considerable powers of seduction,
she threw herself at rancher Jed Caine. Yet instead of taking
her to bed, he made her muck out the pigsty.

It would take the patience of a saint to resist the likes of
Lucy Firr—and Lord knew Jed was no saint. The temptress
fired his blood like no woman he'd ever met. Why she'd
suddenly latched on to him, he had no idea. But the safest
place for her—and her virtue—was out in the barn.

She was supposed to steal his soul, yet here he was...
capturing her heart.

THE DEVIL'S DAUGHTER

ISBN 13: 978-0-8439-6048-8

To order a book or to request a catalog call:
1-800-481-9191
This book is also available at your local bookstore, or you
can check out our Web site **www.dorchesterpub.com**
where you can look up your favorite authors, read excerpts,
or glance at our discussion forum to see what people have to
say about your favorite books.

JENNIFER ASHLEY

Egan MacDonald was the one person Princess Zarabeth couldn't read. Yet even without being able hear his thoughts, she knew he was the most honorable, infuriating, and deliciously handsome man she'd ever met. And now her life was in his hands. Chased out of her native country by bitter betrayal and a bevy of assassins, Zarabeth found refuge at the remote MacDonald castle and a haven in Egan's embrace. She also found an ancient curse, a matchmaking nephew, a pair of debutants eager to drag her protector to the altar, and dark secrets in Egan's past. But even amid all the danger raged a desire too powerful to be denied....

Highlander Ever After

ISBN 13: 978-0-8439-6004-4